PR
Celt

"A haunting tale, a page-turner... DeLima is a delicious new voice."

—Yasmine Galenorn, *New York Times* bestselling author of
Priestess Dreaming

"DeLima's debut is a romantic, suspenseful and rich story about survival and loyalty to those who matter most."

—*Booklist*

"*Celtic Moon* has a great werewolf world... A fun start to a new paranormal series." —USATODAY.com

"A welcome addition to the paranormal romance world arrives with this terrific debut novel from DeLima. Blending Celtic mythology, shapeshifters and magic, *Celtic Moon* is not only an absorbing adventure; it is a story of reconciliation and acceptance. DeLima really brings these characters to life." —*RT Book Reviews*

"Original and compelling . . . a shifter story that stands out from the crowd!" —*GraveTells*

"Not your average werewolf book thanks [to] Jan DeLima's distinctive layered writing style, original mythology and unlikely heroine. A brilliant effort by this debut author!"

—*Rabid Reads*

"A fresh take on wolf shapeshifters . . . DeLima will delight fans with this first in this new series." —*Debbie's Book Bag*

"An engrossing new series . . . Fans of the Kate Daniels series by Ilona Andrews or the works of Patricia Briggs will want to check this out." —*Monsters and Critics*

Ace Books by Jan DeLima

CELTIC MOON
SUMMER MOON

Summer Moon

JAN DeLima

ACE BOOKS, NEW YORK

THE BERKLEY PUBLISHING GROUP
Published by the Penguin Group
Penguin Group (USA) LLC
375 Hudson Street, New York, New York 10014

USA • Canada • UK • Ireland • Australia • New Zealand • India • South Africa • China

penguin.com

A Penguin Random House Company

SUMMER MOON

An Ace Book / published by arrangement with the author

Ace Books are published by The Berkley Publishing Group.
ACE and the "A" design are trademarks of Penguin Group (USA) LLC.

For information, address: The Berkley Publishing Group,
a division of Penguin Group (USA) LLC,
375 Hudson Street, New York, New York 10014.

ISBN: 978-0-425-26621-2

PUBLISHING HISTORY
Ace mass-market edition / October 2014

PRINTED IN THE UNITED STATES OF AMERICA

10 9 8 7 6 5 4 3 2 1

Cover illustration by Gordon Crabb; Celtic symbols © Santi0103 & Leshik/Shutterstock.
Cover design by Diana Kolsky.
Interior text design by Kelly Lipovich.
All interior art by Jan DeLima unless otherwise noted. Owl © Maria Gaellman:
Used under license from Shutterstock.com. Wolf © Holly Kuchera:
Used under license from Shutterstock.com.

In memory of J.S.P.
Not a day goes by that you are not missed.

Acknowledgments

It takes a great deal of research to write a series involving an ancient culture, and I must acknowledge the librarians, educators and historians who have directed me toward reference materials: Christy, Bill Cook, Gary and Professor Ian Bricknell. As always, to my entire family, for their enthusiasm and support. Also, to Kristen, Sue and Wendy, for our many wonderful chats over lattes. Lastly, to Ann Marie, Stephanie and Nancy, who celebrate each of our successes with genuine joy and who gave me the most amazing gift for my debut novel. Thank you!

A Documented Prophecy . . .

Their course, their bearing,
Their permitted way,
And their fate I know,
Unto the end.

Oh! what misery,
Through extreme of woe,
Prophecy will show . . .

—TALIESIN
From *The Mabinogion*
Lady Charlotte Guest translation

An Undocumented Prophecy, Until Now . . .

This union, I shall not revile,
For their fear I know,
Their affliction,
And their gift.

To bear in silence,
Four secrets hidden,
In circles of raindrops,
Cloak death.

Alas, false forfeit gains no vantage.
From deadened earth,
Fevers rise, of lust
And lament.

Thence they plan,
Upon Ceridwen's last fertile daughter,
Eight forsaken warriors
To feast.

For barren not,
Under summer's first moon,
Comes the prophecy
They most seek.

—TALIESIN
A drunken toast from Math and Rosa's wedding feast

One

**CASTELL AVON, HIDDEN WITHIN
THE WHITE MOUNTAINS
AVON, NEW HAMPSHIRE, USA**
Present Day

THREE DAYS AFTER HER HUSBAND'S EXECUTION, ROSA Alban became a traitor to the Guardians of her race.

Oh, she had committed tiny crimes against her late husband—and her keepers before him—throughout the last three hundred years of her life. But none this final or this openly subversive.

If her plan proved fruitful, there would be no explanations needed, or accepted. To openly defy the Guardians, the self-appointed protectors of her dying lineage, was utter madness—and yet necessary for her battered conscience. She would rather live as a traitor than bear witness to one more act of cruelty in silence.

A cool breeze brushed through the muddied courtyard where she stood. Rosa tugged her jacket closed and scanned the area for anyone who might question her morning excursion. Nothing seemed amiss, but she understood more than most that appearances and reality were often quite different.

Regardless, she mustn't linger.

The shadow of Castell Avon darkened her path, her wedding gift from the Guardians, a sad comfort for a false marriage. As its name implied, her home was indeed a castle surrounded by rivers, built of stone, mortar and iron laced with gold; her gilded prison on a foundation of sorrow. The tallest turret heralded the Guardian banner, marking her husband's realm like a medieval hound pissing on this modern age.

Math had not adjusted well to forced anonymity among humans, or to their proclivity for procreation. He had considered himself a god, after all, having walked this earth as both man and wolf for more than two thousand years. Obviously, he'd been wrong—given that the separated portions of his body lay rotting in a casket awaiting shipment to their homeland for burial.

Perhaps she was a tad pitiless, but Rosa felt no remorse over her husband's death; Math had been a vile creature and his execution well deserved. It had, however, expedited her plan to join the very rebels who had so graciously made her a widow.

As Rosa skirted around outer buildings that housed generators, laundry facilities and other modern amenities kept outside the castle walls, she pretended to ignore a female servant hanging bedsheets on a clothesline. Without pause, Tesni pinned three white pillowcases in a row, signaling that all three Guardians who had come to escort Math's body back to Wales were still abed. Not necessarily sleeping, just otherwise occupied.

A bibbed skirt made of wool purposely concealed Tesni's feminine curves. She was of mixed blood, human and Guardian, and bore a combination of her father's soft features and mother's fair coloring. Sadly, Tesni was too human to call her wolf. She was also the most attractive of all the female servants and therefore the one who suffered most.

Tesni's gaze flicked to Rosa with a wordless plea to make haste. Her usually straight posture remained hunched, pronouncing stiffness and misuse from the previous night.

Sorrow-ridden, Rosa knew that Cadan must be in a similar state, and was very likely the reason why the Guardians remained distracted. His room had been empty this morning. She knew because she had checked, even though Cadan had told her not to.

And with that thought in mind, Rosa quickened her pace without looking back.

The surrounding forest was quiet and empty of song. No birds or wildlife inhabited her island, as they recognized death and danger, and the musk of unholy wolves in human skin. Tall trees stood as withered sentries in her path, their roots eroded by water, time and secrets too vile to speak of openly.

Yet for the first time in centuries, Rosa felt exhilaration as she marched toward the only bridge that granted access to modern civilization. Winter's thaw had just ended in the White Mountains of New Hampshire. Melting snow had fed the rivers and cleansed the forest. She sensed vitality in the land beyond, of budding trees and the emergence of life; it called to her inner wolf like moonbeams to a night creature's soul, luring her with promises of power.

On the opposite side of the river, a carriage house secured the entrance to the bridge, constructed of the same stone and iron as Castell Avon, watched at all times by Math's guards. The heels of her boots echoed over wooden planks as she crossed, announcing her approach, even above the thunderous sound of rushing water below. If the guards did not allow her to pass, she would be forced to go upriver, but prudence had prompted her to attempt this route first.

There were six of them watching as she drew near. Four

men and two women, with resentful eyes filled with lust—
or hatred; Rosa preferred the latter. All but one were loyal
to her late husband, but even Gareth shifted his stance as if
uncomfortable in her presence. Normally only two guards
tended the carriage house, but having their eldest Guardian
beheaded within his own home had made the others in residence somewhat paranoid.

She stopped before the gated door, the barrier to her
freedom, and nodded to each of the guards in turn. She must
acknowledge them all equally but not with flirtation. Fur-
thermore, she must never snub them, never encourage
unwanted advances, and *never* dally—or the repercussions
were quite unpleasant.

"Rosa." Gareth greeted her with a slight bow, his voice
deceivingly calm. As her secret ally against the Guardians,
he had been informed of her plan last evening. Gareth had
wanted to accompany her. Judging from his current stance,
he still wasn't pleased about her insistence to go alone.

He had yet to realize that her days of submission were
over, even toward the precious few she considered her friends.

The morning sun did little to soften Gareth's deformed
features. Scars knotted his face and neck, weaving a tale of
torture and unbendable will. Math had destroyed Gareth's
beauty in a fit of rage over an affair with a mortal. Her late
husband had believed that mating with humans weakened
their race.

Gareth's favored jeweled patch covered a deadened left
eye, burned to blindness with ice and rock salt. He kept his
brown hair shorn to his scalp. Math had preferred it long.

"I'm feeling a bit weak," Rosa announced as rehearsed,
adding weariness to her voice that wasn't altogether feigned.
"I need to get off the island for a few hours. I need to go for
a run."

"I'll escort you," Gareth informed her, loud enough for
the others to hear.

She had expected a different response but hid her surprise. Gareth, it seemed, had elected to veer from her instructions. With a slight shake of her head, she met his single-eyed gaze to warn him not to test her resolve. "I think it's best if I go alone." She added for emphasis, "As usual."

If he challenged her now it might raise suspicion. A scowl turned his misshapen features into a grotesque mask, a rare show of emotion from a man who'd mastered the art of indifference, even under the most dire of circumstances.

Arnallt, one of the more observant of Math's guards, shot Gareth a curious glance.

Panic tightened her chest. Thankfully, if naught else, her marriage had schooled her on the art of false composure. One must be duplicitous and enduring to survive under Guardian rule, and she was both.

Rosa continued as if oblivious. "I've been ordered to go with the Guardians tomorrow morning. We are to accompany Math's body back to Wales for burial. I am to stay there through Beltane." A few crude snickers reached her ears, alerting her that they'd been told of the events awaiting her in their homeland. "My wolf is demanding a run before I climb on that plane."

The Guardians in residence might question her request but Math's guards were familiar with her routine. Running as a wolf had been the only freedom Math had allowed her without escort, because when she shifted, many of their kind desired her—and that had angered him.

It was a concession he had allowed after the summer of her seventeenth year. They had married the winter before, and Math had hosted a grand feast the following Solstice. When the hour had drawn late, and the hunt had teased their wolves, Math had brought all his guests outside to witness his new wife transform. It had been a treasured feat, for unmated females of their kind were rare, especially ones who could shift. And Math had always enjoyed flaunting his valued possessions. Like a little caged animal, she had performed, for to do otherwise resulted in the punishment of servants in her stead. She was considered too precious to harm. Even Math had feared the consequences, so he had found other ways.

However, the demonstration had not gone as Math had expected, because his guests had been unable to hide their desire for her.

After that night she'd been allowed to run unaccompanied.

It was, perhaps, the single reason why she had stayed sane. Still, she risked it only when her wolf demanded release, and not nearly as often as she would like. Because, unlike her dead husband, she didn't particularly care for unnecessary physical attention.

Gareth's one good eye, dark gray and direct, searched her face. For what, she wasn't sure, but he must have sensed her determination. "How long will you be?"

"No more than three hours." She kept her tone subdued, her face downcast, masking her relief. "I'm going to White Birch Reserve and will follow the river."

It was a lie, of course. If all went well, she wouldn't return until morning—and with reinforcements by her side as she took control of Castell Avon in her first open act of defiance against the Guardians.

Her neighbors to the north owed her a favor and she fully intended to collect on their debt. Moreover, she knew better than to challenge the Guardians alone. Other than Gareth and Cadan, her only allies in this forsaken place were servants, the *Hen Was* who could not shift.

She needed more wolves.

She needed an alliance the Guardians would fear.

"Fine." Gareth lifted his arm for her to pass.

Her back tingled as she entered the recently restored carriage house where horses once slept. The guards watched her until the outer door closed to block their view. She was greeted with darkness, a place she knew well. Stalls had been removed to afford more space for vehicles, all neatly lined up in soundless mechanical rows. It disturbed her senses. She hated the smell of gas that lingered in the air. She missed the soft breaths of beasts, when the sweetness of hay had mingled with the pungent scent of manure.

As expected, the whisper of a door and a brief flash of light warned of a visitor, followed by the smooth cadence of familiar footsteps. The man who resembled a monster moved like a shade, silent and creeping. It didn't take long for Gareth to find her.

"What has come over you?" she hissed quietly as he drew near. "Go back, or you will ruin our only chance of success."

"I should be with you." He sounded sullen even while refusing to heed her warning.

"I told Dylan's mate I would arrive alone, and I will not go back on my promise!" She barely breathed the words, fearful of detection. Even so, her anger bled through.

"Dylan will forgive an escort. You risked much when you helped his woman escape."

Rosa scoffed. "Guardians under my husband's command infiltrated Dylan's territory and imprisoned his mate. And then, during his mate's capture, had her mother and several others under his protection tortured and killed. And you think Dylan is going to be forgiving toward the widow of the man responsible? *Truly?*"

Gareth ignored her sarcasm. "Dylan took his revenge on Math. Had he wanted more deaths, he would have claimed them."

"Perhaps," Rosa admitted. "But he is not a leader who tolerates dishonor, or deceit. I must stay faithful to my word."

He gave a reluctant sigh of agreement. "Don't mistake Dylan as our ally just because our enemies are the same, nor his brother, Luc. They are not to be trusted."

"You think I don't know this?" She found it strange that he hadn't included the sister in his warning. If rumors were to be believed, Elen was more powerful than both brothers combined. "That is why I need you here to protect the others if I fail."

"You're too stubborn to fail." He gave a crude snort. "That's not my concern."

Her vision, always keen in the darkness, saw his marred features in clear detail. Striations of green and gold bled into his one good eye, revealing a wolf that had dwelled too long under the surface of human scars.

"Then what is it?" She shook her head, suddenly confused. "What has you so troubled that you would detain me here at this time?"

His voice thickened with an emotion she chose not to acknowledge. "I fear that in my absence you'll offer them more than what's already been given."

"I've nothing to offer them other than an alliance with their closest neighbor."

"You're not so naïve." A bitter laugh fell from his withered lips. "And I'm not one of your idiots to be duped by your guile. You're the last pure-blooded, unmated shifter of our kind. You're more precious than any alliance, or parcel of land infested with our vile leaders."

"I'll be no man's breeder," she sneered, "Guardian or otherwise."

Unless she chose to be—but that was *her* decision to make and *her* gift to give.

He began to protest but was silenced when a side door flung open and a shaft of light streamed into the garage, followed by the lewd voice of a curious guard.

"How long does it take to unlock a door, Gareth?" His lanky silhouette identified him as Briog, one of Math's favored guards, not for sexual sport but for his creativity toward torture. "I wonder if there is another task to be done, one I might be inclined to assist you with."

"The woman wants to take the Porsche," Gareth shot back with convincing annoyance. "It's mud season. She's bound to get stuck and I'm in no mood to haul her out."

"Figures," Briog said.

Gareth grabbed Rosa's hand. It took some effort for her not to cringe, more from displeasure than true aversion. She simply didn't care to be touched. It was her bane of existence that most unmated males felt compelled to fondle her in some way, while her reactions to them were altogether opposite.

"Take my truck." He pressed a key into her palm. "And I expect you to bring her back unharmed." His voice left little doubt that it was not his vehicle he spoke of. "There's a winch under the seat if needed."

"I will do my best." She wrapped her hand around the key, grateful Gareth had finally conceded without exposing her mission.

She climbed into the truck and quickly started the engine. The sound was not unpleasant because it always preceded a run, and like Pavlov's dog, she had found her own peculiar bell. The outer carriage door began to open, filtering in natural light; Gareth must have entered the security code and hit the inner remote.

Electricity had been added to the building during its restoration, a convenience the Guardians hadn't dared bring across the river. Her island held secrets, powerful forces that even the Guardians feared, contained only by a moving circle of water. Connections inland were unsafe, especially one as volatile as lightning in a wire.

Tendrils of doubt skittered across her spine, made worse by Gareth's final warning. Was she prepared for the aftermath of what she was about to do? Probably not, and before she had further second thoughts, Rosa adjusted the seat and rearview mirror to her smaller frame and pulled onto the cobbled drive.

As miles separated her from Avon, her tension began to ease. She half expected to be followed, but why would the Guardians suspect her of wrongdoing? Over the last three hundred years, she had given them no cause to doubt her.

She had assumed a lifetime of obedience for this singular act of defiance.

When she crossed the New Hampshire border into Maine, sunlight hit her windshield and blinded her with warmth. It was a beautiful spring morning. Aught not the weather show some sign when one turned traitor? Or perhaps this *was* a sign.

A giggle escaped, an absurdly childish sound for a woman who'd lived as long as she had. *Is this what hope feels like?* she wondered. *If so, this emotion could be quite addictive.* With each hour that passed, burdens fell from her shoulders like seeds from a dandelion, wishes floating on the wind wrought with possibilities.

I can drive away, straight into Canada and beyond. I can be free, truly free, if I choose . . .

The selfish thought lasted only a moment, chased away by the image of Tesni hanging pillowcases on the line—with her back hunched because Guardians had violated her the night before. And Rosa mustn't forget Cadan, as if she ever could, who continued to offer himself, even after Math's death—for this mission.

And there were others who waited for Rosa's return. More than thirty *Hen Was* resided in Castell Avon, forced to be servants because of their inability to shift, and more in the woods. They counted on her to succeed.

At the very least, they trusted her to try. Running away was not an option. She had endured too much—kept silent for too long—to abandon the people who needed her protection at this crucial time.

A war had begun between the Guardians and the rebels who refused to follow their demented ideals, and in times of war it was the innocents who suffered most. She would not leave them stranded, regardless of summer's rapid approach.

Even so, the mental reminder of the upcoming holiday made her stomach churn with dread. For many of their kind, the first of May brought happy celebrations—but never for her. Her husband was gone from this world, and still he had found a way to punish her.

In four weeks hence, the Guardians and their Council were preparing a grand festival. They meant to reenact an old fertility ritual, suggested by Math before his death, to include Rosa and eight unmated Guardians. Contrary to what they assumed, she had no intention of being a willing participant in their desperate plan.

But, if all went well, her neighbors to the north would be a willing participant in hers, bribery notwithstanding.

Two

RHUDDIN VILLAGE, MAINE
240 MILES NORTHEAST OF AVON

LUC BLACK WATCHED HIS BROTHER PACE AROUND THE
gathering room of Rhuddin Hall. A fire had been lit to take
the dampness from the air, but the added warmth served
only to agitate Luc's inner wolf. He felt the stone walls close
in, wanting—no, needing—to get his ass outside and into
the forest.

The room was relatively empty, save for five occupants.
Sophie and Joshua, Dylan's wife and teenage son, sat on the
nearest sofa, while Taliesin, the subject of their current
debate, sulked in the far corner with a withdrawn expression
on his deceivingly young face.

Dylan stopped pacing across the floor and shot Luc a
frustrated glance. "You've been sitting there quiet as a stone,
brother. Come on. Speak up. Let us hear your opinion on
the matter."

Luc would rather clean stalls in the guard's shit house than serve as referee to an argument between a man and his wife, so he stood to leave instead. "My opinion is pointless when you've already promised Sophie that Taliesin can stay. I think my time would be better served having the lake house prepared."

"Bloody hell, you too?" Dylan sighed in defeated frustration. "I didn't think he would actually take me up on the offer."

Ignoring her husband, Sophie gave Luc a grateful smile, one that he welcomed so soon after the death of her mother. Shadows lurked within her soft brown eyes but acceptance had begun to settle, along with determination to move on for the sake of her family.

Absently, Luc fingered a tiny gold charm tied to woven twine around his wrist, two circles that formed a Celtic knot, once worn by Koko, his late wife. He had given her the charm on her fifty-fourth birthday, when her woman's flow had ceased and not returned, and it had become certain that she wouldn't carry his child. Koko had been gone more than sixty years now; she had been the balm that soothed his darker half. Now he felt much like the battered charm, worn and broken with time.

Luc understood the grieving process well and admired his sister-in-law for not showing the sorrow he knew she carried. Time lessened the pain of loss but it never diminished, not truly; it just became easier to hide.

"I'll help." Joshua jumped up, obviously sensing an escape. Gangly and full of youthful energy, he brought much-needed life back to Rhuddin Hall. And, like Luc, he had wolf blood running through his veins. The woods that surrounded their territory flourished with the song of spring, a powerful temptress that beckoned their inner beasts to play. Joshua toppled an antique side table in a hasty retreat to the door. "Er . . . sorry 'bout that," he said sheepishly, righting the furniture before tromping next to his uncle. "I can come, right?"

Luc bit back a smile. "Of course."

Taliesin stretched out his legs before him without standing. His wardrobe looked much like Joshua's, his age hardly much older. He sported ripped jeans, a faded T-shirt, and worn-out sneakers. His fair hair hung to his shoulders, cleaned and combed, because Sophie had requested it. He was more than two thousand years old and could afford a country if it suited him to buy one.

Taliesin was also a Seer, a curse from the goddess Ceridwen, his mother by birth but not much else. Poor bastard had been raised by the *Gwarchodwyr Unfed*, the Original Guardians, also blessed by the goddess to transform into wolves to protect her son. Over the years, Ceridwen's gift had been used for darkness, cruelty and prejudice against humans and weaker members of their race, and therefore, like all misused gifts, dwindled with each passing generation.

It was no wonder that the man was touched in the head. He knew things, and usually not good things. It was a harsh burden to bear, and one that never boded well for the families that housed him. Worse, it was obvious that he had a soft spot for Sophie, like an orphan who had found motherly kindness after centuries of abandonment.

Luc understood the appeal more than most. All the same, he felt for his brother.

With disdain in his tone, as if he'd known his history had been under retrospection and didn't care for it, Taliesin said, "I wouldn't bother preparing the lake house."

That made Luc pause. "Why not? Have you changed your mind about staying?"

"Oh, no, I'm staying. Just not at the lake house." Eyes that belonged on a woman, the color of the sky before twilight, glazed over with what Luc could only assume indicated a premonition. The haze cleared. Taliesin shrugged absently. "You're about to have a visitor."

A chill skittered across the back of his neck, sensing danger in what *wasn't* said. "What kind of visitor?"

By the look on Taliesin's face, very few had the balls to ask about his premonitions, but it would be stupid, and a damn shame, not to use his Sight to their advantage.

After all, if the man was going to stay, he might as well be of some use.

"You'll see." His expression became guarded, then aloof; two protective shields that didn't denote great tidings.

"Are we in danger?" Sophie asked.

Taliesin's features softened to her concern. "No." Then he amended, "Not at this time."

Dylan demanded, "Then who—"

"You know how this works," Taliesin warned, turning stoic. "I can't tell you any more without risking repercussions. I'm not allowed to hinder free will and personal choices. When I do, it never works out well for those around me."

Luc winced for his brother, considering the two people that Taliesin hovered around most were Sophie and Joshua. "That sucks," he said, using one of his nephew's modern phrases.

"You think?" Dylan strode over to Joshua and placed a hand on his son's shoulder. "Stay here while your uncle goes to take a look."

Luc met his brother's narrowed glare, always black, like their Roman father. Or so he'd been told, never having known the man who'd died before his birth. Dylan had assumed their father's role, and Luc would honor him with his own life if necessary for doing so. Acting as second-in-command of their territory was a responsibility that he accepted without question.

Regardless of the fact that it wasn't a position he wanted; Luc kept that opinion to himself. Still, it was becoming increasingly difficult for him to follow orders—even ones given by the man who'd raised him.

As an alpha, Luc was meant to lead his own territory.

And his beast had begun to demand control in physical ways. He had managed, so far, to contain the attacks internally, but . . . *bloody hell* they hurt like a bastard, and he could tolerate a fair amount of pain. His insides were continually shredded, literally and without respite, and the struggle had grown tiresome.

He wanted his own territory, but leaving his family during this dangerous time stunk like a betrayal. He'd rather tolerate the silent torment of submission than that particular stench.

"I'll go warn the others." Luc took the side exit closest to the inner courtyard, and then made his way to the main gatehouse. His scabbard and sword chafed his thigh as he walked. Over the last century there had been no need to carry weapons on his person, but those days of peace had brutally ended less than a week ago—when the Guardians had come for his sister and left a trail of death in their wake.

A mental image of the carnage fully awakened Luc's inner wolf, primed and ready for retribution. Not that his wolf ever withdrew far below the surface of his humanity. He tightened his belt and forced his beast to recede, gritting his teeth against the discomfort that action caused, as though twenty keen blades slashed him from the inside out, tearing sinew from bone to free his more dominant half.

If he coughed, there would be blood.

Annoyed by the distraction, he paused and inhaled deeply. Letting his breath out slowly, he willed his muscles to ease. It was almost noon; the sun rode high above the peaks of their mountains, nurturing and warming the newly budded plants and rows of kitchen garden beds. Every shade of green blended in the forest beyond, deep like the furs, and pale with recent growth that would darken each day toward summer.

Nature thrived in untainted glory, a treasure in these modern times of overbuilt cities and depleted resources. It was a treasure their enemies would soon demand control of, now that they were aware.

I will die fighting before I let that happen. His vow satisfied his beast into submission.

Moving forward, he tapped the rungs of the wrought iron gate as he passed to the outer door, giving the guards due warning of his approach. They were jumpy and there was no need to test their responses. Too many false alarms muddled reactions when true danger arrived.

Sarah and Teyrnon, his newly appointed second- and third-in-command, had been assigned to the area directly around Sophie and Joshua. They stood as Luc entered the small building that allowed or refused visitors to the inner courtyard. Not surprising, there was an edge to their stances and darkness in their gazes. They were clearly troubled with what had transpired less than a week ago in their woods.

Reading their apprehension, Luc shared, "Taliesin informs us we are about to have a visitor."

Sarah began to pace inside the small room. Tall and lithe like all shifters, she had the bright red hair of a Celt, shorn above her shoulders for efficiency. She wore studded leather pants, zippered up on both sides for easy removal before a shift. A scabbard hung from her waist, her hands flexing by her sides, ready. To accommodate her build, her sword was longer than Luc's, thinner and lighter, but she wielded it with deadly competence if needed.

Luc would know. He had trained her to use it.

"Should we sound the alarm?" she asked.

"Not yet," he said. "Warn the other guards but not the villagers."

Their main alarm didn't consist of modern technology,

but rang from the steeple of their local church and meeting hall, where many residents of Rhuddin Village gathered and worshiped. Peaceful faiths were allowed without persecution, a reflection of these modern times, the diversity of their human lineage, and the Constitution of their new country.

They had lived too long in complacency, under the protection of his brother, a strong but fair leader. They had forgotten the cruelty of the Guardians who revered the old ways with self-serving fervor.

Recent events had, however, reminded them.

"Our people are weary," Luc added. "Let's not cause unnecessary fear when Taliesin didn't seem overly concerned. Let's see who it is before we sound a full alarm."

No sooner had he spoken than a gray truck slowed and pulled up to the gate. The female driver turned off the ignition and held up her hands. The gesture was either naïve, desperate—or incredibly bold; his instincts warned that it may be a combination of all three.

Teyrnon growled low under his breath. "That's Rosa Alban. Does the woman think she can just enter our territory without an invitation?"

"We've been expecting her," Luc reminded both guards, a warning not to act without due cause. He and Dylan had discussed in great detail what this woman's motivations might have been for freeing Sophie from Math's dungeon. "It seems she's come to collect her reward sooner rather than later."

"Well, Dylan *did* execute her husband," Sarah pointed out. "*In* her home, I might add."

A snide chuckle fell from Teyrnon's mouth. "Wish I'd been there."

"The Guardians must have swarmed her afterward. I can't imagine . . ." Sarah's somber tone suggested that she could, and did, vividly imagine what Math's wife had endured in the aftermath of her husband's death. "I wonder how she managed to get away."

Teyrnon glared at Sarah, his gaze heavy with censure. He had the rugged build of his Norse father, with tawny hair and a perpetual scowl. "What makes you think she's here without their knowledge?"

The female guard didn't cower. "Because when she helped Sophie escape, she also provided information on secret passages into Castell Avon, information that our leader used to our advantage. Why would she do that unless she's trying to break away?"

Luc let their banter play out, interested in both viewpoints. The two guards paired well together, voicing sound yet opposing arguments. Diverse perspectives were necessary to win battles, and Luc had little doubt that Rosa's arrival heralded a conflict of some sort in their near future, if not an outright declaration of war against the Guardians.

Either way, he was prepared.

Teyrnon widened his stance, turned his head to spit. "Obviously she'd grown tired of being tupped by a rancid husband."

"I'm sure she has others wanting that role." Sarah shook her head. "No, something's off here. It's not typical behavior. Guardians take. They demand. They don't send their precious pure-blooded and unmated females into enemy territory filled with half-human males. I think she's here for our help."

"Don't make assumptions," Teyrnon growled. "They're batshit crazy. You can't rationalize their motives. If you try, it'll get you killed. Guardians have no conscience, especially the ones with tits."

On that note, Luc decided to intervene. "We'll assume the worst until Rosa Alban proves otherwise, but we won't be cruel. That is their way, not ours."

Teyrnon looked away at the reprimand, a slight tic at his jawline the only indication of his ire. Luc allowed him a moment to calm his wolf, aware the Norseman's negative viewpoint toward female Guardians was well-founded.

His homestead had been destroyed by the Guardians in

the late 1600s. For daring to live outside their rules, they had burned his fields and slaughtered his animals. Briallen, a Guardian's wife, had been involved. Her name was common knowledge but not what she'd done to earn the full weight of Teyrnon's hatred. Luc assumed, as did others, that more than a farm had been ruined that day, but only a drunkard or an idiot would venture to ask the full story.

Because on a good day, Teyrnon was an ass. On a bad day, well . . . most knew to keep a wide berth. He had lived in Rhuddin Village for more than a century now, after offering his services in return for being among others of their kind who opposed the Guardians.

Luc had yet to regret granting his request. Regardless of his habitual pissed-off attitude, or mayhap because of it, Teyrnon was a shrewd and loyal guard.

Lifting the iron latch, Luc slid the gate open just enough to walk through. "Sarah, stay with me as my second. Teyrnon, go warn Dylan of our guest, and then the other guards. Check the north and south entrances of our territory first. Rosa's arrival may be a decoy."

The Norseman gave a sharp nod. "Understood."

After the guard had gone, Luc motioned with his hand for Rosa to step out of the truck, while keeping the other on his scabbard that hung from his waist. She complied slowly, but he sensed her cautious approach was for his benefit and not out of fear on her part.

"I am unarmed," Rosa announced. Her voice was formal but pleasant, like the sound of a soft Victorian wind. And if he were to be completely honest, so too was the rest of her. This held no importance to him, simply an observation, because oftentimes the vilest of creatures hid under a shell of beauty.

"Then you are stupid, Rosa Alban," Luc said. "Remove your coat."

"Just call me Rosa." She shrugged out of her wool jacket,

folded it neatly and placed it on the hood of her truck. "And I would only be stupid if death frightens me . . . which it does not. You are free to search."

Her hair was the color of golden wine, pulled back into a long plait. She wore snug-fitting black trousers underneath, common boots and a plain green sweater that hung loose to midthigh. Her boots were the only items that appeared purchased rather than handmade.

"Lift your arms," Luc ordered.

She observed him with unblinking regard—*not* an act of submission, even though she lifted her arms above her head as instructed.

"You are Luc Black, are you not?" she asked with a curious tilt to her head. "Dylan's brother."

Her eyes were a notable color of blue edged with purple that bled to burgundy, reminding him of Elen's garden in bloom, beautiful in nature but peculiar on a woman. The burgundy, he suspected, was a good sign her wolf was close to the surface, rising, as any of their beasts would, in enemy territory.

"My brother has been expecting you." Luc chose not to deny her accurate assumption, but grinned instead, aware of the stories that must have reached her ears about him. "We have a few questions."

He patted her down. A faint hint of vanilla clung to her skin that he didn't find unpleasant. Most Guardians had a stench about them, like corpses with trapped souls, fetid and unholy. He didn't sense that from her, which was an intriguing discovery. If memory served, her parents had been the last mated Guardians to produce a pure-blooded female heir. She was a rare and precious commodity indeed, and one who should have succumbed to the darkness that surrounded her.

More interesting, he discovered nothing other than soft curves and a lush give of extra flesh beneath her clothing, a telltale sign that Math's widow didn't run often. Shifting produced a higher metabolism that left little fat to be stored, no matter what form one assumed, wolf or human.

As Luc stepped back, he wondered at that oddity. Being the youngest female shifter of their kind, she should have flaunted her wolf, but had contained it instead.

Her control, he realized then, must be great. And a wolf with that much control was more dangerous than most. He knew, because it had taken centuries to learn how to suppress his own; it was a constant struggle that never relinquished. And this woman was what? Three hundred years or so?

A baby to their kind.

Though, he had to admit, she did not look like a baby, but rather a woman who had seen too much brutality in her lifetime. A beauty who exuded power and sensuality, despite her demure guise.

She gave a small nod to Sarah, an acknowledgment of respect that surprised Luc, who didn't much care for surprises.

"I'm sure you have many questions," Rosa said. "And I'll answer them as soon as you take me to Dylan."

Luc felt his spine tighten at the insult, quickly followed by a shaft of pain that ripped through his rib cage. Outwardly, he remained stoic, hiding the inner tantrum of his darker half.

She had asked for his brother because Dylan was the leader of the Katahdin territory; he was also the person she had keenly manipulated into owing her, at the very least, an audience.

Still, it chafed his wolf, who wanted to decide Rosa's course in its domain. Two dominants in one territory had always been a challenge. Despite the fact that he was younger, Luc was just as powerful as his brother.

More so, actually, though he kept that secret well hidden. Having been raised by Dylan, he had learned loyalty before dominance. Honor—Dylan's, not his—had made that possible.

And yet, this woman had managed to trigger his baser instincts. And over a perfectly logical request, blatant proof that his control was slipping down a dangerous path.

Harsher than intended, he growled, "Follow me."

Three

Taking note of her surroundings, Rosa trailed Luc down a long corridor toward voices, both male and female. The exterior design of Rhuddin Hall resembled a meld of castle and some of America's earlier defensive forts, with four well-placed turrets surrounded by a catwalk.

Whereas the interior reminded her of a real home, or what little she'd seen of real homes, and even those examples were mostly from books and magazines she kept hidden within her secret cabin.

Wooden floors gleamed with frequent waxes, and cream-colored paint brightened the interior walls, while an assortment of overstuffed furniture invited comfort. It wasn't a proclamation of wealth, but rather a place for gathering, a place for family and pack.

The scent of something divine wafted from the kitchens to tease her empty stomach; it decided at that moment to grumble, to her utter embarrassment.

Luc turned to stare. His eyes were pale gray ringed with black, an eerie likeness to liquid mercury, poisonous and yet strangely compelling. "When was the last time you've eaten?"

If she wasn't mistaken, his question held a note of concern. How strange?

Oddly flustered under the full weight of his gaze, she said, "I'm fine." Although she hadn't eaten since the night before, which was also unusual for her; food was her only enjoyment in this life and she rarely denied herself its comfort.

To be honest, as she often tried to be with self-reflection, Rosa admitted that she felt unsteady in his company. Not frightened—*that* would have been a more normal response—just off balance.

Conceivably, it might have something to do with the fact that his touch hadn't bothered her. She chewed her bottom lip while contemplating that anomaly. His hands had run down the length of her sides, under her sweater and over her stomach, then up her inner thighs, efficiently—and without lingering.

Another oddity, at least for her.

And she couldn't help but acknowledge that perhaps his exploration had been *too* indifferent, when, for the first time, she had almost enjoyed the sensation.

More disturbing, she sensed his wolf. She *felt* it, as if his beast lingered just under the surface of his humanity.

Keeping a few paces between them, she stared at the wide expanse of his back and actually shivered. If Luc was as primed in wolf form as he was in human, then he must be something magnificent to behold.

Her own inner wolf rubbed along her spine in complete agreement with that assessment. The reaction surprised her. Her step even faltered until she righted herself, hoping he hadn't noticed.

What was wrong with her?

She should be afraid.

She should be, at the very least, detached, as she planned to negotiate the future protection of her people. Instead, she wondered what it would be like to run with him, to let their wolves free and just run . . .

Shaking her head, Rosa redirected her thoughts to a more useful purpose. She considered what little she knew of Luc, quite certain that some of her information was untrue given the source.

Math had called this man the Beast of Merin on more than one occasion, a moniker coined by the Guardians upon Luc's birth. Having been born in wolf form to an Original Guardian, Luc was the youngest son of Merin, one of the more influential, and frightening, members of the Council.

Stories were told by kitchen fires about the Beast, in whispers from the *Hen Was* reminiscing about their homeland. Merin had attempted to kill her son upon his birth, sensing weakness like a predator who suffocates their runts. Cady, Luc's aunt and Merin's sister, had attended the birthing bed and saved the infant cub.

According to the stories, and they were too consistent not to hold some truth, Luc had been raised by his older brother in the camps of the outcasts, rebels of their kind who had hid in the forests to protect their families from Guardian cruelty. Much later, Dylan and his siblings had journeyed across an ocean to settle in a new land. Along with their sister, Elen, they had formed a new territory in the valley of mountains. More than a thousand years and they had stayed united.

A true family.

Rosa envied them, and that wasn't an emotion she allowed herself often, for envy only promoted self-doubt and weakness, two qualities she couldn't afford if she wanted to survive.

Nevertheless, she felt compelled to study Luc further.

He wore faded jeans with his sword, a modern and medieval contrast that would have made her smile if that peculiar tightening in her abdomen hadn't occurred. His black T-shirt hugged his back, doing little to hide the mass of muscle that rippled underneath as he moved. Where the cotton ended, black tattoos continued to cover his neck and arms; the pattern resembled wings of some sort. An animal, maybe? Or an angel?

Not many shifters sported tattoos, since the ink expelled from their skin during the change—unless they were skilled. If not, they had to reapply it each time.

Luc, she sensed, was one of the skilled.

His hair was kohl black, as if absent of light, and tied at his nape by a strip of leather. The thick tail reached below his shoulders. According to records, his father had been human, of Roman and Egyptian descent, a warrior during the Roman occupation of Britain around AD 300. He must favor his father, because Merin was pure Celt, blond and pale like many of their kind.

Luc halted under an arched doorway. "Rosa Alban," he announced, holding out his arm for her to enter the room, while he remained at her back.

It took some effort for her not to balk, recognizing the effective trap. "Just call me Rosa," she reminded him.

His brow creased in response. "Your surname displeases you?"

"It represents my marriage to Math," she said. "I despise it more than you'll ever know."

His expression wavered. She might have thought her proclamation had softened him somewhat. However, now that she'd met him in person, *soft* wasn't a quality she would associate with the Beast of Merin. Stern, perhaps. Alert. Powerful, to be sure. Lonely too. She didn't know why she sensed the latter, yet she did; she had lived with loneliness long enough to know when another bore its weight.

But definitely not soft.

Granted, his gaze did seem less harsh. Though only a little, since he continued to regard her like a predator would its prey, as food and not anything that might hint of more pleasurable intents.

She knew the difference.

His left hand rested on his sword. "You are safe," he said in contrast to his stance. "Unless you threaten us first."

"I've no intentions of threatening you. Regardless of what you may think, I'm not an idiot." She gained a certain amount of satisfaction voicing her true opinion in open company. "Besides, I've not been safe since the day the Guardians executed my parents. And I doubt I ever will be again, so save your comforting words because they are lies."

MISFORTUNE HAD NO LIMITS, AS FAR AS LUC WAS CONcerned, and he was reminded that even Rosa had felt its ragged teeth on more than one occasion. Hardly surprising, having been married to Math her entire adult life from the age of sixteen. A sudden repulsive image invaded his thoughts, of Rosa on her wedding night to a Guardian.

Apart from the fact that Math had been too old for a union with a mere girl, he'd had a disturbed mind to match his withered body. Math had been an elder when he'd been granted the ability to transform into a wolf. Two thousand years hadn't helped his cause. Even Original Guardians aged, although much more slowly than humans.

It was also rumored that Math had preferred the company of men. While Luc didn't give two shits about the sexual preferences of willing adults, binding a young woman to a hopeless union was unfortunate, especially if it had followed the recent death of her family.

He shook the thought from his head, apprehensive that Rosa had made him feel sympathy toward her, a dangerous skill of any enemy.

Focusing on his primary concern, he took a quick assessment of the great hall. Taliesin, Sophie, and Dylan remained, but Joshua had been removed and replaced by Porter, the head of security within Rhuddin Hall. His position blocked the opposite door that led to the kitchens. All perimeters were guarded and prepared against one average-sized woman with eyes the color of flowers.

Porter stood with his legs braced apart and arms resting by his sides, a deadly stance for those who knew him. A former Jacobite, he kept his head shaved bald to expose a tattoo of a Celtic cross that covered his bare cranium.

Rosa scanned the occupants of the room without comment until she found Taliesin lounging in the corner. *"You!"* she exclaimed, losing much of her reserved posture to what could only be construed as unmitigated anger.

Luc's eyebrows rose in surprise.

"What are *you* doing here?" Rosa's hands clenched by her sides. "They said you had resurfaced but I didn't believe them."

"Sin is our friend and guest," Sophie answered for Taliesin. She stood and walked toward her husband. "We have been expecting you, Rosa."

Dylan put his arm around his wife and hugged her close to his side. "Before I ask what your demands are for helping my wife, I must thank you for what you did. I'm in your debt. My concern, as I'm sure you're well aware, is what you want in return. If it's achievable without bringing danger to my family, or to the people I protect within my territory, I'll honor it."

Rosa made a valiant effort to calm herself, but her eyes, now pure burgundy, continued to sneak glances in Taliesin's direction. Her shoulders lifted as she took a deep breath and let it out. "I want to join your alliance against the Guardians."

"Ah," Dylan said. "And that raises a second question . . . Who informed you about our alliance?"

Luc gritted his teeth to remain silent, and the submissive act didn't go unpunished. He tasted copper at the back of his throat and swallowed the blood-soaked bile. Though Rosa may not realize it yet, for Dylan to admit to the existence of their alliance revealed his intentions to grant her request.

Rosa nodded slightly, as if she'd been expecting the question. "I'm sorry but that information was given to me by someone who knows my loyalties are not with the Guardians, and who also knows that I can be trusted. I will not break their confidence."

Porter let out a crude snort, crossing his arms in front of his chest. "You'd best be remembering where you are and be telling us what we're wanting to know."

"Rosa won't break her word," Taliesin said with a wave of impatience. "I'll give you the information you want. Drystan told her of the gathering. They are"—he paused, searching for an appropriate description—"friends. Drystan would entertain a more intimate relationship, as Rosa is well aware and uses to her advantage."

Luc filed that information away for future consideration. Drystan was the leader of the Blue Ridge Highland territory of Virginia. He had recently joined their alliance against the Guardians, and had conveniently failed to mention his "friendship" with their enemy's wife.

Rosa glared at Taliesin, her lip turned in a sneer. "You are such an asshole."

A bark of laughter erupted from Dylan. Even Luc was hard-pressed to contain a grin, unsure whether it was her disregard for Taliesin that amused him, or hearing the crude word expressed with such proper cadence.

She ignored their amusement. "Drystan and I are allies, no more. And I don't want"—she glared at Taliesin—"*him* here for this. Please make him go away."

"Believe me," Dylan muttered, "I would if I could."

Sighing at her husband's comment before turning to Taliesin, Sophie said, "For some reason, Rosa doesn't like you. I think we need to know why."

Porter added, "The lady does seem to have a righteous bee up her arse where you're concerned."

"I'm *not* righteous," Rosa interrupted. "Nor have I ever been a lady." Her chin rose in haughty defiance, the very action refuting her claim. "My parents were common black-smiths before they were executed for wanting a peaceful life away from the Guardians."

"No," Taliesin corrected, his voice unnervingly calm, "your parents were executed for hiding you. And they were hardly common, considering I still carry one of your mother's swords."

Her narrowed gaze raked him with hatred. "My parents trusted you. And you did nothing to help them. *Nothing*. You waited until their execution was over before coming to our aid."

"You survived." Taliesin earned a disapproving frown from Sophie for the insensitive comment.

Rosa winced as if slapped. "Only because my father forced me into our hidden room. He locked me in, as you must have known, and I couldn't get out when I heard . . ." Her voice trailed off. After a moment, her shoulders rose and fell on a breath as she gathered her composure. "But you found me." The words flowed now, cool and controlled, and therefore more unsettling. "Oh, yes, the all-knowing Taliesin found me where the Guardians hadn't. I thought you had come to help." Rosa regarded him with such disgust that even Luc felt some pity for the man. "How had I ever been so naïve? Instead of helping, you delivered me to my aunt. You knew what Aunt Neira had planned for me. I was sixteen years old . . . and you knew."

Taliesin said quietly, "If I had intervened, you would have died along with your parents. And you have a greater purpose to fulfill."

"Right," Rosa sneered, "to be a feast for eight forsaken warriors. Believe me, I've not forgotten. The Council refuses to let me."

The acrid stench of fear permeated the air, like acid on flesh.

Luc shifted his stance. Her distress disturbed him, as did the image of a sixteen-year-old girl locked in a room while she heard the murder of her parents. Taliesin's lack of denial was as damning as his attitude, leaving little doubt that Rosa's tale was more accurate than he cared to admit.

Regardless, what concerned Luc most was her last comment, because it was the one that had produced real anxiety and not just distress from a memory. Remaining silent was no longer an option. He stepped between Rosa and Taliesin, blocking her view in order to gain her full attention.

Dylan shot him a questioning glare that Luc ignored. In response, a snarl of pleasure whispered down his spine.

His beast was pleased that he'd undermined his brother's authority.

"Rosa . . ." Luc paused, not for lack of words but because the absence of pain left him momentarily disorientated, as did those otherworldly eyes when they met his. "What are you referring to? A feast for eight forsaken warriors? What does that mean?" Although he had a good suspicion, he preferred to hear her explanation. "And how is the Council involved?"

Porter grunted. "Any mention of the bloody Council of Ceridwen makes my arse itch. Thank the good Lord there's only ten of them left."

Luc couldn't agree more, even if Merin was one of them. There had been forty-eight Original Guardians in the beginning. Regrettably, the ten that remained formed the Council of Ceridwen, a self-appointed governing body whose main mission was to maintain the purity of their race, and therefore their power to shift. They believed one related to the other.

It was all bullshit, of course, born of desperation and arrogance.

"Nine," Rosa said quietly.

Luc frowned. "Excuse me?"

"Nine," she repeated. "There are only nine Council members left." When rapt interest greeted her, she shared, "Modlen was executed last summer for drawing attention to our kind in the human world. The Council is well aware of how much our numbers have dwindled. They believe exposure is our greatest threat."

Luc couldn't help but interject. "Even greater than the mixed-blood rebels who have scattered across the globe and continue to mate with humans?"

A hint of a smile turned her lip. She had a full mouth, he noted, when not pinched in displeasure. "Well, as you know, they don't much like that either. But, yes, they fear exposure more."

"What did she do?" Luc asked, curious to see how much information about the Council Rosa was willing to share.

"She modeled for a photographer named G. B. Smith." She shook her head. "He was human."

"Was?"

"They killed him too, of course."

"Of course." Luc found this odd banter disconcerting, or possibly it was just his growing awareness of her that made him uncomfortable, as well as her easy acceptance of death. But that had been her life, had it not?

"He had already uploaded the photos to the Internet," she continued. "I've been told they are very popular. I've never seen them myself. I'm not allowed access to modern technology. The Council is still livid about the betrayal."

Luc looked to Taliesin for confirmation. "Is this true?"

"Modlen was always a vain creature," Taliesin explained in a derisive tone. "The photos are spectacular. If you haven't seen them, you should take a look. Not worth losing her head over, but—"

"If you are going to live with us," Dylan interrupted, his voice too calm, a telltale sign to those who knew him that his patience had ended, "this is the type of information that you need to share."

"Why?" Shaking his head as if confused, Taliesin pointed out, "I knew Rosa was going to."

Having his suspicions proven, Luc veered the conversation

back to his original question. "Warriors' feast? What does that mean, Rosa?"

Dylan pinched the bridge of his nose as if his head had begun to ache. "I don't know, but it sounds like one of Taliesin's drunken prophecies."

In a sheepish tone, Taliesin confessed, "I may have overly indulged at Rosa and Math's wedding feast."

"Aw, hell," Porter groaned, his black brows narrowed over sharp blue eyes. "I'm thinking we might not want to hear this. They be the ones that usually come true."

"I sincerely hope not," Rosa said. "He was so intoxicated that it took four servants to carry him from the room and put him to bed."

"It was the only way I could get through the atrocious thing," Taliesin mumbled.

Tension along his spine warned that he wasn't going to like the answer, but Luc asked anyway, "What is the prophecy?"

"Basically, in one month, under summer's first moon, the Council is planning to re-create a fertility ritual because of *his* asinine prediction." Rosa tilted her head toward Taliesin as if the occupants of the room hadn't already known whom she blamed for her current situation. "A ritual with eight unmated Guardians and the last unmated—and pure-blooded—female shifter." She smiled and it wasn't a pleasant smile. "That would be me."

Four

This union, I shall not revile, for their fear I know,
their affliction, and their gift.

ROSA FELT LIKE A JESTER AT A FEAST, ONE WHERE HER
act amused the audience not with cleverness but rather with
a lack thereof. Disgust permeated the room like fog over
snow, cold and bone-deep.

Luc's displeasure was the most noticeable, probably
because he stood the closest. Worse, she also sensed his pity.

She looked to the exits for an escape but found none. She
tried to control her rising panic, even as her wolf unfurled
under her skin, demanding release.

Yanking at the neckline of her sweater, she said, "I need
to get some fresh air."

Ignoring her request, Luc asked, "Have you voiced your
refusal to participate? The ceremony will fail if you're
unwilling."

His logic might be amusing, if she wasn't the subject
under debate. He must practice the old ways of the just Gods,
where kindness was returned with favors, cruelty with punishment, and sexuality was valued only if consensual.

That had never been her experience.

"You obviously haven't had much interaction with the Council," she said. Had life among the Guardians made her too cynical? Perhaps. But her disdain had kept her alive, for the moment, and that could always change. "I've learned to keep my opinions to myself, but on this matter I failed. The Guardians believe my reluctance is selfish. They are good at twisting our ways to suit their ambitions, and then wonder why our race is dying and we live in darkness."

Luc appeared calm but there was a stiffness to his stance that suggested otherwise. "Who has volunteered to participate in a ritual that is against your will?" Anger leeched from his voice.

She took a quick assessment of the room. Judging by the collection of similar expressions, they were all of the same mind-set—which only strengthened her resolve to join their alliance.

"Why does it matter?" she asked.

"If you don't want to discuss who the Guardians are—"

"I don't know who they all are," she lied. "I suspect William, Edwyn, and Rhys, because they've made references." And Pendaran, the head of the Council and the Guardian who concerned her most, but offering his name might not help her cause with these rebels.

"What do they hope to gain?"

She laughed bitterly. "Me." Glaring at Taliesin, she dared him to refute her claim. "More important, an heir with a pure bloodline." The fact that they thought this child would be the next *Beddestyr* need not be mentioned at this time.

There were only four *Beddestyr* left, the Walkers who'd once been able to travel to the Otherworld, a place of magical creatures, pixies, giants, and all things Fae, and of restorative gifts for their kind. This place was a legend of Celtic lore, as far as Rosa was concerned, for she had never seen a sign of its existence in her lifetime, or of the creatures who dwell within.

Although, Math had been convinced that Sophie's pet hound had come from the Otherworld. It was an intimidating animal, to be sure, but not unexplainable to *this* world— and thankfully absent from the room at present.

And what remained of the former *Beddestyr* could not be called magical by any sense of the word, or restorative; they lived in death. They were shells of a former existence in a coma-like state.

As their keeper, she would know.

Allowing a child to be conceived to follow their fate was not on her agenda.

She would even barter with men who obviously despised her to prevent it. "I know that you have little reason to trust my motives. I don't share the Guardians' beliefs. I've seen many of our kind needlessly suffer under their authority. This is my only chance to gain control of my territory, but I cannot do it alone. I have two allies within Avon who can shift. The rest are—"

"Slaves," Dylan supplied. "I was in your castle. I saw who resides there."

"Yes." She did not deny the reality of her home, hoping to support her cause. "The *Hen Was* have enough of our blood in their veins to exist alongside us throughout the ages, but without the ability to shift and heal. They are tormented shadows of a forsaken race, hunted if they try to escape, and punished if they don't obey. I'm here to help the ones who have served me, the ones who are my friends. This is our only chance."

Luc leaned forward, close enough that she could smell his scent, clean like moss in a healthy forest, and rich with the power of his wolf. "You would champion them?" he asked, not concealing his doubt.

"I wouldn't be here otherwise," Rosa assured him. "I've already offered them freedom but they have refused. They don't wish to run. Nor do they wish to live separate from our kind. So I'll give them safety instead. Or," she amended, "I'll at least try."

"Why?" Luc had the audacity to sound confused.

But then, why wouldn't he? She was the widow of his enemy, after all. Humility, she suspected, may be a better persuader—and a good dose of honesty might not hurt either.

Sadly, she wasn't good at either virtue, but she could try.

"Because they have protected me from my husband where all others have failed." She met the gaze of every person in the room, beseeching them for help. All but Taliesin, who had ignored her pleas once before. Why would this time be any different? "They have taken beatings meant for me. They have fed me when Math ordered me to starve. They have offered their bodies in place of mine. They have given me love and loyalty and I can do naught but offer them the same in return."

Not one person responded, except for a few exchanged glances. Had the importance of her mission finally registered? Or were they contemplating the obvious advantage of retaining control of the territory that directly bordered theirs? "Nor do I wish to be a breeder for another Guardian."

The bald man with remnants of an Irish lilt spoke first, an indication of his respected status in Dylan's territory. "And if we choose not to help you?"

"Then I will fight alone." Rosa would rather die in battle than submit to the demands of the Guardians one day longer. Moreover, walking off her island this morning had guaranteed her impending punishment when they discovered her betrayal.

She had no other choice but to fight.

"If Drystan lived closer," she continued, "I would have made him this same offer, but Math's death has accelerated my plans. I've little chance of success without your help. Either my aunt Neira or William will retain control of Castell Avon, as both have already petitioned the Council on this regard . . . despite certain steps I've taken to discourage them."

A low growl came from Luc. "That can't happen."

The sound sent a secret thrill skittering across her skin. Her wolf *liked* that his beast had demanded a voice, and that he understood the threat that her losing would bring upon them. "It can and it will if you don't help me. There are three Guardians in residence at the moment, and sixteen of Math's guards who are loyal to the Council. I'm supposed to return with them to Wales for Math's burial tomorrow morning. It would not take much to force them out, but it's the judgment of the Council that I fear. When they send more Guardians, and they *will* send more, I need to have reinforcements by my side."

Sophie looked to her husband as she asked, "Has anyone ever taken control of a Guardian's territory?"

"Not successfully," Dylan confirmed. "There have been a few who have tried. For the most part, we've defended our own lands. We've defended our own people when threatened, but we've never gone after them."

Rosa pointed out, "You came into my home and executed Math."

"I did," Dylan admitted without reservation. "But only after his men, under his orders, brought death into my home. Had I not retaliated, it would have been viewed as weak. The Council would have immediately demanded control of my territory. I will not allow my people to live, or die, under their sadistic leadership."

"Then our goals are the same," Rosa argued. "We are allies, whether you wish us to be or not. And," she added for leverage, "you owe me."

Dylan gave a sharp nod. "As I'm well aware." He ran a hand through his hair, the gesture filled with angst as he looked down at his wife. "If we help her," he explained. "If we do what she's asking of us, if we openly take control of a Guardian stronghold—it will begin a war."

A mangled sound came from Luc. "A war has already

begun, brother." His voice was oddly low, as if he struggled to contain his patience, or something more menacing. "We can no longer hide in the woods and expect them to leave us alone. They have felt our power."

"Luc's right," Sophie said to Dylan. "If you're hesitating because of me . . . please don't. Rosa freed me from that place. We must help her now."

Another voice filtered into the conversation, cleverly unobtrusive, and yet managing to attract full attention. "There's another way," Taliesin said, coaxing a room filled with uncertainty to turn in his direction.

Like a perverted ray of sunlight in a charred forest, Rosa thought, promising warmth and growth while all she offered was destruction. Except she didn't trust this light, having followed it once before only to learn that some secrets were better served on burnt toast. "There is no other way."

"There's always another way." A smug smile spread across his too-pretty face. "And from what I can foresee . . . this one could work in your favor."

"Please," Rosa seethed. "Spare me your foresights."

"One day you'll learn that I'm not your enemy." Taliesin paused as if waiting for a response, then sighed when none was given. "Prophecies can change, Rosa, and yours has never been entirely clear to me."

"And why would that be, I wonder. Has your penchant for wine finally pickled your brain?"

Her mockery earned her a sneer. "I find vodka far more effective toward achieving that goal, but I have not partaken in that luxury for many years. I must admit that I am feeling the urge now." Taliesin shook his head in self-disgust. He swore under his breath. And then again, only louder. "Fuck me to hell and back . . . but when I'm around you I talk like a Victorian sot and feel like an ass."

Rosa shrugged. "Maybe that is because you are one."

"And maybe you should've snuck out of your castle more

often, Rosabea, and joined the modern world. It may have opened your eyes to another perspective."

"You are not my family, or my friend, and have not"—she paused to combine the word—"*haven't* earned the right to call me by that name." Current dialects felt foreign, because she *had* lived in forced isolation, and in part because of *him*. But sometimes, when no one was around to listen or make fun, she had practiced. It was becoming more natural to combine words—but occasionally she reverted back to her learned way of speaking, especially when agitated.

"Enough!" Dylan interceded, giving Taliesin a pointed glare. "You were about to say something, useful I hope, before you'd begun to antagonize our guest."

Taliesin smirked. "She started it."

"Just tell us your idea," Dylan said with a mixture of weariness and censure, "before I regret asking."

"A contract."

"What sort of contract?"

"A *marriage* contract."

Rosa fisted her hands until her nails dug into her palms. She'd sensed victory until *his* interruption. Unfortunately, she'd been coveted for far too long *not* to assume this notion might surface, as Gareth had alluded to earlier.

She wanted to avoid adding herself as an option to these negotiations. But if given no other choice, she would be forced to consider it.

Hoping she sounded indifferent, or at the very least bored, she let out an exaggerated sigh. "I've no interest in entering a second unwanted marriage."

Unless the terms are to my advantage.

Sophie frowned. "From my experience with the Guardians, I doubt they'd respect a marriage contract anyway."

"They might," Dylan said, sounding too interested for Rosa's comfort. "It's one of the oldest institutions and bartering tools of our kind. There is a chance they'll go along with it. For a while, if Rosa chooses a potential mate the Council has no grounds to refute. At the very least, it may buy her some time."

"She has other bartering tools at her disposal to convince them her plan is in their best interest." When Taliesin spoke everyone listened, and all she could do was cringe at his not-so-subtle referral to the *Beddestyr*.

"You're the reason this is happening." Rosa lifted her hands and let them fall back to her sides, losing much of her anger to desperation. "You could change it all with just a word . . . if you went to the Guardians and recanted your prophecy."

"You'll not believe me when I say this, but my interference would only do you more harm than good." Taliesin's gaze held hers with a mixture of emotion, bluish-green like spring and dead like winter. "These events must stay in motion as they're meant to be."

She'd heard him give similar cryptic warnings in the past, enough to know not to push him further. "And Dylan gets control of my territory through marriage."

Through me.

"I'm already married," Dylan pointed out.

"And mated," Sophie added, earning a look of approval from her husband. "I'm learning that their marriages are equal."

"Forgive me," Rosa said, "but that's not been my experience."

Having met Math while chained in Castell Avon's dungeon, Sophie's expression softened with understanding, but then she ruined the effect by asking, "Is there anyone here who the Council would accept as Rosa's husband?"

The Irishman took a step forward. He had a stalky build, wide shouldered, and was undoubtedly lethal or he wouldn't hold a position in Dylan's household. Except Rosa suspected he was also human, or mostly so, having never come across his description or lineage in the Council's ledgers.

More obvious, he sported tattoos, but unlike Luc's, they

had faded with time and permanence on skin that never stretched and morphed between shifts.

Human or not, he must have some wolf under that inked skin of his to be drawn to her. She recognized the look in his eyes, having seen it countless times before. "Take another step toward me and I will . . ." She carried no weapons, none other than her own wolf, but it was enough if given free rein. "Take another step and I will bite you."

The man had the gall to chuckle. "Please tell me that's a promise. It's been a while since I've had me a good nippin'."

"I don't have time for this," Rosa said, but soon regretted her impatience.

His stance stiffened and his eyes lost their mirth. Apparently, he'd rather be bitten than slighted. Flirtations were as tedious as men's egos.

"Ease off, Porter," Luc warned.

Porter? Rosa thought. *How curiously discreet.* He'd disguised his features with ink and taken the name of his title. *Why?*

Porters were the protectors of homes, the heads of security where masters and alphas slept; a prestigious position. Gareth was her porter, once Math's, but his loyalty had always been hers.

Now she wondered at *this* porter's given name, and would wager her right pinky toe that it was in the Council's records. She might even have asked if his embarrassment hadn't turned to spite.

"I pity the poor bastard who'll be taking this one to their bed," Porter muttered under his breath. "I'm betting she'd be killing them while they slept."

"Were that the case," Rosa felt compelled to remind him and everyone else in the room, "Math would have been dead long before now." Still, amends were in order. "I didn't mean to cause offense. I've come here for your help and I'm running out of time. At this moment, the guards have become aware that I've not returned from my run. A search party will have been sent out. By morning, or sooner, the Guardians will begin to torture the *Hen Was* for information. Knowing my aunt Neira, she'll be anxious to begin, so I would like to be back in Avon before that happens."

A red flush crawled up Porter's neck and mottled the patterns on his skull. His eyes shone feverish blue, made more prominent by arching black brows. Those brows appeared to be the only unshaved hair on the man's body. Well, at least on his head; she wouldn't begin to presume what grew in his nether regions.

Without giving it much thought, she acknowledged that Porter was handsome, or would be to other women—as well as a few men. Cadan might even refer to him as *delicious*, her cousin's favorite endearment of late toward men he found attractive.

Porter gave a slow nod in her direction, which only served to reveal more of his cranium than she cared to see, but it was an apology of sorts, or at least an acknowledgment of poor behavior.

And for that, she was grateful; it made an inevitable surrender less distasteful. If she'd sensed even a hint of wolf under the Irishman's tattooed skin, she might have considered him further for her plan. No doubt he'd be more manageable than the one whom she intended to barter a piece of her freedom.

Having arrived at a decision, Rosa ran her hands over her face, refusing to look in Taliesin's direction when she fulfilled yet another one of his predictions. Regrettably, she wished she could do this alone, but wishes were for dreamers and her dreams had turned to nightmares a long time ago.

She was a realist. And these negotiations had gone on long enough. She needed to be in Avon, with reinforcements by her side, by any means necessary. Putting selfishness aside, she made an offer. "I would entertain an arrangement with Luc."

Silver eyes landed on her, not as pretty as Taliesin's, or Porter's for that matter, but far more unsettling. The weight of his gaze felt like a physical force. He gave little indication of his thoughts, other than a brief flash of surprise that also hinted of curiosity.

Tension filled the room, made worse by Luc's blatant assessment. In a few strides, he loomed above her. His hand reached out and lifted her chin. "You know who I am."

"Of course." Had they not already established routine introductions?

His grip remained firm while awaiting a better answer.

"I know what the Guardians call you, if that's what you want to hear." She felt inspected like cattle so wasn't kind with her words. "You are the Beast of Merin, the first of our race born in wolf form. You are loathed as much as you are feared. The Council will not be pleased with our arrangement—if you agree to my terms."

He leaned forward and whispered next to her ear, "Do you think I give a fuck about the Council's opinion?"

"If I'd thought that . . ." She paused, suddenly breathless as the edge of his jaw brushed against her neck. "I wouldn't have proposed an arrangement with you." Flutters unsettled her belly—which was a result of her not eating, and had nothing to do with the fact that his scent was glorious. It rolled over her like a river after a storm, fresh like rain and just as destructive. "If you agree, they will try to kill you."

He snickered. Men, in her experience, found the oddest things amusing. "And that would be different how? They've been trying to kill me for centuries."

"I'm sure that they have," she said without doubt. "Even so, they haven't been successful." Her conscience made her add, "But that was before you took something that the Guardians consider theirs."

"If you were theirs to steal, Rosa, then you wouldn't be here now."

"True." It was her turn to smile. "But I was referring to Castell Avon."

That made him pause. Dark interest exuded from his stiffened stance. It seemed rock and mortar held more temptation for him than bone and flesh.

Five

LUC STEPPED BACK AND SEARCHED ROSA'S FACE FOR deceit, only to find a serene smile and downcast eyes. It was a guise he'd seen on Elen often enough, a mask of indifference honed for survival.

Like with his sister, he had an urge to rip it off to expose what stirred beneath. "I think you are a talented liar, but I'll hear the truth from you now . . . Is your offer of marriage genuine?"

"I offered an arrangement," she corrected him, "not a marriage."

"You mock me with semantics." He sliced the air between them with his hand, impatient with her wordplay. "Calling a marriage an arrangement won't change the outcome, not once vows are given and the Guardians assume we're husband and wife."

"Forgive me," she said with bite in her tone, "but since it's only been three days since my last one ended, I will use any tactic at my disposal that helps me cope with the idea of another."

His gaze narrowed with concern. Her façade had slipped to reveal her dislike of men, or maybe not men in general, just a binding contract to one. Understandable, given her circumstances.

But knowing the root of a challenge only made it easier to defeat. He would need to be gentle with her. "If I accept your offer, if I choose to give vows, they will be real, and they will be honored. Do you understand?"

"Oh, yes . . ." Her voice all but seethed venom. "I understand all too well. I'm negotiating carnal obligations to one man instead of eight."

He scowled at her choice of words but didn't deny them. "Yes."

"You would have to agree to my terms first," she returned.

"That won't be necessary," Dylan interrupted. His voice was low and heavy with displeasure. "This is my debt to pay, not my brother's. We'll help you—"

A guttural growl erupted from Luc before he could contain it. "Don't speak for me!" He whipped around to face his brother. "I'll hear her terms before we agree to help her."

Dylan stilled at the verbal challenge. His stance emanated authority. This time Luc refused to back down and gave a small taste of the volatile power he'd buried for too long.

Energy gathered along his skin, called from nature through glass windows. The scent of elements swept through the room, like a breeze in a moonlit forest, where shadows danced and prey fled, and alphas fought for the right of first kill.

His beast howled in silent triumph, echoed by indrawn breaths.

Dylan's black gaze bled streaks of green and gold as he fought to contain his wolf. "You cannot seriously be entertaining this idea. The Council will execute you as soon as they learn of it!"

"They can only try."

Taliesin cleared his throat, not keeping silent as he should. "This union will cause an outrage, but also dissension." He sounded enthused by that prospect and Luc began to understand Rosa's dislike. "You have allies in places that may surprise you."

Sophie put a hand on her husband's arm, a cautionary gesture before she addressed Rosa. "I believe we should hear what you have to offer." Her voice was strained.

Appeased, Luc's wolf paced with restless anticipation, too content to cause much internal damage. Little did Rosa realize that her territory was the perfect solution to his personal dilemma, with it being close enough to his family so as not to feel like a betrayal, and challenging enough to pacify his darker half.

And all the while he would gain access to a territory that the Guardians must not repopulate, especially now that they were aware of the power that bred in their neighbor's untamed wilderness.

He would have Castell Avon.

And if the beauty who resided within was a part of the contract, marriage, or *arrangement*—call it whatever she damned well liked—then so be it.

Rosa lifted her chin, preparing for a battle that she hadn't yet realized she'd already lost. "I would like to ask Luc a question first."

"Then ask," he said, assuming her concern related to liberties for herself.

"How will you treat servants under your command?"

He concealed his surprise—*and* his approval that her final appeal had not been a selfish one. "I don't believe in servants. Employment will be voluntary and compensated fairly. Your *Hen Was* will have their freedom, land to build if that's their choice, and our protection if they do."

"I've seen your town," she said wistfully. "With its quaint houses and tidy gardens, your people are free to live normal lives, while your secrets have remained secure."

"Avon will be the same, once we expel the filth."

She worried her bottom lip in deep contemplation, while

wearing the look of someone who'd never received a gift, hesitant to open it for fear the unwrapping would reveal an empty box, or worse—a curse.

But she was determined, this Rosa with a castle moated by rivers, willing to use her thorns to make that first tear. "In return for your support," she offered, "I propose an equal partnership for Castell Avon and the surrounding territory. As long as your decisions are rational, made for the betterment of our territory, and with compassion for the people who choose to stay, I'll support you, and any allies who take a stand against the Guardians."

His lips turned slightly in appreciation. She'd kept her offer vague, no doubt, for leverage later on. "I accept the terms."

"You do?" Again, Dylan tried to voice another solution. "Teyrnon might be willing—"

"No." Luc kept his tone firm with conviction. "I'm the one she chose, and I accept."

His brother scowled. "You can't be interested in this woman." He sighed, softening his stance as his gaze fell briefly to his wife, perhaps remembering why he owed Rosa a debt. "Before last week, she's always done the Council's bidding."

"I'm interested in Avon," he said without compunction.

Throughout their scrutiny, Rosa stood poised like a wolven queen. Proud and unrepentant, she'd lain with a monster king, and would do the same with a beast if it meant protecting the people she loved.

Her burgundy gaze met his, stricken with her wolf yet fiery with challenge. "I must warn you that I'll not be submissive."

"Good." A slow, predatory grin tugged at his lips. "I've no interest in a submissive wife."

Indeed, Luc found this whole bargain less distasteful than he ought. And for the first time since Koko's death, the idea of a woman's flesh wrapped around his was more tempting than his conscience cared to admit.

"You truly want to leave Rhuddin Village?" Dylan asked, his voice raw with disappointment. "This is your home—*our* home."

"It's time." Luc searched for the right words. Even his wolf quieted out of respect. Most brothers would have tossed his beastly ass into the barren forests of their homeland to starve and be exterminated. But Dylan, only thirteen years his senior, had cared for him, fought for him—chose isolation for *him*, and raised him as a father would a son. "Was it not you who taught me that not all battles need end in blood, for the ones who pay that price are often the innocents? And if given a choice, choose the option that will spare more lives."

"It must be divine influence," Dylan muttered thickly, "that my one sibling who has sought war for over sixteen hundred years would now come to understand my lectures."

"Even a beast can grow tired of death." The gravel in his voice had nothing to do with his aforementioned animal. He cleared his throat. "With Rosa's cooperation, we'll bring Avon to our side in a way the Guardians are too arrogant to expect. If they hunt anyone, it'll be me, and I'll be prepared. A war has begun, but we can forestall an outright declaration for a breath longer—"

"And possibly turn the advantage even more in our favor," Dylan finished, mulling over the idea with a frown. "Even if the Council doesn't immediately decide to abolish this marriage agreement, are you ready for their politics?" He paused, lowering his voice. "Are you ready for who you're bound to see?"

Merin. Even when left unspoken, her name hung in the air like a poisoned memory.

Luc never thought of her as his mother. For wanting his death she didn't deserve the sentiment. "I think the better question may be"—his mouth twitched with irony—"is she ready for me?"

Dylan studied him for a long moment. As always, his assessment was thorough and he saw too much. *"Bloody hell . . .*" He let out a frustrated sigh. "The White Mountains will suit you well. And truth be told, I could use you there, but . . ." He shook his head, looked away. "Guardians and Gods be damned if I'm not going to miss you."

"And I you," Luc said with more emotion than he liked to show in open company.

AN HOUR HADN'T PASSED BEFORE ROSA WANTED TO KILL her soon-to-be-second husband. Well, not *kill* exactly, but cause him an equal amount of unpleasantness. He'd brought her to his sister's cottage—to meet Elen, which was intimidating enough—but then, right after a brief summary of events, had left her and Elen alone to "get acquainted" while he'd deserted her to gather supplies.

If possible, Elen seemed more annoyed. "My brother should've stayed." She tucked a golden strand behind her ear and forced a smile. "Luc told me you're hungry? Are cucumber sandwiches okay?"

"Please don't trouble yourself," Rosa said, hiding her disappointment. Cucumber sandwiches might appease a rabbit. And after this morning she needed a buffet, with meat, and gravy, and buttered bread. "I'm fine."

"It's no trouble at all." Elen busied herself making petite triangles with thin bread while preparing a licorice-scented tea.

Wishing she were doing something productive, like planning for tomorrow's strike, Rosa stood in the center of a stranger's kitchen instead. She felt like an intruder in someone else's space, or an eavesdropper on a secret that she didn't want to know.

Elen's garden grew up every vertical surface within its green reach. Trees, fence posts and arbors had all fallen victim to its twining vines. The interior of the cottage was much the same. The power of nature breathed from its very walls and whispered temptation along her skin.

Yet a deep sense of solitude and sadness lingered amid the enchantment. Merin's children knew strength and unity, but loneliness too. Was it a curse of their race, Rosa wondered with some resentment, for those who had a conscience to suffer its consequence?

"My home frightens you," Elen said.

"No." *Not exactly.* "It calls to me." With some relief, she turned and considered her host. "I'll assume polite conversation is over, then."

She gave a delicate shrug. "If you don't mind, I'd like to hear more than just pleasantries from the woman who's just convinced my brother to marry her. Not a small feat, I might add."

"I have heard about your gift," Rosa replied in return. "I was skeptical, until now."

Elen's ability to pull life from one source and give it to another was of great interest to the Guardians. Plant or animal; if it grew, it was rumored that she could control its life force—or take it. One of Math's guards had been stripped of his wolf by Elen's hand, or so the others had said upon their return. Math and the Council had orchestrated that battle, no less than a week ago in these woods. Blessedly, they had been given a bloody comeuppance in return, with two Council members and eighteen other Guardians now dead.

And all for this woman, who, amazingly enough, if the accounts were true, could not shift.

"It's not a gift." Elen resembled her mother, tall and lithe like many Celts, with golden hair and deep blue eyes of summer, but unlike Merin she had a gentle demeanor.

"The Guardians disagree." Walking to the nearest window, Rosa pulled back the curtain and looked outside. A row of aspen trees had been planted for shade alongside the back porch; their leaves danced like faeries at twilight. If faeries did indeed exist, then this was a place they would want to play. "As do I."

Elen looked away. "Let's discuss other things while we

eat." She placed a steaming pot of tea on a small pine table, arranged chocolate cookies on a plate and cut sandwiches on another, and then finished the meal with tulip-shaped teacups. "Please . . ." She pulled out a chair. "Come sit."

The cookies, Rosa admitted, had potential. She slid into the chair and snagged two. "I would like to know more about Luc . . . if you're willing to discuss him with me."

"I'd be concerned if you didn't." She paused a moment to nibble at her sandwich, or contemplate how much to reveal. "He was married once before. Did you know?"

"Yes." But Rosa hadn't given it much thought until his sister's melancholy warned her that she should. "I've only read what the Council recorded in their ledgers."

"Ah," she said with some amusement. "So the Council's still keeping records of us. I'm not surprised. But they can only gather facts. The subtle details of life are always more important." She took a sip of her tea, an innocent enough gesture until she asked, "How curious are you, Rosa? Would you like to know some of those details about Luc? The ones the Council may have missed?"

"Of course." Rosa paused in midreach of another cookie. "But why do I now think that knowledge comes with a price?"

"That depends."

"On what?"

Elen rested her arm on the table, palm up. "Whether or not you're brave enough to take my hand?"

"Why?" Rosa eyed it with open apprehension.

"I'm a healer, among other things. I won't harm you, but I can sense if your power is tainted . . . *or not*."

"I heal when I shift," Rosa pointed out. "I don't need your services."

A golden eyebrow rose in challenge. "Do as I ask and I won't question your intentions toward my brother."

Rosa needed to reevaluate her original assessment of this woman's demeanor. "I've nothing to hide." On her person, at least; her tainted power rested in tombs at Castell Avon.

"Prove it." She wiggled her fingers. "Come, now, what would I have to gain by causing you harm?"

What did anyone have to gain? And yet there were still people who did it for sport . . . *and pleasure*.

However, Rosa didn't sense that kind of malicious interest from her host. For survival, she'd learned how to tell the difference.

With resignation, she offered her hand.

"Ummm . . . *nice*," Elen hummed when they touched. "Luc will be—" She flinched. "You're hurt!"

"I'm not," Rosa immediately denied the other woman's accusation. Warmth washed through her like an autumn breeze, carrying winter's bite on summer's last breath. Invisible hands found and stroked her injuries, a sensation of both pleasure and pain that twisted within her abdomen. "Whatever you're doing . . . I would like you to stop."

"Oh, hush and be still. I'm almost done." Elen's eyes fluttered closed, then opened again, only this time they carried certainty in their soft depths. "The damage is internal. Your reproductive organs are burned."

She could tell that with just a touch?

Okay, Rosa silently admitted, *perhaps I do have other secrets to hide. Not to mention, the Guardians have good reason to fear this woman.* She yanked her hand out of Elen's grasp and tucked it under the table. "You're mistaken."

"No, I don't think so." She shook her head slowly. "You're hindering your fertility. With poison, I assume, since human contraceptives don't work on our kind. Well, besides condoms. I'd be interested to learn the ingredients. I've never had anyone request a tonic of that sort. Our children are so rare. Why would you do this to yourself?"

"Would you want to be mated to Math Alban, or any other Guardian who forced his seed into you?" For Rosa, the mere idea inspired nausea. To be joined to evil for an eternity was a risk she refused to take, even to go as far as thwarting the will of the Gods to prevent it.

The bane of their existence came with the bonding instincts of their wolves. Human and animal compulsions united to form an undeniable force; dual natures weaved into one. If a child was conceived, she would desire the sire no matter his morality. She had watched mated couples, and many of them were not as kind to each other as Dylan and Sophie. Worse, hatred did *not* hinder their urges to reproduce.

And if Taliesin's prediction proved true, her child would inherit an even greater torment.

"I understand," Elen said with more sympathy now. "It must reverse to normal fertility when you shift. Do you take the poison every time?"

The process wasn't something Rosa cared to discuss. "You wanted to know if my wolf is tainted. Any other information you found is more than I offered to give." Then a worrisome thought came to mind. "Did you heal me?"

"No." Elen reached again for her tea. "But I could. And you can stop frowning. Your secret is safe. That's a matter between you and Luc, and needs no interference from me."

Her tension eased somewhat. "Thank you."

"Your power is lovely, by the way. It tastes like vanilla and Yuletide cookies." A knowing smile turned her lips, half-hidden by the raised cup, giving her an impish look. "And that, I'm guessing, my brother already knows."

"You were going to tell me about his former wife," Rosa prompted, uncomfortable with this line of conversation.

With a slight nod, Elen went along with the changed subject. "Her name was Koko, a shortened version of *kokokhas*," she explained, "which means owl in Abanaki, the language of our local Native Americans."

"Wasn't her family of Romany descent?" Rosa thought back to what she'd read. According to the Council's records, Koko had been human. More important, she hadn't conceived Luc's child, so therefore she had lived a normal life-span until the early to mid-1900s.

"They were," Elen said with fondness. "Gypsies and

Abanaki often traded goods. The nickname was given to Koko for her golden eyes and spirit, and kept by her parents because it was fitting."

In light of these new details, an earlier observation became troublesome. "The tattoos on Luc's arms . . . Are they owls?"

For Koko? His human wife who was sixty-plus years dead?

Elen stood in haste, catching her chair just before it toppled to the floor. "I think I've revealed more than he'd like. I'll pack some food for your trip, and then we'll go in the garden and pick a bouquet for your ceremony. How does that sound?"

Perfectly dreadful, Rosa thought. Almost as awful as Elen's suddenly chipper voice—and as welcomed as a lifetime with a second husband whose loyalties belonged to another.

$\mathcal{S}$ix

OVER THE NEXT HOUR, LUC MADE ARRANGEMENTS FOR their campaign against Castell Avon. Teyrnon and twenty-six more guards had agreed to go to the White Mountains, the most Dylan could spare without compromising the defenses of Rhuddin Village. And while he planned for war, Sophie and Taliesin arranged a wedding that neither bride nor groom wanted any part of.

Gods be merciful, Luc swore under his breath. He'd lost his faith after Koko's passing, but if there was a time for prayers, this would be it. He was scheduled to leave a few hours after a ceremony that he'd thought never to repeat again. *May this marriage not bring more death onto a family who's already seen too much.*

More wolves were on their way from Ontario and Minnesota. Both Daran and Isabeau, their closest allies to the north, had agreed to help. Securing Avon was as much to their advantage as it was his. They arranged to rendezvous on the Canadian border of New Hampshire in twelve hours, before moving on to Avon by morning.

Llara wanted in as well, but had a longer distance to travel. Her territory encompassed a good portion of the current Russian boundaries. She was prepared to come if called upon.

In the interim, he retreated to his apartments alone, ignoring stares as he walked. Word had traveled quickly to Rhuddin Village, and the townspeople had come for glimpses of Rosa. Luc had little time, and even less patience, for their awkward felicitations. He needed to shower and change, gather a few supplies, and say his farewells to a woman who no longer graced this world but continued to haunt his heart.

His living quarters encompassed the entire top floor of the west outer building. Koko's artwork lined the walls in an assortment of wildlife paintings in both oils and watercolors, her two favorite mediums. In her later years, his wife had moved on to sculpting wood into furniture. She'd been a practical woman, his Koko, who hadn't understood why beauty couldn't also serve a useful purpose.

Luc ran his hands through his hair, ripping it loose of its tie to hang down his shoulders. He allowed himself one last perusal of her work, and then headed to his private kitchen where he dug through his utility drawer and pulled out a thin knife. He gripped the handle and worked the blade under the twine wrapped around his wrist. Normally he untied it with care before a shift, and then retied it afterward.

"My sweet Koko," he whispered aloud, "I'll never forget you."

With one swift stroke the hemp-entwined charm fell to the counter. Setting the knife aside, he scooped the pile into his palm and crossed the hallway to his office. Bookcases lined the outer walls from ceiling to floor, filled with volumes turned ragged with use. He ran his hand over a row of beaten spines before resting on a simple leather-bound journal, a gift he had given to Koko when his denial had ended.

Almost a century later, her handwriting had faded, the pages had yellowed, but her memory held firm, a constant torment to feed his empty soul. Out of both habit and need, Luc opened the journal and read the first passage . . .

September 12, 1922

It is my birthday today. This journal is a gift from my husband. Luc has given me many gifts, too many, but this is the only one that made me sad. I think he has finally come to accept that our time together in this life is limited. Luc, I now realize, wants something more than my artwork to remember me by. It is so little to ask, and yet so difficult to give. I want these final years to be happy ones, but there is darkness in my heart, because it bleeds when I think of Luc alone, without me. I am selfish, too, I think, because I want him to remember me when I should be helping him to forget.

I have lived through sixty-eight birthdays, and while I am grateful for every year with him, my body longs for more, my heart aches for the child we never had. At night, while he sleeps, I pray that our love will be stronger than the will of his Gods. Perhaps that is why my prayers are ignored.

Perhaps that is why I age like his precious gnarled tree, while Luc remains the same, forever young, forever strong. Perhaps I want too much.

Enough words.

I will stop before I blur these pages with senseless tears over something I cannot change.

I think my pen would be put to better use if I draw my husband, for he is more beautiful than anything I could ever write.

~Koko

Luc thumbed the sketch, recalling that winter afternoon with melancholy clarity, as if he could take a walk to White Birch Grove and still find her there, sitting on a snow-covered rock, bundled in a wool coat with her legs crossed and ink on her hands. She'd convinced him to pose, like a dandy dressed in fur. He'd have done anything just to watch her worry her bottom lip while she worked, or the way her eyes glowed when they lifted up from her easel.

Heart-burdened, he placed the twine between the pages, letting the charm dangle over the side, and slid the journal back in its place. Out of respect for another, it would be the final time he read it.

He doubted he could love any woman as he had Koko,

but then reminded himself that Rosa hadn't asked for love. What she had asked for, he could give.

He showered quickly, changed into rubber-soled boots, jeans and a clean T-shirt. Not the wedding attire appropriate for a queen, but somehow he doubted she'd care.

Afterward, he packed a spare set of clothes in a waterproof hunting bag that crossed his chest like a sling. He then added a hunting knife from his armory, his two favorite swords, and an extra one for Rosa, only lighter and longer. She may have come to his home unarmed but she wasn't leaving that way. If her parents had been sword smiths, then they must have given her some training in her youth.

For this plan to succeed she needed to retain that golden head of hers for at least a month, long enough for suspicions to settle—or this crusade would turn ugly fast.

While he prepared himself for battle, he thought of his brother's countless lectures over the years. Time would tell if he'd chosen the least bloody path. He would attempt to rid Avon of its filth without death, but if the Guardians did return for blood, then it would be his hand to spill it and their necks to bleed out.

THE CEREMONY TOOK PLACE UNDER A GROVE OF MAPLE trees with mint-colored leaves of spring. Saplings lined the open trail, nourished by a few fallen trees. The setting sun cast rich shadows of burnt umber and gold in a forest of wonders, where life was continual, unhindered, and too beautiful to be real.

Rosa inhaled deeply, savoring the taste of life and power that clung to her skin and rolled over her tongue.

Could it be this way for Avon? she wondered.

Could this arrangement heal her home? Could it mend poisoned ground and broken hearts, and bring strength to those who have forgotten how to breathe?

She dared not hope for such things, for hope was a dangerous seed, and once planted it could tangle hardened souls with false dreams.

Even so, the magic of the night beckoned her, and humbled her as well, for Sophie and Elen had gone to great trouble to make this ceremony more special than it was.

Lanterns hung from branches, and white candles lined the moss-covered trail, glowing like soft orbs in emerald silhouettes. She held a bouquet of pink roses and white peonies that had bloomed by the touch of an enchanted hand. Twin torches awaited her ahead, placed on either side of the trail, made of stone and topped by fire.

Luc stood between the two flames—the Beast in the flesh, cloaked in human trappings and modern clothes. Ink-black hair hung around his shoulders, wild like the wolf she sensed within.

His family watched from the outskirts, following her approach with wary eyes and a few forced smiles; Dylan, Sophie, and Joshua, their son. Elen was there, Porter as well, and of course, Taliesin would not have missed the show. He had cursed her first wedding with his presence; why not her second?

Other guards lined the trail as she walked, while her gaze remained on Luc, drawn like a night creature to darkness and forbidden things. He wore jeans and a black shirt, with serviceable boots, an insult to tradition, and to her.

He should have been awaiting her nude.

Honor called her to shift, to give witness to her gift, and to stand unclothed before him in the pure form in which she was born. She dared not shift, not here among other unmated men, but the other allowance may make this whole event seem less doomed.

She stopped a good eight paces before Luc and set her bouquet gently on the ground. He frowned at her, impatient to be done, or so she assumed.

He would have to wait, for respect deserved a small measure. And with that thought in mind, she pulled her sweater over her head and let it mingle with overwintered leaves by her feet.

Luc froze . . . *surprised?*

As a child, Rosa had lived during the reign of Queen Anne, when propriety had taken root and nudity was scorned. She'd been raised among humans; men and women who had strutted about in wigs and velvet trimmings, and did their debauchery behind closed doors.

As a result, she felt exposed when unclothed, but Luc was Pagan born and mustn't be allowed to know her insecurities. Kicking off her boots, she shimmied out of her pants and tossed them next to her sweater.

Her underthings followed.

"Okay, then," a young male voice murmured. Joshua, she guessed. "I think I'm going to like this wedding."

With a mortified groan, Sophie slashed her arm through the air in a silent command to stay quiet.

Ignoring the exchange, Rosa reached behind her head and undid her plait, shaking her hair loose to fall around her waist. She looked to the man who was about to become her husband, in name if not in heart. His eyes glinted silver, kissed by fire and cursed by shadows, and dared her to run if only to sweeten the hunt.

"It seems," Luc said as she stepped beside him, "that I've come overdressed."

"That is your choice . . . and this is mine." An evening breeze kissed her naked skin. She felt her nipples tighten in response and willed him not to look down, but to no avail.

His voice took on a husky tone. "Does my being clothed bother you?"

Yes, but more so that he'd asked. "No," she lied. "And if your vows are short then this will be over with soon."

His jaw tightened. "If that is your wish." He placed his hands forward, palms down, and waited until she covered them with hers. "Rosa, *Penteulu* of Avon, I offer you respect, loyalty and protection, as long as you offer the same in return."

She repeated similar vows back to him, simple and uncommitted to love. Blessings were given by their local holy man, and a few in their ancient tongue from Elen as she placed strips of cloth over their joined hands.

Rings were not worn by their kind nor exchanged at ceremonies. However, the assurance in Luc's voice held more meaning than circles of gold. "I enter our marriage by my own choosing. I accept your vows and will honor mine."

"I enter our marriage by my own choosing," Rosa repeated, taking solace in the fact that this time her words were not forced. "I accept your vows and will honor mine."

It was not the most romantic wedding in history, but not the worst, and if kept true, it would serve her far better than her first.

As if he sensed her thoughts, Luc gently tugged her forward and searched her face. Stark eyes simmered with haunted specks of black and iridescent silver. "I won't be unkind to you, Rosa." The kiss he gave her was chaste, hardly a kiss at all, but firm, and warm, and gracious.

She much preferred his kiss over Math's, who had used his tongue to slime her face and to put on a show for their guests.

The moment was disturbed by a mechanical click. An unnatural burst of light followed; they both turned and squinted into the shadows.

Taliesin stood off to the side, sporting a camera and a satisfied grin. "For proof." But why would he need proof, when all the man needed to do was speak and the Guardians listened? No doubt, there were amusements afoot, because Taliesin liked to play games with the people who'd raised him, and she was their favorite pawn.

Afterward, Rosa dressed quickly, picking leaves from the front of her sweater if only to occupy her hands while Luc said his farewells. A few guards offered polite regards, but most spoke of the upcoming battle, for which she was glad. Gareth's truck remained parked on a dirt road just off the trail, the vehicle that would return them to Avon.

Before they climbed into the cab to be on their way, Dylan followed with a final cryptic message. "Be considerate to my brother," he said with an underlying threat, "and you'll be welcomed in our home, with our protection. But if you betray him—"

Clutching the handle of the door, Rosa said, "He would have to betray me first."

Sophie stepped beside her husband. "Her intentions are pure." A loose jacket hung below her waist, but a glint of gold sneaked out to rest on her hip. She wore the Serpent of Cernunnos on her person, a weapon honed in the Otherworld for Taliesin in the form of a whip. Taliesin had given it to her, to Math's utter disbelief. Her late husband's arrogance had cost Avon a few Guardians and several more guards.

Dylan frowned down at his wife. "Did you come to that assumption from instinct, or something more?"

"Both," she replied in a clipped tone.

Having heard stories of the weapon since childhood, Rosa was too curious not to ask, "Does the Serpent speak to you?"

Sophie ignored the question. "Luc is not like your first husband, Rosa. You may find this arrangement could be something more . . . if you open your heart to the possibility."

No, Luc was not Math, but neither was she the innocent girl who'd once believed in love. "Open my heart?" She fought the urge to laugh. "How can I, when I'm not entirely certain I have one anymore?"

"Now, that's not true." Sophie shook her head. "You wouldn't be here now if it were."

"It's time to go," Luc announced, resting his hand on his brother's shoulder. "I'll call you when it's done."

"I should be there with you," Dylan said, his voice laden with concern. "If it weren't for Arnulf's arrival—"

"You must trust me to succeed in Avon," Luc cut him off as if they'd already had this argument and he didn't care to repeat it. "With Daran and Isabeau joining us, I'll have enough shifters backing this siege."

"Arnulf of Salzburg?" Rosa asked. Known for his affinity for reclusion, the Austrian leader's territory was old and powerful.

Dylan turned his heated glare back on her. His look produced a memory, poignant but not unwelcomed. Her father had often worn a similar expression, bleak with concern and troubled with doubts, as if contemplating whether or not to share dangerous information, or run away with everyone he loved.

"Rumors of our alliance are spreading," Dylan said with some hesitation. "The Council has created more enemies than even I was aware of. Arnulf has requested a meeting."

"I know he answers to the Council when they call," she warned.

"As do you."

Point taken. "I pretend my enemies are my friends, and my friends are my enemies, and I never expect either to be true."

"That's sad," Sophie whispered.

"No, that's survival." Luc held out his hand. When Rosa simply stared at it, he prompted, "Keys."

"I'll drive." She ignored his scowl. Having betrayed Gareth enough for one night, there was no need to add insult to injury and let her new husband drive his truck. Gareth was a true friend, the person who had taught her how to drive in the first place—who had convinced Math to let him. He had also procured her a fake license, among other things. He deserved more than what she'd given him in return.

"Fine, you drive." His lips thinned. "I'll give you directions."

"I know my way home," she returned. They both settled into the truck while Luc adjusted the passenger seat to accommodate his height.

"We're not going straight to Avon," he informed her. "My guards are meeting us by the church at midnight. Daran and

Isabeau will join us near Salmon Mountain at four in the morning."

Salmon Mountain sat on the tri-border of Maine, New Hampshire and Canada. She looked to the truck's clock on the dashboard. Fourteen minutes past seven o'clock—almost five wasted hours.

"I had hoped to be there sooner." She gripped the steering wheel, biting back her frustration. Imagining Aunt Neira had reached her volatile point by now. None of this sat well, but beggars couldn't be organizers of other leaders' forces.

"I understand your concern, but Daran and Isabeau needed travel time, and their help is necessary for our strike to be successful. There's nothing you can do for your friends until then, so put it from your mind and prepare for the morning. You'll be arriving in Avon with three armies on your side."

"And a husband." *Mustn't forget the husband.* Of course, acceptance helped dissolve her bitterness. There was no point in regretting what had already been done, or what couldn't be helped. For now, she would follow Luc's lead, at least on this matter—a small forfeit to reclaim her home.

"Take a right up ahead." He pointed to a turn in the road. "We're going to my brother's lake house."

"Why?" Suddenly her concern became selfish. She'd known this was coming, but did it have to happen so soon?

"You know why, Rosa." His low, slightly rough voice was riddled with more guilt than promise. "I'll make sure it's pleasurable for you."

For me . . . but not for himself.

Unsure why that annoyed her so, she blurted out a petty comment. "I don't think I'm built for pleasure."

$\mathcal{S}$even

THE LAKE HOUSE WAS CONSTRUCTED OF FIELDSTONE AND mortar, and supported by large pine beams. Propane lanterns hung from the rafters and braided rugs covered wooden floors. Luc busied himself setting a fire in the cast iron woodstove, while Rosa huddled in a cushioned chair.

I don't think I'm built for pleasure.

The memory of her biting words continued to taunt him, too much of a challenge to ignore. He'd seen her nude, an image he wouldn't be forgetting anytime soon, *if ever*, curved like a goddess in just the right places, and highly responsive to touch, even if it were only from a brisk breeze.

When the fire blazed high, he shut the grate and turned to face his new wife. She watched him over raised knees; the added warmth in the room did little to lessen the chill in her multicolored eyes.

He could not help but give a weary sigh. "Come, now, Rosa . . . Is the thought of lying with me *that* distasteful?"

"It's not you I have issue with, per se," she informed him with bored acceptance, "but your aversion to me. I've been with one husband who found me repulsive, and it's just so, I don't know"—her shoulders lifted in a slight shrug, searching for the right term—"*tedious* to find myself stuck with another."

Taken aback, he could only stare. "I have no such inclination." He needed only to remember her bared breasts, perfectly rounded with fat, erect nipples that begged for his mouth, and was prepared to show her how *little* aversion he had.

"But you don't want me either." Her eyes took on a violet tone, softened by the overhead lanterns. "Not in *that* way."

A bitter laugh escaped before he could contain it. "That's not true."

His conscience may not embrace this woman, but his cock had no such qualms. It pressed against his jeans in eager anticipation of more than seventy years denied. Koko had been frail in her last decade of life and he had refused to force his needs on her—or look to another to serve them. Even after her death, no other woman had tempted unfaithfulness to her memory.

Until now.

Rosa made a soft sound too feminine to be called a snort but close enough. "I know when a man wishes I were someone else."

Insulted by the comparison, he said, "I'll only ask you this once, and then there'll be no need to discuss it again. Is your hesitation because of your experience with Math?"

She dismissed his concern with an absent wave of her hand. "He was cruel but not in that way. It wasn't pleasant, mind you, but there were many times Math couldn't . . . *er*, perform. He didn't like being around me. Eventually he stopped trying. It's been several years since . . ."

Much longer for him, but he'd be damned if he'd share that with her now. "We'll consummate this arrangement, but it only need be this once."

His beast growled in silent outrage, too enamored of this

woman to think straight. *Only need be this once? Only in your delusions!*

From the moment she'd stripped to honor the old ways, his wolf had found its voice. Not even Koko had inspired such mental outbursts.

And that angered Luc as much as it fed his lust.

"Truly?" Her relief was palpable. "Don't promise such things unless you mean to respect it. Otherwise, it's just petty."

"I'll never force you." An oath given with confidence, knowing he wouldn't have to. "Not even now."

This arrangement *would* be sealed with seed and flesh at least once so as not to be refutable later on—by her or anyone else. He had little doubt, like Sarah had mentioned earlier, that she had other men who wanted his role. And that didn't include the Guardians planning a fertility ritual with his new wife.

All the same, a bad taste settled in his mouth. "If you require more time—"

"No, let's just do this." She expelled a defeated breath. "I've always found the interval of expectation to be worse than the actual event. And since it only need be this once, I would rather just get it over with now."

"If there is a child . . ." He let the possibility hang in the air, his crowning betrayal to Koko this night. Simply admitting to the prospect with another woman rejected her as his mate.

"Then the fertility ritual will be good and truly thwarted." Her smile was too practiced, too . . . amiable. Not entirely a lie but not the full truth either.

He was beginning to learn her cues. "If it were to happen," he pressed, "would you accept my child, even if it were born a Bleidd?" A human trapped in wolf form, as he had been for almost six hundred years, until Dylan had smuggled him across an ocean to a wilderness so wild his beast had felt confident enough to recede.

Her guise slipped to reveal compassion of all things.

Remarkable that she still had the capacity, considering her life up until now. She must know his history, after all, and the real motivation behind this inquiry.

"I highly doubt there's even a small chance of pregnancy." Her voice turned serious with respect for the topic. "But if you must know my views on the subject, then rest assured that I would protect my child in the unlikely event, and teach him or her to face any challenge they were born with."

Satisfied, he strode toward her and held out his hand. She eyed it as a hound would a piece of grass, something to chew on for digestion purposes.

"Only this once," she prompted again for reassurance.

"Only this once," he returned. To demand more of her went beyond what was necessary to complete this arrangement. Likewise, it would equal his motivations to that of her former husband's, a comparison too vile to consider further. "The next time," he felt obliged to add, as hunger, decency, and a too-infatuated wolf battled a silent war within his gut, "you'll have to come to me."

And I'll make you beg!

Did she sense his other half? he wondered when she unfolded from the chair to stand, brushing aside his offered hand. Did she know his beast howled in joy while the man watched her hair cascade down her back, picturing his face buried in all those damn silken curls?

"Then it will only be this once," she said without thought, "because I'll *never* come to you for this."

"One day you'll learn it's not wise to challenge me." More important, however, was her continued hesitation; he wondered whether it might ease her qualms if she were to control this first time.

"It wasn't meant as a challenge," she said.

A calculating smile tugged at his lips. "Have you ever taken a man, Rosa?" Her deepened frown proved his assumption true. "No? Then by all means, you should be the one to consummate this arrangement, and I'll be your willing receiver."

"EXCUSE ME?" SHE MUST NOT HAVE HEARD HIM CORrectly.

Rosa forced herself to remain calm, not an easy task as he stalked to the sofa like a primed alpha who had just won entitlement rights in a territory his opponent had never chartered. Gloating as he removed his shirt along the way. A tattoo of an owl in flight spanned his entire chest, down his arms and into the sculpted planes of his stomach.

Luc was hard in every place her former husband had been flaccid, and tanned to the color of aged honey. Math's skin had been a loose, translucent gray.

Was it unfair to compare the two? Probably, but since the other man was dead, what was the harm? Besides, if not for the owl she would have enjoyed the view. Still, she half expected him to demand that she disrobe from the waist down—as Math had preferred—then bend her over the nearest chair, mount her from behind and be done with it. As in the way of wolves, only in their human forms.

However, it seemed this coupling was not to be as easily accomplished—or over with as quickly.

With his jeans still on, but riding loose on his hips, Luc took a seat on the sofa. After a pace of breath his gaze narrowed . . . *waiting for her to move?*

Oh, *right.* She was supposed to be taking him, wasn't she? Sadly, she didn't quite know how that worked. She'd seen it, of course, but observation and participation were two completely different things.

"I'm not sure what you want me to do," she told him.

He patted the cushion next to him on the sofa. "Just come and sit and we'll see where this leads, shall we?"

Sparing him a wary glance, she knew where it would lead if he would just act accordingly. Her current trepidation was *his* fault for not following normal mating procedures.

Taking a deep breath, she reminded herself that this was just an inconvenience, over and done with the sooner she cooperated.

"I can make this easier on us both," she finally offered, bending forward to remove her boots. Kicking them to the side, she straightened and methodically began to take off her trousers—

"Stop!"

Her fingers froze. His command annoyed her but she complied. "Why?"

"Because . . . I don't want you to undress yet. Let's just sit awhile first."

She blinked, trying to acclimate to the mating rituals of a different male. Again, she asked, "Why?" What was the point of just sitting? And while still clothed, no less?

He scowled. "Are you always this obstinate?"

"I can be stubborn," she admitted. "When something prolongs a goal and has no useful function."

"This has a function." His gaze met hers, molten silver and black with impatience. "When I've no taste for fucking a woman I haven't held first."

"Well, then," she clipped, unsure how to respond to his penchant for vulgarities given with acts of affection. It was another conundrum that left her on unfamiliar footing, since she was accustomed to the opposite: malice dispensed with excruciating propriety. "That is a different matter altogether, is it not?" She felt a flush begin to crawl up her neck. "I did not realize that is a problem for you."

"It's not a problem," he corrected in a tone that could freeze rocks. "It's a preference."

"Oh." She felt motivated to add, "I thought I was the one who . . . *er*, would be"—she paused, slipping over *that* word—"*taking* you."

"You will be." The glint in his gaze suggested he was enjoying her missteps.

Her interactions with Math had *never* been this unnerving; they had been a chore, no more. Not so with Luc, *unfortunately*.

Anxiety threatened her composure. "I do not want to do this anymore." He played an unfair game and her lack of knowledge put her at a disadvantage. "I do not know what you want. I have never had to—"

"Hush, Rosa," he said in a smooth tone. Worse, he had the audacity to chuckle.

"I find no humor in this situation." She crossed her arms in front of her chest. "It disturbs me that you do."

"You misunderstand." He attempted to explain, but the smirk that continued to tug at his mouth did not help his cause. "Did you know your speech changes when you're upset?"

Yes, she silently chastised herself. "I am . . . *I'm* learning to talk with modern linguistics. Sometimes I revert." In Avon, she had never risked adapting her speech for that very reason. "It's something I'm working on." Taliesin had callously noted her confinement from modern society earlier without consideration for the reason.

"Don't work on it too much because I think it's charming."

"I don't." She intended to practice more now.

"My goal wasn't to upset you, but to make you feel more comfortable. And now I fear I've made things worse." He may not be a Seer but he was dangerously observant.

"I don't think I'm built for pleasure." Rosa had warned him once, and did so again to explain her obvious ineptness.

"You're wrong." Luc sounded so sure; she wanted to believe him. "I think you've been badly neglected."

"That was a blessing." She didn't insult him by denying the obvious. "I've never had to actually participate in the act. I was only required to be still . . . in whatever position I was placed." She felt compelled to repeat, "While our couplings were passionless, Math was never cruel during the process."

Math had wanted an heir, a son or daughter to carry on his bloodline, and respected the method of conceiving. If he'd known her fertility had been secretly obstructed every time . . .

Well, she shook her head at the thought, happy to still have one attached.

He paused as if weighing the best response, or summoning restraint. A bite of energy danced along her skin, suggesting the latter.

"That's not how it will work with us." He grabbed a blanket from the back of the sofa. "Come to me, Rosa. Let me give you pleasure. If at any time you want to stop . . . we will."

Unwilling to disclose more details concerning her less-than-passionate life, *and* personal fulfillment for that matter, she simply nodded. Walking those few steps, however, was a dreadful experience. She didn't feel well at all. Her stomach became unsettled and other regions began to throb.

He wrapped the knitted blanket around her and draped it like a shawl. Fisting his hands around the corners, he pulled her forward, like a fish caught in a weir. Before she could guess his intent, she found herself on his lap, cocooned in heat and hot male skin, with her legs dangled over his knees.

"Now, is this so bad?" he taunted while tucking her head under his chin.

"I suppose not." Pondering where to place her hands, she ended up curling them in her lap, while her shoulder rested in the crook between his arm and chest.

In truth, it was hypnotic sitting on him like this—dangerously so, like the hush before a storm. The rise and fall of his torso as he breathed lulled like a male siren, along with the weight of his arms and the lure of his skin against her cheek. The most exquisite scent of forest and man weaved around her senses. More tempting, underneath it all lay the hint of musk, of potent wolf waiting in the shadows to protect her if the human failed.

All her tension ebbed like a babe in caring arms. Away from Guardians and wrapped in strength; she'd not felt this safe since childhood. How sad that she'd found peace with a virtual stranger. And how easily she could become addicted.

Oh, yes . . . this was dangerous. "How long do we have to stay like this?"

"Shhhh . . ." His throat moved as he swallowed while his hands trailed up her thighs and under her sweater, but only to knead the muscles of her lower back.

As if she weren't becoming a puddle of goo already.

Before long, her eyes grew heavy, drifted closed. Had he been waiting for this moment of surrender, she wondered drowsily, when her guard had dissolved enough to welcome his gentle game? And did she care? For this was far more pleasant than any others she'd been forced to play. It still surprised her, too, that his touch was not repulsive. Her body practically whined for more.

He shifted to the side and moved his shoulder, leaned a bit, and her head rolled back, only to be caught by the soft pressure of his mouth on hers. So tender she didn't even open her eyes. Were a man's lips supposed to be this soft? Like with other carnal acts, she had little experience with kissing, sadly enough.

Having known only violence or indifference, her perceptions reeled. Indeed, if this was passion, then she didn't know how to respond. But she was curious enough to try. She would admit that to herself, and even to him if he asked . . . She was so hungry to know what others whispered about in giggly tones. How many stories had she heard, from Tesni and others, of their forbidden trysts and naughty secrets, only to feel like a bystander to their private joy?

"Open your mouth, Rosa." The order came on a husky whisper against her lips.

She complied because she wanted to, and his growl of approval made her shiver, which was odd considering . . .

Their cocoon of heat had begun to swelter and she felt moisture gather in embarrassing places. Turning his head to deepen the kiss only made her tremble more. Her insides were a riot of misinformation, a hot, quivery mess of nerves, and she had this distinct urge to rock her pelvis—and how unlike her normal self *that* was.

More interesting, his tongue entered her mouth and found hers. And she relished it. She actually enjoyed his taste, the sounds that he made, and the way his movements turned aggressive and less coaxing. If her wolf had been feline she would have purred.

His mouth broke from hers, and his breathing became ragged. "Now it's time to undress you." His fingers curled around the waistband of her trousers and underwear, tugging them down—and off. His hand tapped her left knee. "Bend this leg."

She complied only to be rudely readjusted.

"Oh," she breathed. The position she found herself in was interesting, to say the least, straddling him like a rider would a horse. It made her feel rather well exposed, with her legs tucked on either side of his.

"Wiggle one more time and you'll be on your back," he growled softly next to her ear.

She thought about that for a moment, a remarkable feat in view of her current state. "Would that not be for the best?"

He made a sound, a word perhaps, but nothing coherent. Grabbing her bared backside, he pulled her even more forward.

And that was when she felt it—a thick male appendage trapped within the material of his trousers, beyond anything she'd experienced before. How his jeans kept it contained, she had no idea. Her former knowledge hardly compared to this; oftentimes, Math had pumped his organ with his fist just to get a semi-rise.

"Luc . . ." She trembled, heard the desperation in her voice and cringed.

"Be still." He rested his forehead in her hair. "*Please*, just be still a moment."

Swearing that word again, he fumbled with the button of his pants. In the process, his knuckles repeatedly grazed against her in the most intimate of ways.

A tightening gripped her insides, a foreshadowing of pleasure she had yet to achieve by any touch, not even her own. If she'd known it could be like this she would have been more persistent with her personal experiments.

"I do not think I can." She wished his attentions would return to the closure of his pants. Instead, he lifted his hips while pushing the item down to his knees. He lowered her back onto his lap and she inhaled a sharp breath. To feel warm skin instead of coarse material was disconcerting in the most decadent of ways.

Once again she pondered where to place her hands and settled them on his chest for balance, awed by the reflexing muscles but disliking the inked patterns under her palms. Was it the tattoos that made her suddenly possessive, or the fact that her trepidation had changed to this . . . *yearning for something more?*

"Are you okay?" he asked as if it hurt him to do so.

I don't know. She felt exposed, never having been in such an intimate position, face-to-face, much like baring her soul while the taker watched.

"I feel achy," she said, only because it seemed he required an answer. "I think I would like to mount you now."

"Rosa . . ." He swore under his breath, then again, "*Fuck!*"

He really liked *that* word.

"Isn't that what I'm supposed to do?" She'd walked in on a coupling pair in much this same position. The logistics weren't difficult to surmise.

"Yes, but—" His chest rose and fell under her hands. "I wasn't expecting a narrative."

"Oh." Her legs trembled as a pulse of pleasure pierced her core. She flexed them around his hips for relief, but that only made it worse. "Well, may I?"

$\mathcal{E}$ight

THANK THE GODS HE WAS HALF BEAST, FOR IF HE WERE a mere mortal he might bloody well die of overstimulation.

"Lift your arms." Grabbing the hem of her sweater, he yanked it over her head. With a quick flick of the clasp, her bra followed and her breasts tumbled out, joyfully freed from imprisonment.

Closing his eyes, he was momentarily overcome by the sight of her. He'd forgotten what it was like to have an aroused woman in his arms.

It had been too long.

"Is something wrong?" She stopped squirming, but now her voice held that note of awkwardness again.

"No," he lied. Years of abstinence weakened his restraint. Or maybe that was what he needed to believe to ease his guilt.

She inhaled a sharp breath when he opened his eyes once again. He knew what she saw.

"Your wolf has blue eyes," she said with too much delight.

"I cannot wait to see him in full form. After we secure Castell Avon, maybe we can run together."

A sound erupted from his throat that he himself didn't recognize. The creature deemed worthy of her admiration postured with contented arrogance. "I'm having a difficult time containing him, so *please* . . . save your praise for another day."

He didn't mention that they would never be running together because of a promise he'd given to another.

She worried her bottom lip, but nodded. His gaze fell, drawn by baser instincts. Her breasts were the most divine things he had ever seen in almost a century of self-imposed deprivation. As if he no longer had the will to steer his own hand, he reached out and thumbed a coral-colored nipple. It puckered immediately under his touch, echoed by a feminine gasp.

Ah, *yes* . . . this woman had been neglected, and he found great enjoyment righting that wrong. Slowly, he let his hand trail down. Her stomach contracted and her eyes widened.

Not built for pleasure? She all but shook with it.

"I'm going to lift you," he told her over the gravel in his throat. "Take me in your hand and guide it—"

"Like this?" She complied before he'd had the chance to lift her. Her hands caressed him with gentle curiosity, soft, and light, and teasingly torturous.

He squeezed his palm over hers, halting her exploration. "Not this first time."

Her bottom lip protruded. "I think I want to go back to your original idea and let me do the taking."

Was she pouting? He prayed for endurance, like some bloody saint or Buddhist. "That's what I'm trying to show you."

Grabbing her by the waist, he lifted her up but the new position put her breast mere inches from his mouth. Nothing, no good intentions, or shadows from his past, could have stopped him from lowering his head to taste her nipple in that moment. He groaned like a starved man and, even to his own ears, his voice sounded raw. "Now just ease down and find the rhythm that is most pleasurable for you."

She was too good of a student, too eager to learn. And Luc realized then the full extent of the deed he'd done this night. The Guardians would come after him, all right, but not for taking Castell Avon. Great men or evil ones, human or wolf—and a few women as well . . . It mattered not. With the look she now held in her gaze, all would gladly fight for the chance to be beneath her.

A possessive growl vibrated through his core. *Let them try. If they do, they will learn I don't share well.*

He felt her stretching to accommodate his size, easing down with soft panted breaths until he was completely fisted by tight, pulsating warmth. One hand tangled in his hair, while the other pressed against his abs for balance, or resistance, or just something to help leverage her position better.

She found the rhythm; up, then down. Slow at first, then frantic, rocking to grind forward while taking him deeper each time. She bit her bottom lip in an attempt to stifle her sounds. Her brow furrowed with rising need and . . . *uncertainty?* She was close to release; he could feel it with each entry, with each gripping of muscle and tremble of her thighs. He reached down and parted her where they joined. Her nub was swollen, painfully erect, like a smaller, yet more beautiful, version of his. He circled it with his thumb a few times because he couldn't resist—gently, since it was close to peaking.

A whimper fell from her mouth. "What are you doing to me?"

"Easy," he soothed. "You're about to come, Rosa."

"I cannot," she breathed in half denial and half plea to prove her false.

"Yes, you can." He leaned forward, pressed his lips under her ear and inhaled her potent scent of vanilla and female wolf rising. It smelled like home. "Tilt your pelvis forward and move faster."

"Like this?" The cadence she found was primal and desperate.

"Harder," he whispered. Her head fell back, baring the long line of her neck, elegant . . . *tempting*. Without thought, he nipped the corded muscle; an act of an alpha to his mate.

It rocked her over that shining edge. She unraveled around him, a woman without inhibition, taking freely of her pleasure. It moved him more than he liked. He swallowed her scream by claiming her mouth while her release pumped him with contracting waves.

His cock tightened beyond the point of readiness, threatening nausea if he dared prolong its release now that she'd found hers. Moved by an instinct older than the creation of his kind, he flipped her over and onto her back, bending her legs as he fell on top of her. The damn cushions gave under his weight when he tried to thrust.

Gripping her ass to halt any resistance, he rode her hard. Harder than he should have but she responded by arching upward to meet his thrusts. Anguished sounds came from his throat. Seized by a tight throb of pleasure-pain, and too gone to care before falling over that sharp threshold of release. He lost reality, became weak to the demand of completion as wave after wave pumped his seed into her core.

After, he collapsed with his face buried in her hair. He thought she may have found pleasure again; he wasn't sure, but the possibility gratified him. "Did I hurt you?"

A soft laugh next to his ear. "No."

If he stayed inside her and rode her again, would it still count as the once? Better not push his advantage this soon, he decided and forced himself to rise, easing out. The cold air on his wet flesh was unwelcomed.

Resting on his elbows to lessen his weight, he watched his new wife. Golden curls tangled about her face, flowing over the arm of the sofa and onto the floor. Her eyes fluttered open, deep blue and satisfied, normal—*human*. A soft smile curved her lips.

She was a woman awakened.

And too exquisite for words, he thought as guilt drove like a spike through his heart. Now that his seed was spent, another face swam before his mind's eye. Only this one was dark and not pale, warm, not cool—and produced instant, futile regret.

Koko . . .

Rosa stiffened, lost her pliancy. Her smile faded, and then dissolved completely, as if sensing his sudden emotional distance. Blue eyes bled to violet. Not to the full burgundy of her wolf; hurt but not afraid. "You're thinking of her, aren't you? Your first wife."

The question caught him by surprise. His private life had been kept just that . . . *off-limits to anyone but family.* Apparently, the time she'd spent with his sister had also included learning about him. The notion didn't sit well. "No."

Her gaze narrowed. "You're lying."

While justified, he was in no mood to address her disapproval. "My past is none of your concern."

A practiced actress, her mask of indifference appeared like a plastic veil. "Of course it's not. And now that we are done with this sordid business, I *won't* be tempted to breach your privacy again."

It had been a while since he'd had to dance around a woman's mind-set. They were complex creatures. Evidently, he'd insulted this one. "Rosa—"

"No, I don't need false sentiments." She pushed at his chest. "But I do want you to get off of me."

With a sigh, he leaned enough for her to roll out from under him and land in an unceremonious dump on the floor.

She remained on all fours for only a second. Like the wolven queen she was, she rose before him naked and proud. "Does this place have a bathroom?"

Luc nodded toward the door. "I'm going for a run and may not be here when you get out." He needed to placate a very angry inner wolf who wanted to follow Rosa and show her how to work the shower. He also needed to run alone because it was a promise he had given to Koko. "Try to rest, if you can. We'll be leaving in a couple of hours."

"You can regret that I'm not your first wife while you're gone." She scooped up her fallen clothes on the way to the bathroom. "But don't punish yourself too much, because unless you deceived me earlier like you did just now, this will *not* be happening again."

Her parting words before she closed the door, echoed by a slash of sinew from bone so brutal he limped to the front door before his wolf took full form.

GRAVEL DINGED THE BOTTOM OF GARETH'S TRUCK AS Rosa spun away from the lake house. Headlights guided her over a pitted dirt road that meandered through dense-growing trees. Night had fallen to full darkness when Luc had finally returned in human form, dressed and armed for a shifter war.

He reclined in the seat beside her, smelling like forest, contentment and too much vitality for one man to possess. Gripping the steering wheel, she had the distinct urge to kick him in soft places but pressed down on the pedal instead. If her tolerance didn't deserve an award, then she didn't know what did.

"The road curves up ahead," Luc said in a lazy tone. "You might want to slow down."

Easing off the pedal, Rosa silently berated herself. To show emotion meant she cared, and she must never give any man that power, *especially* not the first one to give her pleasure.

Oh, but the memory of it. Even now she felt a quickening in her belly. In many ways she wished he hadn't shown her, wished he'd been more callous—or, at the very least, less adequate.

Her anger was petty, she knew, but when his thoughts had turned to his first wife it had exposed their encounter for the sordid affair it was. Although he had denied it, his guilt had been too raw, too . . . *intimate*. She'd been spurned by Math after every session but never by someone whose company she craved.

For recompense, she'd taken an obnoxiously long shower. Hot water was a luxury at Castell Avon. The generators supplied a limited amount but that had been reserved for Math and his lovers. After Luc had left for his run, she'd taken hedonistic advantage, staying under the cleansing stream until her skin pickled.

"Stop the truck!" Luc ordered, jarring her away from ridiculous musings.

A shadow moved awkwardly in the middle of the road and she slammed her foot on the brake; the back end of the truck glided off traction, she turned the wheel to correct while skidding to a halt. Headlights cast the figure in stark light and harsh shadows. He lifted his arm to shield his eyes.

"Do you know this man?" Her heart slammed against her chest but she stopped in time.

"I do." Luc flung open his door.

"Why is he walking like Frankenstein's monster?" Like a man-child who struggled for balance on unused legs.

"He was falling on his ass yesterday. I think he's doing pretty damn good, considering . . ." Luc jumped from the cab in a smooth leap on gravel, leaving the door ajar.

"Considering what?" Rosa followed him, turning off the ignition but hitting the switch to keep the lights on. Her steps faltered as she neared the stranger, in part due to the hatred that greeted her in his cerulean blue gaze, but more because she'd seen its female counterpart. "You're Cormack," she guessed. "Siân's brother."

"And Taran's brother as well," Luc added, his scorn unnecessary. She felt its weight as heavily as they did, if not more. "Both his sisters were killed by Math last week, so I'll ask you to give Cormack some allowance."

"I thought he was a Bleidd," she blurted before understanding dawned. The man walked on unsure legs because he was learning how to be human after centuries trapped in wolf form.

Luc stiffened but didn't deny it.

She stepped closer, too curious not to explore this anomaly. A familiar scent cloyed her nostrils, of death and decay, and of Iwan—the Guardian rumored to have lost his power to Elen's hand. "He smells like a Guardian."

Cormack bared his teeth, behavior of a wolf in human skin.

"Sweet Mother," she inhaled a reverent breath, arriving at a startling conclusion. "Is this the work of your sister?" Luc's continued silence was her answer. "I heard what took place here last week." Again, no response. "When Math's guards returned with Sophie, they claimed Elen consumed Iwan's power." Her voice dropped with awe. "Elen gave it to Cormack, didn't she? She took a Guardian's ability to shift and gave it to another."

"My sister is suffering from this." The threat in his voice was a stark reminder of who held his true loyalty. "I'll consider anyone who speaks of her involvement an adversary."

"Our enemies are the same," she reminded him. "If Iwan is gone, it will give someone who is very dear to me peace from his torment."

After a moment Luc said, "The Guardian you speak of, this Iwan . . . he killed Sophie's mother and wanted Joshua's death as well. He is dead."

"Did he suffer?"

A pause. "The separation of man and wolf didn't go well."

"Guardians have already begun to fear Elen. If they knew the full extent of her abilities—"

"They must never know, unless my sister wishes them to."

A garbled noise erupted from Cormack, a growl perhaps,

or a curse to draw their attention. He took a wobbly step forward. His sharp gaze didn't match his disjointed movements, filled with malice directed solely at Rosa.

She lifted her chin, unwilling to accept blame where none was due. "Your sister came to Castell Avon last week requesting sanctuary because Dylan banished her. I don't know what Siân did to earn such a sentence from your leader; nor do I care. I refused her twice. She came a third time and found Math . . ." She let her voice trail off because Siân's fate need not be shared aloud. Math tortured her for information, only to end the sessions after she spoke of Elen's gift. "I couldn't help her without putting others in danger, but I'm sorry for what happened to her. And to Taran as well."

Rosa assumed the second sister had died in the battle, not by Math's hand but by his order—one of many shames that blackened her dead husband's soul. If divine justice did indeed exist, then he would return to this world as a cockroach, forced to scurry from light into dank walls.

Cormack beat his hand against his chest, then against Luc's, made another strangled sound, and then stamped his foot. She noticed his feet were bare. The man wore loose pants with an elastic waist. His gyrated movements exposed hip bones and a trail of hair that thickened each time he stamped his foot and the waistband fell a bit lower. Obviously, he was natural under that one item of modern clothing. Did he not even know how to dress?

Luc frowned with concern. "Are you sure?"

"Sure about what?" Her question went ignored.

Nodding, Cormack growled a low gurgle of half wolf and half human.

Luc gave a heavy sigh. "Have you gone to Elen yet?"

Cormack shook his head, too violent not to relate his vehemence, even without words.

"She misses you," Luc pressed.

An anguished sound fell from his mouth. Cormack lifted his hands in a helpless gesture.

"Then go to her as a wolf."

A growl this time, heavy with self-disgust. His gaze was that of a beggar, pleading for something he wanted but couldn't have.

"I understand," Luc said, not overly pleased.

Excluded from the odd conversation, Rosa assessed both men. The light washed out Cormack's coloring, but thick hair curled at his nape, hinting of brown dusted with red. He had a fair amount of hair on his chest as well. There was no fat on his body, just muscle and hard angles from centuries confined as a wolf.

Luc stood a few inches taller and broader. He wore dark pants with side pockets and a cotton shirt, but she remembered him all too well unclothed. In comparison, his torso was larger and more defined. Having moved as both man and wolf, his muscles were dually honed.

Thankfully immune to her thoughts, Luc gave a sharp nod. "Come with us, if you wish, but I'll have the wolf who can fight." He waved his hand toward Cormack. "You are of no use to me like this. Not yet, at least."

Rosa blinked in surprise. "You're not serious?"

"I am." His tone warned her not to argue. "I was Cormack once. I can help him."

"Shouldn't we gain control of Castell Avon first? He can come to us afterward."

"As a wolf, Cormack is a worthy warrior," he informed her. "He's welcome to stand by my side in any fight. As a brother who lost his entire family to Math, he has the right to be in this one."

"Fine," she said with a shrug. Rosa reserved her arguments for respective causes. But the satisfied smile that turned Cormack's lips warranted a stern warning. "I feel your need for vengeance. I even understand it. If you want to join us, then do so, but if you harm anyone in my home who does not deserve your wrath, then I'll kill you myself."

Holding his hand up to stop Cormack from stepping closer, Luc gave her a curious look. "I'll advise you not to make threats unless you have the skill to follow through."

"And what makes you think I don't?"

Nine

As midnight fell to the waking hours, the sky lost
its sapphire hue, giving way to the iridescent shimmer of a
new day. This was the usual time of day Rosa drove, when
the roads were clear, the drunkards had found their beds,
and police officers were back at their stations after a long
night enforcing their human laws.

She'd been allowed out of Avon so rarely, and interactions
with mortals had been forbidden by Math. Early mornings
were the safest to travel unnoticed. More so, she admitted,
with Luc by her side and Cormack lurking over her shoulder.
Luc had ordered the man to shift before entering the truck.
In wolf form he was intimidating, to be sure, with more than
two hundred pounds of angry beast on a mission of retribution.

"Take a right at the next turn," Luc said.

The Salmon Mountain marker was a welcomed sign, the
small rest area chosen well for their rendezvous. It was far
from any major roads, with only a small section of lawn
surrounded by a dense forest, and darkened by broken lights.

As she pulled into the paved lot, figures began to emerge from parked cars. Luc's guards followed in separate vehicles, parking off to the side and on newly mowed grass.

Scanning the line of trees, Rosa counted thirty or so shadowed silhouettes and a dozen wolves, guards and warriors who had followed their leaders to help with her campaign. She sensed more in the woods who chose to remain unseen. Anticipation tightened her spine. She tasted success in the air, or at least the potential, and that was more potent than fear.

A petite woman sat on a nearby picnic table with her legs dangling over the edge. Isabeau, she assumed, the leader of the Minnesota territory, since her guards formed a wide but protective circle around her. Isabeau had been the only child born to her family with the ability to shift; the others had been killed in the house of Rhun, an Original Guardian.

Regrettably, Rhun had been Math's partner in all things but flesh. Both, thanks to Dylan and Sophie, were now dead. It was no wonder Isabeau fought on the rebels' side of this secret war.

The second leader to join this gathering stepped from his car and approached Isabeau. Rosa had met Daran briefly in her youth; he'd once purchased weapons and other wares from her parents. He now resided in Canada, where his territory encompassed much of Ontario and the surrounding woodlands.

Turning off the engine, Rosa opened the door and jumped to the pavement, hitting the latch under her seat. It lifted to reveal her sword wrapped in cloth, kept hidden for too long.

Luc quietly watched her movements. "You said you came unarmed."

"I held no weapon at the time I told you that." She met his guarded glare with one of her own. "Now I do."

"Your threat earlier, to Cormack . . . Can you use that sword? Or was it just a ruse as well? Don't lie to me," he warned. "Not on this matter. I'll know your skill now and be prepared to defend, or assist, whatever the case may be."

His concern was a valid one; therefore she answered in kind. "Before the Guardians came for me, my parents were . . ." *Neurotic. Diligent. Obsessive.* ". . . adamant with my training. I'm unpracticed, but I have full confidence my skills will return."

Immortality for our kind is a curse. Her mother's words, repeated throughout her childhood. Rosa had been loved, gratefully so, but her younger years had been ruled by strict parents bent on her survival. They'd moved to the country by then, to live among farmers. While human children climbed trees, fished in rivers, and chased one another around pretty fields, Rosa had trained.

But there are ways around our inhuman longevity, her mother would say. *No creature who walks this earth is infallible. You must be strong, Rosa. Not even Guardians can survive without two vital organs. Always go for their head first, and then their heart.*

In dark moments on loathsome nights, when the lock turned on her bedroom door, she would recall her mother's words and plan for this day. Math had several guillotines constructed for Avon's dungeon, but they weren't as portable as swords.

Unaware of her deadly musings, Luc waited for Cormack to leap out, and then shut the door. He walked around the truck and held out his hand. "May I?"

She lent a possessive shake of her head. "My cousin Cadan gave this to me. It was a gift to him from my mother. It's the only thing I have of hers."

"Cadan is your aunt Neira's son," Luc said.

Apparently the Guardians weren't the only ones keeping records. "Our mothers were sisters." One was intemperate and evil, the other stern but kind. Their stark differences had always puzzled her.

"Is Cadan at Avon now?"

She didn't care for his tone. "Yes, but my cousin isn't loyal to the Guardians. Without his help, I wouldn't have been able to leave. You *will* be kind to him."

Luc's eyebrows rose at the order. "Why wouldn't I be, if he's our supporter, as you say?"

She pondered over how much to reveal, but decided to prepare him. "You should know that he was Math's lover. They were together when Dylan claimed his revenge."

He cocked his head to the side. "By choice?"

She answered with care. "Cadan prefers to be with men in that way, but he wouldn't have chosen to be with Math were it not for our circumstances. I'll not tolerate him being judged for his sexual preferences."

Luc offered an affronted scowl. "I judge people by their actions and who they choose to protect." He slashed his hand through the air, apparently angered. "I don't bloody well care how willing adults find their comforts." He paused to make one stipulation. "As long as it doesn't harm others."

"Well, then know that Cadan is my protector." He was the only member of her family left who cared about her. Vehemence bled into her voice. "And I am his."

"Are you sure he'll choose your side over Neira's?"

Allegiance seemed to be his only concern—which was good.

"I could ask the same of you," she said quietly, only to remind him not to condemn a child for their parent's actions. Merin and Neira were both Council members. "Very few people have earned my trust; Cadan is one of those few. After my wedding to Math, he traveled with me. I consider him more a brother than a cousin, and he's the only family I have left who values my safety over the Council's dictates."

Cadan had accompanied her on their journey to Castell Avon because she'd wept through his farewells. What had started out as an adventure, at least from her cousin's perspective, soon became a nightmare. Once across an ocean, he never returned home. Cadan's compassion became his curse—because of her selfishness for not hiding her sorrow on her departure day.

She hadn't shed a single tear since.

Luc gave no indication of his thoughts, and as the silence stretched, Rosa felt compelled to fill it. "I was Math's come-uppance for leaving his homeland to resettle in America." Her words rang true because they were, just absent of the reason why.

He frowned slightly. "That seems like an overly generous gift to be given just to keep an eye on us." Luc, as she'd noted earlier, was dangerously observant.

She knew that he, and the other rebels, thought Math's presence during the Americans' war for independence was to stop them from having similar notions of their human compatriots. They couldn't be more wrong. Soon, she would have to enlighten her new husband about the Walkers.

"Math was an Original Guardian," she reminded him. The Originals of their kind took what they wanted and were rarely challenged. "I've never been able to understand their mind-sets, nor do I ever want to."

He accepted her explanation. "And Math allowed Cadan to join you?"

A bitter sound fell from her mouth. "Math *wanted* Cadan on our journey." She now understood what his dark looks had meant—but she hadn't then. "Once here . . ." An unpleasant memory came unbidden to her thoughts and she pushed it away. "Math used our isolation to his advantage."

His expression hardened even more. "And your cousin didn't try to leave?"

"No." Guilt sat heavy on her chest, as it always did. "He protected me from my husband the best way he knew how."

Luc offered no reply. After a long pause, his gaze fell to her sword. "It's built for a man," he noted. "I brought you one that will suit you better."

If he'd meant to distract her, he succeeded. "You brought me a sword?" The rapid beat of her heart echoed her surprise.

He gave a sharp nod. "And a scabbard designed for a woman's build."

"Truly?" She swallowed past a sudden lump in her throat. "I wasn't allowed weapons at Avon." Prisoners weren't allowed such privileges. "May I see it?"

"Later," he said, "after we meet with Isabeau and Daran." Did her doubt show, she wondered, when he leaned forward to whisper in her ear. "Let's wait for them to leave, when there are less curious eyes watching us. You'll hold them both and decide which one feels better."

"What if I want them both?" she challenged.

"Then you may have them both."

A burning sensation spread through her stomach—those blasted tendrils of hope again—like holding frozen hands over a hot grate, pulling life's blood back to deadened limbs; it hurt, but she couldn't pull away. The seed of hope had begun to grow and she was too tempted by its warmth.

A few minutes later, with her mother's sword tied rather poorly with a crude rope around her waist, Rosa walked with Luc and Cormack toward the two waiting allies who had come to help. This was a dubious position for her, unaccustomed to generosity without an underlying motive.

Isabeau hopped off the picnic table. "Luc." She greeted him with a nod. "And Cormack . . ." Shaking her head at the wolf, she exclaimed, "It's extraordinary, I must say, to see you faring so well after your ordeal."

She had a frail quality about her, or perhaps waiflike was more apt, as her stance exuded dominance, petite but lethal. She wore modern clothes, jeans ripped at the knees and a sweatshirt with block lettering that spelled *Holli* on one line, and *Ster* on another. Her dark hair was tucked under a hood, possibly tinted since it was naturally red. The Council ledgers had two paragraphs describing its color, penned by a dangerous admirer.

"Rosa Alban." Isabeau regarded her with hooded eyes. "If you are leading us into a trap, it will be your last betrayal in this life."

Thankfully, Rosa was adjusting to frankness. Isabeau's guards shared her opinion in grumbled whispers and wary glances.

Luc stepped forward in a protective stance.

"No," Rosa said before he spoke for her. "I'll address this now and end it." She faced Isabeau but raised her voice so all could hear. "I understand your concern but it's unnecessary. Like you, my entire family was murdered by the Guardians. I, however, didn't have the luxury of escape afterward." Bile filled her voice like poison and she let it spill out with her words. "I believe we were orphaned at the same age, you and I, but imagine if you'd been forced to wed the man responsible—"

"I'd have killed him the first time he tried to crawl into my bed," Isabeau spat.

"Really? At seventeen? Alone? With forty-plus guards waiting in the hallway to protect him, or to take their own turn? When rebels and outcasts kept to their own woods? What is one woman worth, after all, if helping her brings destruction to *their* families, to *their* people?"

"You could have run away," she challenged, but her voice had lost much of its scorn.

"There are servants in Avon whom I care about. *Hen Was*, like your family had been. They would have been tortured for information. My freedom has never been worth their pain."

Silence.

"You don't have to trust me," Rosa continued. "Or even like me, but know that I've been waiting three hundred years for this day and I appreciate anyone willing to stand by my side as I reclaim my home. And if a day comes that you need my help, I'll stand by yours in return."

"Our home," Luc added when the whispers subsided. "As of this afternoon," he announced, "Rosa Black is my wife."

Daran exhaled a low whistle. "No shit." He appeared older than she remembered, early thirties by human standards, the price of responsibility as much as time. With fair hair darker than blond but not quite brown, cropped short, he was less jovial, more cynical. But weren't they all?

Isabeau barely blinked. "Well, that was fast. I'll assume the Guardians are unaware."

"My aunt Neira will learn soon enough," Rosa said.

"So, is that your plan, then?" Isabeau didn't hide her skepticism when she addressed Rosa. Her guards encroached to hear the conversation, more curious now than threatening. "Are you just going to walk into Castell Avon and introduce your new husband?"

"It's my property by modern law," Rosa pointed out. "And my territory by Guardian rule, just as it's within my right to remarry an unmated shifter. We'll use their laws against them, openly at first."

"It will give us some time." Luc repeated the same argument he had given his brother earlier. It was as persuasive the second time as it was the first. "Llara is ready to join us if needed. Arnulf is meeting with my brother tomorrow, and Hagen from Landstuhl has also reached out expressing interest in our alliance. Russia, Austria, Germany—"

"And the Himalayas as well," Daran added. "I've been in contact with Mabon and Sioni. They've joined our cause."

Isabeau shook her head as if overwhelmed. At first Rosa thought she would protest until a slight dimple appeared on her cheek, hinting of a suppressed grin. "I've been waiting too long for this day to come." Her gaze briefly landed on Rosa. "Far more than your three hundred years. Let's have some fun, shall we?"

Relieved, Rosa said, "The river forks around Castell Avon. There is a shallow end that's easily crossed but I suspect it will be watched."

"We know of this section you speak of," Daran replied. "We were there with Dylan less than a week ago."

"Good," Luc said. He had discussed his plan briefly on their drive over. It was sound, but even good plans could fail without warning. "Rosa and I will enter at the gates as if nothing is amiss, with Teyrnon, Cormack, and our other guards. Isabeau, we would like you to stand with us. Daran, you'll circle from behind if . . ."

"If our news is received as expected," Rosa finished for him.

LUC ENJOYED THE VIEW FOR MOST OF THEIR JOURNEY, with winding country roads that followed a wide river's natural path. Snow lingered on the highest peaks of the White Mountains while spring bloomed in the valleys. His first inkling of concern began with a few lifeless trees where no natural occurrence seemed plausible. Before long he saw more brown than green, and wildflowers became dead grass and ragged weeds.

When the narrow lane merged into a graveled drive, he felt a wave of malevolence, like desperate fingers of death reaching for life, or shadows lingering in a dormant forest. Darkness had swallowed Avon; of that he was sure, reminiscent of a winter without snow, with no blanket of white to cover the bleakness beneath.

"We've arrived," Rosa announced with false cheer, parking a few car lengths behind a gated door. A carriage house designed more for grandeur than security declared the entrance of Castell Avon as clearly as her words.

That would change, among other things.

"What's happened here?" Even from where he sat, enclosed in metal and glass, he felt starved earth on the island . . . *and parasites?* He could think of no other explanation for a land that appeared sucked of its very life force. "Your forest is dead."

Her hands clenched the steering wheel. "It's suffering

from misuse under a distorted leadership, but it's not dead, not yet." She spoke the truth, he believed, but not all of it. "I want to bring life back to my island. I want Avon to be like your Rhuddin Village, once we expel the filth."

It didn't go unnoticed that she'd used his precise words against him. "I hadn't been aware the extent of damage when I made that promise. My brother's territory has been nurtured for centuries. This place is overwhelmed by desolation."

Soft light outlined her profile in quiet disappointment as she turned off the truck's engine and placed the keys in the center console. "I only need your help to reclaim Avon, which, if you'll remember, was my original request when I came to your home."

"Isn't that what we're doing?" He shook his head. Her suddenly distant behavior puzzled him more than the topic at hand.

"Afterward, if you wish to revoke our personal arrangement, I won't object." She turned to him then. Her violet gaze filled with assurance made more poignant for the sincerity he read within. "We both know you married me for Avon. Now that you've seen it's no great treasure, no one need know our arrangement was consummated."

Ah. Now he began to understand. She was giving him one last chance to default before announcing it to whoever waited inside. How many promises had been broken in her life, he wondered, to reject his so easily? Indeed, Avon wasn't the treasure in this arrangement, a point of distinction becoming stronger the longer he spent in her company. No, that sat before him with her hands fisted by her sides, evidence of her first real emotion since beginning her little speech.

"I'll know, Rosa." He reached over and enclosed her hand within both of his, coaxing it open to entangle their fingers. "Once given, I keep my vows. I only need to reassess how to keep this one." He gave her hand a gentle squeeze. "We *will* restore Avon."

Her eyes closed briefly and her fingers returned the slightest bit of pressure. "I hope . . ." Her voice broke on that simple word. "I hope so."

"And you'll not mention ending our marriage again."

She tugged her hand from his grasp. "If you don't give me cause, then I won't."

Letting her withdraw for the moment, Luc began a mental list of what needed his immediate attention. He began with simple mechanics first, noting that the electrical lines stopped at the carriage house. "Is electricity run through the bridge?"

She shook her head. "Math kept everything relatively feudal, except for the plumbing. Bathrooms were added about a century ago. There are generators on the island to heat water and run the laundry facilities."

"How have the locals not noticed?" Environmentalists should be rightly screaming. Even remote territories were bound to have humans happen upon them by chance.

"Oh, they have. Locally, Math was known for his eccentricities and generous donations. Anyone stupid enough to investigate further was terminated."

Her practiced responses only provoked more questions, ones that would have to wait as two Avon guards walked around the building. The scarred one with a patched eye relaxed his stance before schooling his reaction.

"The guard on the right is one of mine," Rosa said. "His name's Gareth. He's also my porter and I don't want him harmed. The other is Briog. Do with him as you wish."

"Briog is a shifter, I assume." Both guards frowned at Luc but Gareth's single-eyed gaze held an edge of intimate displeasure.

"So is Gareth. His disfigurement was a punishment from Math."

He heard regret in her voice. *For kinship? Or for some-*

thing more? He also noted the porter's possessive glare. "Is Gareth your lover, Rosa?"

She stiffened slightly. "No." Her vehemence was as candid as her denial. "I've never been tempted enough to endanger another's life for a fleeting moment of pleasure."

His tension eased. He'd suspected as much but wanted her confirmation. *Why* he cared about her former lovers was better left for later deliberations. For now, Luc assessed the extensive damage done to Gareth's face. "What did he do to deserve such a punishment?"

"Gareth had an affair with a mortal. Her name was Rachel, a widow who had lived in the next town over. Math was of the same mind-set as many Council members who believe mixing with humans is weakening our race. It isn't tolerated."

"Math had Rachel killed," he assumed by her tone.

"Quite brutally," she confirmed softly. "Then he destroyed Gareth's face so no other humans would be attracted to him. At the time Gareth was our envoy to the local governments. Others served in his stead during the 1900s, but Gareth was reinstated fifteen years ago and Math reapplied the scars."

"He hasn't shifted for fifteen years?"

"No. He likes his freedom, as meager as it is, and the locals now know him by his scars."

"The forced seclusion will end," he clipped. Banishment had always been his brother's punishment, one that was taken seriously because Dylan provided a safe and fair environment for their kind. With time and trust it would be the same for Avon.

A black Chevy suburban pulled up beside them, one of the few vehicles large enough to accommodate Teyrnon's size. The Norseman scanned the property, then met Luc's gaze and held. The tinted windows didn't hinder his silent message: *Something is amiss on this island surrounded by rivers, more than just a Guardian lair.*

Luc returned a sharp nod of agreement. Cormack and three other guards had ridden with Teyrnon from Salmon Mountain; doors opened as they spilled out, stretched and readied themselves for a potential battle. Isabeau's sedan and other cars followed, parking in a haphazard cluster so as not to block one another in.

"Are you prepared for this?" Luc asked.

"Oh, yes." Rosa opened the door and jumped to the gravel. She belted the sword and scabbard he'd given her around her waist, adjusting it to settle on her hip. Her former weapon and makeshift rope remained in the truck. Favoring her right hand, his gift rested on her left side, accentuating her curves like a warrior queen. She'd been taught to reach across her chest to release her weapon. They hadn't had time for a decent sparring session, but she held her posture with confidence as Luc walked with her, stopping a few paces before the two Avon guards.

Rosa looked to Gareth first. "Has anyone been harmed in my absence?"

"Mae," he confirmed without apparent emotion. Up close, his disfigurement revealed a graphic story of torture, while his one good eye scanned Luc with suspicion. "Cadan tried to intervene, but—"

"Where are the other guards?" A slight frown marred Rosa's otherwise calm features, as if this news was commonplace.

"A handful are watching the shallow side; a few are searching for you. The rest are in the castle."

Luc remained silent for the moment, allowing Rosa to collect information, taking his cue from her lead. Soon enough, his good intentions were thwarted, as they often were in the company of fools.

Briog spat on the ground next to his feet, twitching nervously as more cars pulled in. "How dare you come here, Beast?" He had a wiry build, brown hair made darker by grime, eyes gaunt and sunken. He turned to Rosa with a sneer. "What is this? What have you done?"

A smile spread across Luc's face, one he practiced for enemies. Most knew to run. "I'm Rosa's husband and your new leader. Show disrespect one more time and you'll lose your head."

Ten

ROSA REFUSED TO COWER UNDER THE FULL WEIGHT OF Gareth's accusing glare. His one eye held the heat of two, daring her to confirm or deny Luc's claim. What he read in her stance distorted an already maimed face.

"Tell me he lies," Gareth demanded with an underlying plea.

"I cannot," she confirmed softly. Gareth may not have been her lover—but he'd made a few dangerous flirtations over the years, all of which she had ignored, hoping he would desist without the inevitable anger. "As of yesterday Luc Black is my husband."

"Was it consummated?" Though Gareth's posture exuded only casual curiosity, anguish leaked into his voice.

Rosa hesitated, sparing one final glance in Luc's direction. "I don't wish to discuss the—"

"Thoroughly," Luc interrupted, putting the final verbal seal on their arrangement. He also earned several chuckles from the guards who'd begun to gather behind them.

His arrogance should anger her, but it was difficult to hold such an emotion when something eased from her chest.

An unseen weight had lifted. Her seed of hope, the one she dared not wish for, had sprouted within her darkness of doubt. Comparable to root vegetables in a dank cellar, it had made do without sun. Perhaps it had happened when Luc confirmed his intentions to keep his word—or sooner, when he'd given her a sword.

Now it spread its first leaf.

"This marriage—" Her voice dropped off when Luc had the gall to wink at her, but she recovered by turning her back. "This *arrangement* is the most sensible solution to our needs," she explained to Gareth. "I've returned with three armies to help us maintain Avon."

Gareth had gone quiet, watchful of their exchange. A distorted growl broke the air—from Briog, not her friend. With more impudence than intellect, Briog lunged toward her with his fist raised. Luc reacted in a blur of motion, of leather and steel, and the bite of his beast's power. He had his sword unsheathed and poised before the blow landed, removing Briog's arm in the process.

Rosa reacted as well—but not in time to counter the attack. Her new sword, though lovely, was longer than her mother's and caught on its sheath, a slight hesitation but an unacceptable one. "My speed needs work," she admitted with self-censure over Briog's outraged screams. "I'll practice more . . . now that I can."

"You will die for this, Beast!" Panting in outrage, Briog cradled his bloodied stump against his chest.

"Shut your vile mouth, Briog." Gareth found a target for his frustration and released it without restraint. He, too, had unsheathed his sword. As Avon's porter, he was one of the few allowed to carry one. "Or I'll remove what can't be healed with a shift."

Briog stilled. Deadened eyes landed on his supposed comrade with disgust. "You knew about this," he accused. "You will be named traitor along with them. I will make sure of it."

With steady purpose, Rosa approached Briog, allowing him to witness what she'd kept hidden all those years under his torment and unwanted flirtations. His eyes widened at her aggressive posture, at the power she pulled from a frail forest.

The weapon she raised this time was an invisible one, but just as formidable as forged metal, and far more comfortable in her grasp. Trees groaned with their sacrifice as weakened branches cracked, a sound much like gunshots and breaking bones. Such an eerie resonance and a sad reminder of her cause, cries of nature carried on the wind.

But the power felt good, too good. She took more than needed. Her inner wolf paced, impatient and ready to run. Rosa coaxed her other half back with a thought. *Soon, but not yet. This is for proof of our authority . . . This is for our right to be free.*

Elements flooded her senses, wind kissed by circles of raindrops from the mountains. Her river was her balm, her equalizer and her defense, as pure and resolute as melting snow.

"What are you doing?" Gareth took a protective stance beside her, a show of faith despite his unease.

"If you're my friend, I'll ask you to trust me now."

"You know I am," he said. "And I do."

Briog began to squirm, expecting her to shift at any moment and attack. The longer she resisted the urge, the wider his eyes became. "You are an alpha," he whispered with disbelief.

Only an alpha could hold this much power without succumbing to the change. It singed like lightning under her skin, burning her blood and oozing from her pores—but she held it, promising her inner wolf a grand feast this evening for her cooperation.

Briog hedged backward, stinking of fear and prey. Even Teyrnon and Isabeau sent wary glances her way. A growl pierced the air—a war cry—from Cormack.

"Yes, I am alpha, but more important, I am your queen."

She delivered her proclamation with the authority of one, as if Briog were a flea sucking blood off a fat rat, and that rat was three—no, make that four—days dead.

"Rosa . . . ?" Luc gave a warning growl by her side. Like in the truck, his voice held questions, so many questions. He would receive his answers, *after.*

She turned to her new husband, who stood with his legs braced and chin lowered, ready to charge. "I warned you I wouldn't be a submissive wife." *And I gave you your chance to renege . . . You chose not to accept my offer.*

After a long pause, Luc said, "So you did." His silver gaze sparked blue, heated by dancing flames. His wolf was pleased and wanted to play, but the human in control held it back.

Rosa circled Briog. "It's within my rights to take any man or husband I choose. Luc Black is an unmated shifter. His family has proven their power. We are a good match and I have full faith the Council will come to terms with my new arrangement." She made an impatient motion with her free hand. "Go tend to your wounds while I show my husband our home."

Luc offered her his arm. A slow, predatory grin tugged at his mouth as he gave her a brief, if not teasing, bow. "Shall we, my queen."

She grinned despite herself, too drunk on power to resist his antics. "It was a bit much, I think."

"No." He spoke low, only for her ears. "It was necessary. The Guardians only respect power."

Briog's eyes darted to the crowd, then the woods, hedging backward for several paces before turning to bolt on shaken limbs.

"We should kill him," Gareth said as he watched the man scuttle from view. "He'll find the guards searching for you and they will return."

"I *want* him to carry my message to the Guardians." In the past, Rosa would have posed her order as a request, but her docile days were over. She *was* a queen, by birth, alpha blood and her first marriage. Math had ruled over kingdoms in both human and Guardian realms. It was high time she claimed her proper role. "No deaths unless we have to. Let us play their game for a while and perhaps avoid casualties of our own in the process."

"You've thought this through, it seems." Gareth's voice held more surprise than anger. "Without us."

She sighed. "No, I've thought this through *for* you, and for Cadan, and Mae, and Avon, and everyone else who has protected me all these years. I've much to explain, Gareth, and I will, but first we must reclaim our home. Where's Neira?"

"In the great hall," he finally answered. His stance remained guarded but she had confidence he would adjust. "With William. They have been questioning Mae since last evening when you didn't return."

"And Gweir?" she asked.

"He flew Math's body back to Wales this morning as scheduled."

"That's good," she said. "Only two Guardians remain."

"Neira and William are to follow when they find you." His single-eyed gaze fell to Luc. "You've no idea what you've done."

"Oh, I have a good idea." Luc's voice was full of carnal knowledge—and dominance. To prove his claim on her? Or a suggestive promise of spousal privileges?

Either possibility confused her. Besides, now was not the time for such things and she reminded him of that fact. "Luc, have you ever met my aunt?"

WITH ROSA BY HIS SIDE, LUC MARCHED ACROSS AN ELABO-orate bridge made of stone and wood, leading the procession of wary guards. Boot heels echoed in a scattered rhythm on wide planks. Death clung to the air like rotting vegetation and coated his nostrils, worsening as they neared the shallow island. Stranger yet, the bridge didn't meet land; it ended on stone parapets so water flowed freely around the shore, leaving Castell Avon eerily disconnected from the mainland.

"What is this?" Luc asked Rosa with mounting unease.

"It's just a small jump." She descended off the bridge in a smooth leap to prove her point.

"I understand the concept," Luc clipped. "Just not the reason behind it."

Frowning, she sent an absent wave toward the river. "Ice can build on the shore in winter."

The weak explanation didn't fool him. "Even more reason to build a steady foundation on both sides of land above water."

Her tongue reached out to moisten her lips. Her eyes fell to Isabeau and the line of guards listening behind him. "I will answer all your questions, I promise, but can they not wait until after?"

"A brief explanation is all I need for now." He kept his feet rooted to the bridge. "I'm not moving until I have one."

She cast a nervous glance in a direction he assumed led to Castell Avon. "Fine," she said on a defeated breath, her voice washed away with the sound of rushing water. "The river is the one element we've found that effectively contains the *Beddestyr.*"

"Excuse me?" Luc asked, hoping the rushing waters had skewed her words.

"We came to this island because it's surrounded by moving water." She nodded toward the river. "It nulls their powers."

Teyrnon hissed beside him. "Did she just say the Walkers are here?"

Luc held up his hand as more voices rose behind him. "I thought Math was sent here by the Council to watch us?"

"Please," Rosa scoffed. "Why would you think the Guardians care about this place, or you? They care only about themselves. And Cymru. They protect our homeland because it's where our kind began."

"I always knew there had to be more to it," Isabeau said,

unable to stay quiet by Luc's side. "What happened with the Walkers to bring them here? And how many are there?"

"There are four of them left now." Once she revealed a secret, Rosa was generous with her answers. "You must know about Fairbryn."

"Of course." Luc had lived in the area once, when it was inhabited only by outcasts of his kind in camps away from Guardian rule, long before humans had formed a town and named it Fairbryn.

"Then you know what happened there," Rosa said in a way that suggested they should.

"I was born a little over three hundred years after the modern calendar lists the birth of Christ," Luc reminded her, calling for patience. "Much happened on that land over the last two thousand years. You'll have to be more specific."

She prompted, "In the late 1700s."

"Are you referring to the typhoid outbreak?" Isabeau asked, earning a nod from Rosa. "Most humans died from it, if I remember. But that was a while ago, around—"

"Around the time we settled here," Rosa finished. "The fact that the Americans wanted independence at the same time was just a coincidence."

"It wasn't typhoid that killed the humans in Fairbryn," Luc guessed.

"It was the Walkers," Rosa confirmed. "Or that's what the Council assumes. The Walkers were in Fairbryn at the time. Not surprising, Taliesin was there as well." Wherever that man traveled, bad things happened—and the Walkers had never been far behind to fix his misdeeds. Many of their kind believed that the Walkers had once been messengers to the Otherworld and that they had acted on Ceridwen's orders to guard her son. "An outbreak of a rampant disease was a convenient way for the Council to cover the human deaths, and keep others away. They chose to move the Walkers to an isolated area far away from our homeland."

"We're a dumping ground for their problems." Luc ran a

hand through his hair. "With Math sent to keep watch and be rewarded for doing so."

"Essentially, yes." After a pause, Rosa added, "The Council doesn't want the Walkers harmed. We can use their problems, as you call them, against them."

"You say that as if they're incapable of defending themselves," Isabeau pointed out. "And yet they drained a village and its inhabitants of life, not to mention this island."

"Not consciously." Rosa lifted her hands up only to let them fall back to her sides. "The Walkers are in a coma-like state, like shells without souls. The Council believes their spirits are trapped in the Otherworld, the Land of Faery, and that they are trying to come back to their earthly forms."

"Is that what you believe?" Luc asked.

"I'm not sure what I believe . . ." She let her voice trail off for lack of an appropriate answer. "It's better for you to see and decide for yourself than try to explain."

Teyrnon made another suggestion. "Wouldn't it be easier if we just killed the poor bastards and let their spirits rest where they are?"

"I've often wondered if they would welcome that, but it feels—"

"Cowardly," Isabeau supplied.

"No." Rosa shook her head. "Wrong. I feel like they want to return. Also," she warned, "we did have one guard who entered a Walker's tomb with malicious intent. Later he rigged himself up to a guillotine in Math's dungeon and cut off his own head."

"We'll discuss this more later," Luc said and jumped from the bridge. "Once we control Avon."

The others followed. One by one, Isabeau, Teyrnon, and the rest landed on dry ground covered with rust-colored needles. *One day this river will be lined with moss and grass, and wildflowers in spring.* A silent vow as Luc made a motion for Rosa to walk ahead and guide the way. They followed her through a well-traveled path colored in sepia and muted browns—not the lush emeralds, blues and golds of Rhuddin Village.

No saplings lined the forest edge, too malnourished to survive tender beginnings. Only the elder trees provided minimal shelter, with roots exposed by years of erosion. Many grew around rocks and boulders and stretched their gnarled feet into a barren forest floor—survivors, like Rosa, he realized, refusing to die under the rule of a greedy king.

Castell Avon soon came into view, with several stories of stone, stained glass and classic turrets. Another gift from the Council, he expected, for guarding their mistakes. "The yard is empty." He stopped Rosa before she crossed under a stone archway that led to the outer bailey. "Could the Guardians not have spared even a few watchmen? And where are your *Hen Was*?"

"How many guards do you think Avon has to spare? Many of them died in your woods a week ago." She nodded toward Gareth, who followed at the end of their procession. "Our best one is with me. My aunt will have her personal protectors close to her. And my friends will have gone to the woods as soon as trouble began." Her gaze lifted to his, still red from what she held within, the only indication of her wolf. "It's the Guardians who will come after that we need to prepare for, when Neira and William inform them of what I've done."

A possessive instinct gripped his gut when he looked at her like this, discussing the defense of her territory with power bleeding from her pores. Admiration too. And pride.

His wolf added another thought. *Mine.*

"We'll be prepared for whatever counterattack the Guardians bring upon us," he promised. Still, he wondered where her people had gone. "These woods cannot provide enough shelter to hide." If they did, he couldn't imagine where.

"We have another place," she said vaguely. "Across the river."

"I see." More secrets. Having learned of the Walkers, this one could wait.

They crossed the courtyard in silence, as if tromping over the grave of a powerful witch, expecting a curse to attach and follow them out. Despite their foreboding, Teyrnon and a few other guards gave reminiscent sighs as they entered the inner bailey. Unlike Luc, many of his warriors had spent their youths in places such as this, learning to fight and play in stone-enclosed yards.

In spite of Rosa's claim and because it was beyond comprehension, Luc expected at least a few Avon guards to greet them. But no, even the front doors stood ajar over wide steps made of stone, thick oak panels framed by wrought iron hinges. Once inside the castle, caged gas lanterns lined the walls, drawing them down a long hallway toward an assembly of hushed voices.

With whispered movements and soundless signals they approached. The throughway opened to a great hall two stories high, with a circular balcony that led to upper rooms. From above, stained glass windows cast colorful beams that met at a central point on a stone floor. A small crowd gathered in the disjointed light. The Guardians' numbers were few, a dozen—if not less, and only if he included their guards in the tally.

Pitiful, Luc thought, that these were the leaders whom many of their kind feared—whom *he* had once feared. At the moment, these Guardians were too enthralled by perverted amusements to notice an invasion.

In the center of the gathering sat an older woman tied to a chair, her head bowed forward, unconscious. *Hen Was*, he assumed, given that healed scars mapped a trail down her neck, not quite hidden under fresh-cut flesh. A younger man was tied with her, or rather, *to* her. He remained untouched, at least visibly, since blood caked the woman's shirt but not his. Regardless, he drew attention with his long red hair and eyes that burned with hatred.

Neira walked a circle around the pair, blond and fair like many of their kind. A tiny woman in knee-high boots, leather pants and a red vest, swinging a thronged whip—she was a demented bully, a performer dressed in circus garb. Not only finding joy in causing pain, but also making it a show. Worse, if the man was Cadan, then she'd been punishing her own grown son.

He felt an instant affinity for Cadan in that moment.

And, yes, Luc had seen Neira once, from afar, standing beside his own mother, wearing clothing far more primeval than this. There had been a time when he had wanted Merin's acceptance, before Dylan had forced him to board a ship to a new world. The Guardians had loved their festivals, had flaunted them far and wide, with games, music, bards and roasting meats, while non-shifters served them or starved.

Slaves had been more valued than Luc; as a Bleidd, he should have been killed at birth. If not for Dylan, he would have been. Even so, even knowing they despised his existence, he'd watched from the woods, hiding under the cover of trees, longing to be human, to be a man—to be a wanted son.

He'd dared to be seen that day, to step away from the forest edge, if only for a moment, to let his mother know he wasn't dead. The two women had laughed at him, like friends. The wind had carried their voices, enough to know he'd been the source of their amusement. He'd slunk back to the shadows. The Beast of Merin who lived in the forbidden forests of Cymru, the black wolf who could not shift had not deserved to play in the light among their gilded throngs.

Drowning with unwanted memories, Luc waved a signal to proceed. Reflexively he gripped his sword. He'd found the weapon in Rhuddin two months after his first shift, before more outcasts followed and requested sanctuary from Dylan. Like Cormack was now, he'd barely been able to walk. But he'd understood the world like any other man. He'd wanted like one, and bled like one, even if the wounds had not been of the flesh.

Neither Dylan nor Elen could confirm who'd placed it there, but they'd had their suspicions. Both had seen their father carry it, and then their mother after his death.

Swords, for their kind, were the most precious heirlooms to bequeath. Because their generations were so few, most kept them for life. He understood why Rosa cherished hers. His had been given to him by less pure hands. As his own retribution, he used it when facing Guardians, the people who had wanted him dead. Even his own mother had been willing to kill him to protect her other children from their scorn. Later, her only acknowledgment of his existence had been to laugh about him with her friends. Giving birth to a Bleidd weakened her in their eyes, and only the powerful survived under Guardian rule.

But then, why leave him a gift such as this? If indeed it was Merin who had. And if she despised him so, why not give it to Dylan, or Elen? Luc shook his head to clear his thoughts. He had stopped seeking Merin's acceptance a long time ago. Still, even though it galled him to admit it, there were times when her rejection festered like an unhealed wound.

Koko's Journal

August 12, 1928

I cannot sleep. It is one of those hot nights when the air is thick with moisture and the sheets cling to my skin like spiderwebs in the rain. I prefer autumn, with cool nights and warm blankets.

As I sit here with pen in hand, I wonder if it is not the heat that keeps me awake, but rather the images that haunt my thoughts. They race around my head like pesky ghosts, as if calling me to put them to paper and bring them back from death.

Strange, how the image that haunts me most is of Luc's sword, the one he keeps behind our bed and believes I know not of it. Sometimes he forgets, I think, that Gypsy blood flows in my veins. Secrets are like shadows and my people know shadows well.

I believe the image is a warning; it flows fast like a river, only to be felt and seen, but not held. Luc's sword is entangled in the knots of a Celtic Moon. It waits for him in a violet grove surrounded by broken trees.

I fear it is a vision of his past and future, and has naught to do with his present, or with me. I will paint it now to expel my ghosts.

I only wish I could expel his.

~Koko

Eleven

Alas, false forfeit gains no vantage. From deadened
earth, fevers rise, of lust and lament.

Aunt Neira stood in the middle of the great hall,
wearing an outrageous costume spattered in blood, and a
well-fed smile distorting an ageless face. Blond hair, blue
eyes, tepid features and a taste for pain—her victim's as well
as her own—she resembled an angel of death in the biblical
sense, only without the mercy bit.

Rosa swallowed her fury, even though it burned like
embers stoked by a drunkard's breaths, threatening to ignite
on fumes alone. Mae and Cadan were bound to chairs, and
to each other, back-to-back and facing opposite directions.
Neira circled with one of her many toys, like a circus han-
dler breaking in misbehaved animals.

Mae's eyes had swelled shut from Neira's beating. Her
face, already bearing too many scars, would have more after
this. Rosa wanted to go to her, to pull her from that chair,
but to show any sign of favoritism would only make her a
target for future torture. Knowing Neira would suffer for
this deed helped Rosa hold her ground. Oh, yes . . . Mae

couldn't shift but she possessed other skills, knowledge of alchemy that had felled more than one wolf.

Cadan faced the entryway and noticed their entrance first. His hair hung loose around bare shoulders, soft red like a fox's pelt against pale skin. His curse was beauty where hers was fertility. She gladly accepted her affliction over his, because hers could be secretly controlled.

Green eyes lifted to meet hers; torment bled to relief, absent of his usual candor. Cadan would rather feel pain than have another take it in his stead, a weakness his mother had known and used well.

Luc found her free hand and squeezed briefly before letting it go. The gesture was alien to her, a form of comfort, offering strength with support.

"Let me go in first," she whispered. "It's me they want."

Together, Luc mouthed in return.

Rosa felt the gentle pressure of his hand on her back as she stepped forward. "Aunt Neira, what's going on here?" Her announcement echoed through the cathedral-like room. "I have some happy news I want to share."

Her aunt jumped, issuing a small squeak as she turned. "Rosa Beatrice Alban, you naughty child, where have you been?" Neira had a singsong voice, rising and falling on the cadence of her breaths, like a twitter bird in flight. Recovered from her surprise, she barely glanced at Luc, or the rebel warriors filing in to form a half circle around Rosa. "Why have you brought these people here?"

"We must have a feast," Rosa proclaimed in forced joviality. "I'm married once again."

Neira sniffed, clucking her tongue. "If what you say is true, then your selfishness has reached new heights."

William cleared his throat, rising from a chair located under the balcony to declare his presence. The second Guardian wore a dark suit, dressed for a journey among humans, with his fair hair cropped short; he presented an image of a formidable businessman. He was one, after all, for the Council.

"Your disregard for the Council's plans has now become an issue, Rosa." The Guardian gave a bored sigh as if annoyed by this slight delay. His pale gaze scanned the rebels, shrewder than Neira's. "You will cease whatever juvenile plans you had by bringing these"—his nostrils flared with disgust—"*Drwgddyddwg* in my presence."

Evil Bringers. The term was the equivalent of *Hen Was*, only much less kind, created by the Guardians when the first non-shifters were born, fearing their loss of power.

Cormack gave a warning growl by her side. He'd weaved his way to the front of the crowd. She rested her hand on his side, a show of support in front of the Guardians, one that did not go unnoticed.

"And a Bleidd," William added with a sneer. "We could charge admittance for this freak show."

"Aunt Neira is dressed for the part," Rosa mocked. *Never* had she dared such disrespect.

Her aunt's lips peeled back when the insult registered.

Confirming her intent, Rosa curled her fingers in Cormack's fur. He allowed the intimate gesture; perhaps for the purpose it was given.

"We also have the Beast among us," Neira returned with petty insults and perverted words. "Merin's runt. You are the image of your father, did you know?" Greedy eyes scanned Luc in a long perusal that left little doubt of her thoughts. "My, oh, my," she hummed, "does your human skin ever fit you well. I will have fun removing it."

For Neira, pain was her pleasure.

Luc laughed at her, a deep chuckle of belittling amusement.

Neira hissed as if slapped, accustomed to having her victims cower in fear. Lowering her chin, she gripped her whip, poised to lift her arm when a shrill sound came from her waist, echoed by another from William's lapel, intrusively modern in the medieval gauntlet. Her expression went from savagery to glee in the time it took her instrument for flagellation to fall, forgotten in a black serpentine heap.

If not for Mae, who had yet to move, Rosa would have laughed at the absurdity. "I believe you both have a call." She had seen a human using the portable device, enough to recognize the sound, and had read about them in the magazines she snuck to her secret cabin across the river.

"Sin sent us these cell phones as a gift," Neira boasted. "He is coming home to us."

Only a select few called Taliesin by that name. Rosa wondered whether the man would welcome its use by her aunt, but then tried not to waste much of her mental energy when it came to him.

"It is a message," Neira preened. "Oh, look at this," she breathed in her twitter-bird voice. "Sin sent me a photograph." Her hands fumbled with the phone. "Why can I not see it?"

"Just touch the screen, Neira," William snapped, impatient with her antics, and her ineptitude. "Like this."

Neira mimicked his motion, viewing whatever message she received. Her smile froze. William merely turned to Luc for a more calculating assessment.

"Explain this to me!" Neira marched over and shoved the phone at Rosa, holding it up in front of her face.

Rosa blinked at the small rectangular box with an image of her standing nude next to Luc, recalling the flash of light and Taliesin's grin after taking it. "That's a photograph of our wedding."

William's gaze narrowed. "Taliesin was there?"

"Actually, if you must know, it was his idea." Whatever Taliesin was about, Rosa might owe him a kind word for this, if only a small one.

Neira appeared stunned by this news, wide-eyed and pale, like Rosa's own expression in the photograph. Another chorus of modern music echoed from both phones. Neira fiddled with hers for a bit. Her breath caught over what she saw. A muscle clenched on the side of William's jaw before he shoved the phone in his pocket.

What an amazing device. Rosa wanted one, if it could produce such responses. She couldn't help but lean over for a peek. It was a picture of Taliesin. Well, to be truthful, it was mostly of his middle finger.

"Math's funeral is scheduled for tomorrow evening," William announced to Rosa. "You will come with us for the service."

She gave him her sweetest smile. "I would rather die."

He sent her a look suggesting that he could easily arrange her wish. "Neira," he announced, "we are leaving, for the moment."

"I do not take orders from you, William. We cannot let them—"

"You can stay," he interrupted with an elegant wave toward Luc and Rosa, arching his arm to include the warriors that now surrounded the Guardians in a circle of unsheathed swords and feral grins. "But I don't share your taste for pain." He pivoted for the stairs. "Taliesin's messages must be discussed with the Council before we continue with any drastic measures," he warned. "Once I retrieve a personal item, I will be gratefully gone from this cursed place."

If she didn't despise them so, Taliesin included, Rosa might feel empathy for the *Gwarchodwyr Unfed*, the Original Guardians who had lost the respect of their foster son. A mere sighting of Taliesin warranted an assembly of all Council members. Math had been called to attend meetings over unsubstantiated evidence rather than actual contact from the man, much less photographs.

Once-powerful creatures of Celtic lore were now Guardians of a dying race, created to protect the son of a goddess— and the very purpose of their existence spurned them at every opportunity. Desperation may well become their eventual undoing.

Cadan cleared his throat and spoke for the first time since the rebels stopped his mother's interrogation. "Check his rooms before he leaves." His voice was hoarse from abuse.

His gaze searched for Rosa and held. "Trust me. Just check his rooms."

And then, true to her experience, a reminder would come of why the Guardians didn't deserve compassion. Rosa searched the crowd for Gareth.

"I'm on it," he said without being asked. Gareth headed for the balcony, lunging up the stairs while Luc gave a nod for Teyrnon to follow.

Neira frowned as if confused. "Cadan, you are coming with us. There is no need for you to stay here now that Math is dead."

A bitter laugh fell from Cadan's mouth, looking down at his tied hands. "To quote my dear cousin, Mother, I would rather die." His words rang as true as Rosa's.

Neira pursed her lips. "I am sorry I had to punish you, but all is forgiven now that I know Sin is involved. I am sure he has a reason for all of this. Maybe even another prophecy."

Cadan ignored his mother. "Is it true, Rosabea? Did you wed our neighbor's brother?" There was hesitation in his tone. His only interaction with Dylan had not been a pleasant one.

"I did what needed to be done," she said without remorse.

Cadan's gaze searched hers. "I had hoped it wouldn't come to that again."

She wanted to tell him of Rhuddin Village, how rich it was with life and freedom, but would save that for when they were alone. After a pause, she admitted what she could in front of Neira. "So far"—heat crawled up her neck—"my second marriage hasn't been entirely unpleasant."

The first touch of mirth turned the corner of her cousin's mouth, and she almost breathed a sigh of relief to see even a minimal sign of his normal self. "Then let us accept that blessing at least," he teased, as he often did to lighten a tense situation.

Luc strode to the center of the room and released Cadan's ropes with a flick of his sword. "What's in William's room?"

Cadan gave him a wary glance. "I don't know, but he feeds it." He stretched his arms, then turned to Mae and began working the knots that held her upright in the chair. "And it cries."

Rosa rushed to catch Mae as she fell forward, unconscious still. She scanned the crowd for anyone who might help. Her eyes fell on Tesni; she wore the same bibbed skirt Rosa had seen her in the day before. Had it been only a day? It felt like a year since she'd first walked off this island.

Tesni stepped forward, followed by two more *Hen Was* who had stayed with Cadan instead of escaping with the others. "Bethan and Tobias," Rosa called them out. "Come here if you will and carry Mae to her bed and tend her wounds. Tesni or I will find you when all is secured."

GARETH AND FIVE OTHER GUARDS REMOVED WILLIAM AT the points of their swords, along with Neira and the rest of their ensemble. The Guardians were escorted across the river and allowed to leave in the vehicles they'd arrived in. Isabeau and her men circled the island and set up camp around the outskirts, prepared to warn and defend if necessary.

Once the castle was secured, Luc made his way to the second floor. He needed only to glance at Teyrnon to know he wasn't going to like what he found.

With lips pressed in a tight line, the Norseman gave a wary shake of his head, his legs braced in front of the door, standing sentry in a bedchamber of painted ceilings and carved wooden panels until Luc arrived.

Cadan and Rosa pushed by him only to halt a few paces in. Like gawkers in a sick room, they simply stared. Tesni followed, but not before giving him a thorough scan. She was bold, this *Hen Was*, and comely—and loyal to Rosa by the dangerous glint in her narrowed glare. Like the others, morbid curiosity eventually drew her gaze toward the open armoire.

A thin woman sat huddled within the ornate closet with her arms wrapped around a female child.

"I heard them in the bathroom earlier," Cadan informed them. He seemed to have bounced back from his ordeal. No doubt, like his cousin, he had his own guise of filtering cruelty from the mind.

Rosa ran her hands over her face. "I won't ask how you know that."

She was fighting fatigue, Luc knew, and her wolf. She needed to run and then rest.

"It is not like that with William," Tesni said in a defensive tone. "He refuses to touch any of us. He thinks we are all tainted. Cadan served William's meals to protect the others. That is how he knew someone else was in here."

Slowly, Luc approached the armoire. "We mean you no harm."

The woman unfolded from the cabinet and stood, leaving the child huddled within a curtain of coats. "Is William gone?"

"He is," Luc affirmed. "Is the child yours?"

Affronted, the woman scoffed, "I'm its tutor, no more. The creature is a Wulfling."

"A Wulfling?" Rosa frowned with disbelief.

Luc swore under his breath. "Where the hell did William find a Wulfling?"

Wulflings began as infant shifters, often deserted by the deaths of their parents while in hiding. The few he'd known had been discovered in isolated forests, no doubt because populated areas posed different hazards; children were too innocent to conceal their true nature, even among humans. The parents brave enough to keep their young from the Council were almost always hunted and killed for their cause. And some, like this one's parents, built secret places to hide their child during an attack.

And sometimes, though it was rare, the child wasn't found. They were left alone to fend for themselves, and without the company of humans they were unable to learn by example. Survival instincts of their wolves often became more dominant than their humanity.

When the woman refused to answer, Luc took a step forward and unsheathed his sword, lightly resting the tip on the woman's shoulder. He had no patience when it came to the mistreatment of children. "Tell me the Wulfling's history and how she ended up in William's care."

The Guardian gave a haughty sniff; she may be a teacher but her disdain of a child revealed her loyalty to the Council's bigotries. "After hearing suspicious reports, William hunted and retrieved it from the Black Forest this January. I tutored future kings and queens," she sneered with pride. "I tutored the children of Guardians. And he took me from my home as if I were no more than a servant. He forced me to be a caretaker to a . . . to a *beastling* worse than you. He'll kill me now that his secret's exposed."

Luc lowered his sword, sensing the truth in her story. "What is your name?"

She hesitated a moment. "Lona Blackwell."

Obviously, it wasn't her real name but it was something to address her by. "Are you requesting sanctuary, Lona Blackwell?"

"In Avon?" Lona scoffed as if she found his offer amusing. "Never!" Her gaze fell to the open door. "Do not doubt that William will return for it." A final warning before she dashed toward the hall. "And I will not be here when he does."

"Let her go," Rosa ordered when Teyrnon made a motion to follow. "If she can leave a child, then let her run away like the coward she is."

Teyrnon looked to Luc for confirmation.

In support of his wife, he nodded. "Make sure Lona leaves the island and doesn't try to return."

"A Wulfling," the Norseman muttered under his breath as he strode from the room. "Will the surprises of this day never end?"

Hearing the scrutiny, the girl scuttled back in a tangle of clothes, with her face tucked deep like a ball. She appeared to be around four or five years of age. The aging process for their kind equaled humans' until adulthood, when it slowed.

The armoire stank of urine and fear. Not surprising if she'd heard William being dragged from the room by several guards while her caretaker fled soon after.

"We will not hurt you." Cadan tried to coax her out. "You are safe now. William is gone."

"You lie." Her reply was muffled by her arms. "He wouldn't leave me here."

"You must be hungry."

Her face lifted with lips peeled back from tiny teeth, a dominant gesture with a gaze to match. Hair the color of hay framed a pixie-like face, albeit a feral one. "Go away or William will kill you."

"He can try." Cadan reached into the closet, attempting to tug her out gently, but the process was like watching him untangle an angry kitten from a padded box, spitting and clawing at his attempts.

Before someone got hurt, Luc removed the hanging clothes and dumped the piles on the bed. Once exposed, the child rolled out with an enraged cry, looked about with wild eyes and made a mad scramble to the bathroom, slamming the door in her wake.

If possible, Rosa's expression became more fatigued. "I thought Wulflings were just tales my mother told me to keep me from wandering too far into woods."

"No, they're real. But I haven't seen one for . . ." Luc had to pause to search his recollection. "A thousand years or so, and not since leaving Cymru."

More important, his nephew wasn't the youngest shifter. Dylan and Sophie would find some relief in that information.

Luc shook his head over this new development, as surprised as Teyrnon. "The fact that she retains her human form, and can talk, is an accomplishment. William obviously wanted her educated."

Rosa fisted her hands by her sides. "He was fostering his potential future breeder."

"I suspect you're right." He shared her ire.

"What are we going to do with a Wulfling?" Now that the situation had begun to register, Rosa began to pace. "For that matter, what are we going to do with a child?" She sounded more perplexed by the latter notion.

"Give her a bath, for starters," Tesni suggested. "Then feed her."

"This is not the place for her." Rosa acted panicked, eyes wild and spooked like a horse in a barn full of shifters.

"What else are we to do?" Cadan challenged. "Should we send her back to William?"

"Of course not!" Rosa paused when a loud crash came from the bathroom. "But what if we do the Wulfling more harm than good by keeping her here?"

Cadan relaxed his stance. "Must you always fret so? Sometimes you are worse than Gareth," he scolded in a way a brother would an overprotective sister.

Luc watched the exchange with interest and began to understand Rosa's affinity for her cousin. "I would ask Dylan and Sophie to take the child in, or my sister." But he suspected the tutor's final warning was an accurate one. "The girl also comes with William's obsession to get her back. I won't put that on my brother's family after what they've just been through, or any other."

Rosa started shaking her head before he finished, regaining her composure after the first initial surprise. "We should handle this responsibility within Avon."

Luc agreed. "We have much to do to strengthen the defenses of this place. The child will need constant supervision for a while."

"And protection," Rosa added.

"Yes." Luc turned to her cousin and Tesni. "Are you both willing to help watch the Wulfling? This is going to take a group effort during an inconvenient time."

Cadan seemed taken aback by the question. "Did I not already say that I would?"

Luc sighed at his defensive tone, realizing the air needed to be cleared of misconceptions before it became a problem. "I know your encounter with my brother was an unfortunate one." He didn't defend Dylan's action because Math's atrocities needn't be aired among those who'd lived through worse. "I am your ally, not your enemy, and I hope we can move beyond that incident and work together to rebuild Avon."

Cadan was quiet for a long moment. "I will help with the Wulfling while she's here. And if we have a chance to rebuild Avon, I will march on the bloody wall."

"If need be, I'll march with you." Luc didn't make light of the offer because a day might come when it was necessary.

A smile greeted him when he chanced to look in Rosa's direction. It tightened his chest, as he suspected her smiles were rare gifts.

"We've never had a child in Avon," she said softly.

With one problem addressed and another delegated, Luc walked to Rosa and placed his hand on her shoulder. When she didn't pull away from his touch, he moved his palm up to cradle her neck. Touching her skin was like holding a live current. "You need to run."

"I know." Her burgundy gaze bled into the whites of her eyes.

"Avon is secure for the night, and I'll help Tesni and Cadan with the girl while you're gone."

That earned him another smile. "You're going to give a Wulfling a bath?"

"No," he teased because suddenly he couldn't help himself. "I'm going to amuse myself by watching them try."

Twelve

STANDING ON THE SHORES OF THE RIVER WYE, TALIESIN tossed his cell phone into the murky waters, letting the currents carry away this latest indulgence with so many others. Even now, with his deed done, her violet eyes haunted him. Rosa saw him for what he was: a monster. May the Gods not punish her for his latest interference?

When William traced the call he would find that it had come from the proximity of his own home, one final insult after the loss of his young Wulfling ward.

He would be livid.

And Merin too—for not being warned. A regrettable necessity; her reactions over the next few days must be pure and absent of previous knowledge. The future of her children depended upon her performance on the Council's seat. Dylan, Luc and even Elen believed their mother despised them. One day they would know her love was so great that she had sacrificed her heart to keep them safe.

Taliesin let his head hang forward as images flooded his

mind's eye: the past, present and future—one mangled mess of free will and destiny, of piety and lust, honor and wickedness. And pain. *Fuck*, so much pain—because of his existence. Sometimes the weight of it robbed him of air.

Running his hands through his hair, he needed a good, stiff drink. Sadly, he'd given up that balm shortly after condemning the Walkers to their lifeless state during a rather satisfactory binge. Poor bastards, indeed—to suffer such a fate. And Rosa, with her violet eyes that saw too much, forced to be the keeper of his sins.

Turning from dark waters and dangerous thoughts, he made his way back to his rented Mazda. Wind and rain snapped against his face, calling him to stay home, pulling at his coat with whispery fingers and humid tears. Like his vodka-scented siren, he resisted their pull. More than three hundred years now he'd remained brutally sober, from the morning after Rosa's first wedding feast.

His flight back to Maine was scheduled to leave in a few hours and he would be on that plane, despite his ability to travel in any form. For him, humankind had their own strengths, as did Luc, Cadan, Rosa, Elen, Isabeau, just to name a few of the many descendants of an ancient race created to protect him; of all the vile curses of the world, that one may well be the worst.

Yet within their dysfunction and weakness he had seen the greatest acts of courage. They did not deserve to be pawns of forgotten Gods, for in their presence he could almost believe the world was less doomed.

And for that alone he must fight for their cause.

WITH SHAKING HANDS, ROSA UNDRESSED AND PLACED her sword and clothes in the hollowed trunk of a tree. Once naked, she collapsed to her knees, bracing her fall with her palms. Pine needles and dirt clung to her sweat-soaked skin as the power consumed her. Head bent, she rode the wave in a rush of breaking bones and re-formed fur over skin. The change was less painful when done quickly, like bathing in her river during winter; easing in only prolonged the torture—and freedom when her other half took form.

Everything was brighter as a wolf, better, uncluttered by useless thoughts and dull senses. She padded her way around secret trails, searching her island where Luc wouldn't know to look. Satisfied to find it clear, she crossed the river at the shallow edge to her own forbidden forest, meandering in circles, and turning back several times to make sure she wasn't followed.

Like Fairbryn, her people had their own place to hide when Guardians were close by, a land trust secretly purchased by the *Hen Was* from many years of combined treasures, then donated to the state of New Hampshire with stipulations to keep it undeveloped.

It was an hour journey at full run. The camp was quiet at first, its small cottages hidden under thick vines and dense trees, like hobbit holes covered in moss. Rosa's own cottage lay nestled over the next bend, built in the shelter of a weeping willow, with just enough room to hold a bed, a cabinet and two bookshelves.

A crescent moon smiled down from a clear sky as Rosa sat back on her haunches and waited to be seen, taking in the sweet sounds and crisp smells of an untainted forest.

Caron was the first to step from the shadows. "It's done," she announced on a reverent breath, trusting Rosa wouldn't be there otherwise. "The Guardians are gone from Avon."

Rosa gave a deep nod, then returned from whence she came, her message delivered. Those who chose to follow did so of their own free will, knowing that the worst battle was yet to come.

AFTER FINDING A BRIBE FOR THE WULFLING, LUC WALKED the halls of Castell Avon, clearing rooms and learning the lay of his new home. Now that control of Avon was accomplished, and the Guardians scurried home to their own beds, he gave orders to his guards to find unoccupied quarters other than the master wing. All rooms were connected on the upper floors, a puzzle of doors and passageways. He claimed the apartments that smelled of vanilla. Afterward, he put Teyrnon in charge of alternating shifts on the island, and Gareth in control of the bridge and surrounding woods. While a third of his guards slept, the others kept watch.

No one had yet dared to venture toward a graveyard of aboveground tombs, once they'd learned the Walkers slept within. Rosa would guide the macabre tour come morning.

Until then, Isabeau and her men met with Daran, making camp on the opposite side of the river. Both leaders planned to return to their own territories after a few hours' rest, leaving some of their guards to assist Luc with strengthening his defenses and the training of Rosa's people.

As always, when leadership changed and armies merged, personalities conflicted. More so when they were wolves. But for the moment, all was calm.

Luc stopped briefly to check in on Mae, and found Rosa sitting on the woman's bed, spent of her wolf but slumped with fatigue. Another *Hen Was*—Bethan, he recalled— bathed Mae's swollen face with a cloth.

He leaned against the doorway. "Your run went well?"

Rosa's violet eyes met his and suddenly he wanted to see them blue once again, vulnerable and human and consumed by passion.

And as quickly as the thought came, another followed— only these eyes were golden-brown and long gone from this world. Guilt roiled in his gut but it was fleeting, less painful, a whisper around a violet grove with blue skies. Whispers were like memories, transient and empty. Selfishly, the idea of a warm woman in his bed after seventy years of cold nights compensated his regret.

"Mae hasn't regained consciousness," she said.

"I know. I'm sorry. I heard when I was in the kitchens. They're well stocked," he pointed out with some relief, because well-fed guards made a more peaceful night. "And your chef is competent."

She shrugged. "We have many depravities here at Avon, but worldly wealth isn't one of them. You'll find this castle is fit to serve a king."

He scanned the small but clean bedchamber, and the woman lying still as stone on the bed. Mae should have awakened by now. The *Hen Was* may not have the ability to shift, but they were more resilient than mortals. "Do you have a healer?"

"Mae *is* our healer," Rosa said, her voice solemn.

"I'll call my sister if she doesn't awaken by morning," Luc offered. "Elen will know what to do."

"Truly?" she whispered. "That would mean a great deal."

"Consider it done." He tipped his head toward the doorway. "Will you join me? I'm on my way back to see how the Wulfling fares. Your Tesni is watching the child while Cadan is finding clothes, and I went in search of a bribe." He held up the bribe, a sack of sugar cookies wrapped in a cloth napkin. "I'm hoping we can get the child settled for the night and then find our own bed."

She frowned. "I thought . . ." Her voice trailed off as she looked to Bethan. With resignation, she rose and told the other woman, "I'll be back in the morning."

"Tobias is relieving me in a few hours," Bethan said. "Go with your new husband; there's naught you can do here." She gave a slight bow to Rosa, then to Luc. "Please know that we are all grateful for what you have done. May your marriage be blessed and these halls echo with the laugher of your young."

Rosa remained silent by his side as they made their way to William's old chambers, now apparently the Wulfling's.

Luc eased open the door to find Tesni stripping and remaking the bed while the girl watched from the bathroom. Gas sconces illuminated the room in a warm glow; though electrical lights had been added in each room, the castle ran mostly on natural resources. Bathrooms were the exception, and most likely the main draw on the generators.

"I told Cadan to get some rest." Tesni spoke directly to Rosa. "I'll keep an eye on the child tonight. A change of clothes wasn't necessary." She paused. "I found something you should see."

Luc looked over Tesni's shoulder as she opened the door to an adjoining closet the size of a small chamber. Toys and books lay scattered across a makeshift bed lined with pillows, with an open bag of clothes for the child shoved hastily in a pile.

"She's eaten a sandwich," Tesni said. "And I drew a bath, but I think we should just let her be for the night."

"I hate to leave her like that." Rosa turned toward the bathroom, concerned and unsure.

"We're not going to." Luc kept his tone at normal levels, knowing the Wulfling listened to every word. "She smells of urine and should be groomed by her new pack. It will ease her fears."

Human children may have different needs, but wolves responded to leadership, and grooming was an act of affection and comfort. The *Hen Was* should have known this, even though she lacked her own wolf.

Assessing the bathroom as he walked in, he removed one cookie from its sack, took the first bite and placed it on the floor within the Wulfling's reach. "What is your name, child?"

"She will not tell me." Tesni moved to the doorway, regarding Luc suspiciously. "And she has already eaten," she reminded him as though he hadn't heard the first time.

"I'm sure she has room for a cookie." *Or four.*

The girl eyed the cookie, Luc, and then the cookie again. He pretended to look away. By the time he turned back she had the entire thing shoved into her mouth; her cheeks puffed out like a chipmunk after finding a bowl of sweetmeats.

He gave her time to chew and swallow before holding up another. She went to grab it but he moved it from her reach. "For your name," he said. "I know you speak English well, and that you understand what I'm asking, unless you don't have a name."

But he suspected that she did.

She ogled the cookie with indecision. "I'm called Audrey."

"Thank you, Audrey. My name is Luc." He handed her the reward and swung the rest of the sack back and forth. Her head moved with the pendulum motion. "These are all yours if you do just a few things for me. We are going to wash you because you are part of our family now. Then you'll dress in fresh clothes. And then you'll be sleeping in this room. Do you understand what I'm telling you?"

Her gaze moved from the cookies, brownish-green and too old for her age. She gave a tiny nod. "William's not coming back."

"That's right." Luc kept his voice calm but firm, kind but dominant. "You'll be staying with us from now on. Tesni will sleep in your room tonight. If you need anything she'll help you."

"William said you stink like humans. He said you were all filthy pigs who slept in hovels. He said I needed to keep quiet or you would eat me for breakfast and suck my bones for dessert."

Rosa slid into the bathroom and crouched down next to Luc. "You smell worse than we do, Audrey. And we eat cookies, not children. And bread with thick cream and strawberry jam. And roasted tarts with gravy fillings. And we sleep in beds with fluffy pillows and warm blankets."

Honesty had a scent and Rosa's was as sweet as her words.

In true Wulfling form, it didn't take Audrey long to decipher friend from foe, even if her senses were hindered by her human skin. "And if I take a bath, I get to have *all* the cookies?"

Rosa nodded. "All of them. And then afterward, if you're still hungry, we'll make you something else."

"A roasted tart with gravy filling?"

"If you like."

The girl looked down. "Can I change?" she whispered. Luc could hear the frantic beats of her heart for daring to ask what she obviously wanted most, to change to the form where she felt the safest. "William gets mad when I change. I go in a dark room and I get so hungry. He says I must be like the *Hen Was*. He says I mustn't change so the Council will not take me away."

Startled, Rosa looked to Luc for advice. William had kept Audrey's ability to shift a secret from the Council. To protect her? Or to keep her for himself? Maybe both. Lona, if indeed that had been the tutor's name, had good reason to run for knowing William's secret.

Luc couldn't help but wonder about the identity of Audrey's parents, though he had little doubt they were dead. "You'll never go hungry here." But he didn't want her to revert to her other form entirely. "I have an idea. Why don't you stay as you are now while the sun is up, and change to your wolf when the sun is down?"

Audrey heaved a sigh larger than her chest should hold. "I can do it." She padded to the side of the tub, stood on her toes and reached her hand into the water. Her stern expression faded into curiosity. She picked up a bar of soap, smelled it, and went to take a bite.

Snagging the bar, Rosa said, "We use that to make bubbles to wash you with."

Audrey frowned. "Smells like food."

"It's made with rosemary and mint." Rosa turned to Luc. "Don't ever use the soap made with lavender."

Curious, Luc asked, "Why?"

"It has an extra ingredient in it from Mae. She makes it special for the Guardians. It will cause sores on your skin."

"Noted."

As if handling a sack of golden eggs, Rosa gently removed Audrey's soiled clothes and tossed them in the corner. There were no welts on her body, or shyness—a blessing in light of how she'd been found.

Rosa lifted the girl into the water, lathered soap in her palms and worked on the child's hair. Audrey allowed the process with attentive eyes, testing the bubbles with her tongue and wrinkling her nose, while Luc stood back and watched his wife.

He recalled Rosa's initial reaction to the Wulfling; she had faced Guardians without fear and yet an innocent child caused her to panic. Instinct tightened his spine then; an assumption, but one he suspected was true. Something, or someone, had been harmed in Avon, an innocent that Rosa had been unable to keep safe.

After the bath, they wrapped her in a thick towel. The child's eyes fluttered closed but she was determined to finish all her cookies. By the time they tucked her into bed, she had succumbed to sleep.

"I will watch her through the night," Tesni said, nodding to Luc. "Cadan will relieve me in the morning and bring the child her morning meal." Her expression was still guarded though less critical.

Rosa went to leave but paused as Tesni grabbed her hand. A meaningful look exchanged between the women. "All is well," Rosa reassured her.

With a nod, Tesni dropped her hand. "Then try to get some rest." The last comment came with a teasing note, although a slight one.

Once in the hallway, Rosa turned to Luc, her eyes wide

with awe as she whispered, "Where did you learn to do that?"

"Do what?"

"Handle children."

A grin tugged at his mouth. "We do have a few in Rhuddin Village." *If only eight.* Children were rare blessings for their kind. He cherished every one, with their bright eyes and curious questions. "And you handled her well. They are resilient little creatures. With love, our Wulfling will be okay. You'll see."

"Our Audrey," she said, sparing one last glance toward the tiny form on the bed before softly closing the door. "The Guardians are gone and in their place we've been given a child." Concern and awe weaved through her voice, as if awarded a gift she dared not accept for fear it would be taken away—*or destroyed*. "We have a child in Avon," she said again in disbelief. "A child without being mated to a Guardian." Her haunted gaze lifted to Luc. "We must protect her."

"We will, Rosa." He wanted to say more, but hesitated. Now was not the time to pry into her secrets; nor was he ready to talk of his.

A silence stretched.

"Yes," she whispered. "Yes, we will." And then her whisper became hushed laughter and it was a glorious sound. "I don't want to go to bed for fear I'll wake up and this will all be a dream."

Watching her like this, spontaneous with joy, triggered other desires. "There's more to do in a bed than just sleep." He immediately regretted his words when her posture stiffened and her laugher vanished like skipping stones on a lake, their circles dissipating into a smooth surface, leaving the turbulence hidden beneath.

"You promised only the once." Now that they were alone, she let her accusations flow. "I didn't think we would be sharing a room."

He had surmised as much earlier. "We'll share a room and sleep in the same bed. You trust your *Hen Was* but I don't. There may be spies in our midst. For all eyes but our own, we'll appear to have a healthy and active marriage. What goes on in our bed behind closed doors is up to you."

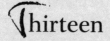hirteen

Luc's words tempted her more than they should, and as Rosa made her way toward Cadan's rooms, she couldn't help but picture the night to come. She had never slept in the same bed with a man, let alone one she was attracted to. Likewise, her infertility regimen needed a re-application since she had shifted and was now fully healed.

Cadan's rooms remained next to Math's old chamber. She knocked and waited. When there was no answer, she tested his door, finding it unlocked. Decorated simply in shades of black and gray, his bed remained empty while steam wafted from the bathroom, fogging the terrace doors.

"It's just me," she announced from the open bathroom door before peeking her head around the corner.

"Over here." His voice came from the direction of the vanity where he sat with a thick towel wrapped around his waist. Clumps of red hair formed a tangled pile on the marble floor. His eyes found hers in the mirror, haunted and challenging, with shears held midair as he hacked away his beautiful hair.

Walking over, she covered his hand with hers and gently pried the shears from his fingers. "Let me."

This was Cadan's first act of freedom and she would assist him in any way she could. And as he sat quietly on a carved seat before her, she removed the tresses Math had cherished.

Afterward, she combed her fingers through his shortened hair and smiled at his reflection. "If possible, I think it makes you look even more handsome."

"Better," he whispered thickly. "Mae hasn't woken yet."

"I know." Setting the shears on the vanity, she rested her cheek on the top of his head. Before Luc, Cadan was the only other male whose touch didn't bother her—because it was brotherly and pure and came without demands.

"The Council will return for me," she eventually said. "But one of us can be free. Take anything you want from Math's vault," she offered, knowing Cadan had always wanted to live in the mortal world. "And I have some modern currency—"

He stiffened, and she sensed both temptation and regret. He didn't belong within stone walls to serve the whims of kings and Council. Like an exotic animal, he deserved to fly without broken wings, to live as he chose, and to love whom he wanted.

"I'm not leaving you, Rosabea. Not until after summer and I know you're safe."

"Cadan—"

"Has your new husband been kind to you?" he interrupted, changing the subject. "It's only us now, so be truthful with me."

Looking up, she met his gaze in the mirror. She noted, too, that he made an effort to lose the formality of his speech. They were a pair still, were they not, taking their freedoms in the steps of babes?

"Luc has been very"—she searched for the right explanation—"considerate." Heat crawled up her neck then, remembering *how* considerate.

"Didn't you just return from a run?" Green eyes darkened with alarm when she nodded. "Your wolf has risen again."

"I like Luc," she admitted. "And my wolf . . ." She let her voice trail off, shaking her head as she caught the burgundy reflection that had warranted her cousin's worry. "My wolf wants him . . . *that* way. It's very disconcerting."

A teasing glint entered his gaze but he swallowed whatever he was about to say when a dark shadow loomed in the doorway. "Gareth," he greeted.

Silently, the guard assessed the situation, his scars stark around his features as he checked his frustration. "It suits you," he offered in reference to Cadan's shortened hair.

"We did it," Rosa said with triumph, holding out her hand. Was not a small collaboration in order with the three who had begun this journey of defection from the Council? "The Guardians are gone from Avon."

Taking her hand, Gareth pinned her with a single-eyed glare. "But at what cost?" His concern softened his censure.

"I'm satisfied with the terms of my second marriage," Rosa assured him once again, squeezing his fingers briefly before letting go of his hand. He knew her reasoning behind the arrangement and she wouldn't waste words trying to justify her actions. "We need to prepare for the Council's retaliation. I've made this decision and I'll answer for it. But I'll understand if you want to leave before—"

"Don't insult me," Gareth snarled. "We began this together. We'll end it together." In a softer tone, he added, "And Avon is my home . . . such as it is."

"Such as it is," she agreed. "I wish you could see Rhuddin Village." A meager offering in face of his continued loyalty, she described the town and the fairness she witnessed under Dylan Black's leadership. Cadan and Gareth listened intently, wanting the same for Avon, united in their goals—just not in her methods of acquiring them.

They remained silent for a while, a quiet harmony in a

small space—and her seedling of hope reached out a few more branches.

"Luc asked me to remain on as porter," Gareth eventually conceded. He hadn't referred to him as the Beast, which was progress.

It had been her request. "As you should."

"The Norseman is watching me," he added with a grumble.

"As I know you're watching him," she returned. "Concessions must be made to strengthen Avon. And respect won't come in a day."

"No," Gareth agreed. "You *will* tell us if he's unkind to you."

She smiled at an order similar to Cadan's. "I will."

"You need to run," he said.

"She already has," Cadan supplied. "Her wolf has risen again."

Gareth scowled with suspicion over the cause.

"Good night," she said, squeezing Cadan's shoulder as she left, not willing to discuss at length her wolf's apparent admiration for Luc. That was a private matter, as was the unpleasant task of what needed to be reapplied in light of her ill-timed attraction to her new husband.

GRIPPING THE EMPTY VIAL OF MAE'S POTION, ROSA leaned over the toilet and tried not to retch. Her mouth filled with saliva, thin like water, forcing her to spit or swallow.

Stay down, she prayed with watery eyes, because it was her last dose. She sagged in a miserable heap, resisting the urge to cool her forehead against the sweating porcelain of the tank, and this was just the first phase of destroying her fertility; the second phase was much worse.

In the bedroom beyond, she heard Luc walking about, opening drawers, touching her things—*invasive man*. He seemed perfectly comfortable in her room while she swallowed poisoned vomit behind a closed door.

Her wolf pranced and rolled, stirring up the nausea, because the disobedient creature *liked* Luc—as did Rosa. Even she would admit that Luc was becoming a dangerous temptation, and now that Avon was secured, reminders of their time in the cabin weakened her resolve.

Luc made her want impractical and womanly things. But staying fertile was too much of a risk among all these new guards, and until summer's first moon waned, the prophecy mustn't be discounted.

When—*or if*—she ever conceived a child, she would choose the father.

In stark contradiction to her vow, another roll twisted her intestines. The potion burned like firewater, making a slow crawl back up her throat.

The gag came all at once. Her stomach muscles clenched in wave after wave, emptying its contents. She tried to be silent, but liquid heaving into liquid made a distinctive splash.

"Rosa . . . ?" A brief knock, that was all he gave before shoving open the door. "You're sick."

She wiped her mouth with the back of her hand and snapped, "It happens."

His nose turned. "What's that smell?"

"Vomit," she offered in her most sarcastic voice. Math had never come to her room before midnight; he had never been this close to the process. If he had, perhaps he also would have scented the malevolent contents of the potion.

"It's more than sickness," he persisted. "It's aberrant. It's . . . *unnatural.*"

"Do you mind?" Rosa huffed, hoping to keep his attention away from the counter beside the wash sink where the second dosage waited in plain sight. "I deserve privacy in this room."

Ignoring her outrage, Luc's nostrils flared. He reached out and grabbed her hand, prying the empty vial from her fingers. Scowling, he brought it to his nose, snarled—then sneezed.

When his gaze lifted to hers, it burned bright with indignation. He might not know for sure the potion's intent, but he had made a good guess. "What is this?" He threw the vial against the wall. It bounced and rolled on the mosaic-tiled floor. "What have you done?"

She lifted her chin. "What I put into my own body is none of your concern."

"If it makes you ill, it is!" His eyes landed on the second item that destroyed all possibility of her carrying a child, the one administered through a different portal. He stalked toward it, gripped the bladder with a growl and contracted his hands. For a moment she wondered whether his claws might actually emerge.

She rushed over in a frantic grapple with his arms. "Don't—"

But it was too late. The bladder ripped and the contents spilled across the marble countertop in a pale greenish hue.

Luc tested it with a touch, rubbing the concoction between his thumb and forefinger. "It burns, like acid."

"It is acid." Denying it now was pointless.

"You would put this inside you? *Why?*" But then he stilled, like the air around the Walkers' tombs, cold and unmoving around living graves. "Is carrying my child so repugnant that you would burn your insides to prevent it?"

"How dare you look at me with scorn in your eyes, or think this is about you," she spat, "when you have never felt the heat of Guardian leers."

"I'm the Beast of Merin! I've been judged by Guardians far longer than you."

"I'll take their judgment over their lust any day." Rage threatened to consume her, fueled by mounting fear as the consequences of his actions swam before her with vile possibilities. "You've never lived among them. You've never had to stay silent while they whisper putrid threats in your ears, while they tell you how they're going to tie you up and shove their cocks against your womb so hard that their seed is bound to take root." She advanced on him, daring to poke her finger in his chest, which was bare, because not only had he barged into her space, but he had done it half-nude. "And you've never had a fertility ritual planned where you're the main event."

He grabbed her wrist and held it midair. "You are my wife," he ground out. "I *will* protect you." His gaze bled blue. "I don't share what's mine." The last was spoken with a low growl, as if the wolf spoke through the man.

They stared at each other, a battle of wills and inner wolves, with her wrist held high in his grasp, his eyes flashing like diamonds in a blue flame.

She wanted to say something rash; she wanted to whip words against his arrogant face like Boadicea might have done, the Pagan warrior who had led an army to battle. Or Joan of Arc, who had done the same, later burned at the stake for heresy and then canonized a Christian saint.

I can defend myself was ready to roll off her tongue, but Luc had destroyed her last potion and Mae had yet to awaken to make her more. Until then, pride be damned, she would accept any protection offered.

The consequences of failure were too great.

Caution had always been at the forefront of her survival. She had lived too long among the Guardians to make false boasts or tempt fate. More important, she did *not* ignore prophecies given by drunken demigods.

"You must understand . . ." So weary now she could barely stand, she relaxed her arm and yielded her stance. "This isn't about you. I'll accept your offer of protection, but I'll not ignore Taliesin's prophecy, either. I cannot be mated to a Guardian." She let her forehead fall to rest against his chest; such an intimate gesture but it felt right, and she needed to touch him. Or her wolf needed her to touch him. "I cannot . . ."

He exhaled and she swayed into him with the release of

his breath. Perhaps it was her final fear that had registered, turning insult to understanding. She felt his hand loosen and his lips brush the sensitive skin behind her ear. "Then be mated to me," he offered in a husky voice filled with promise. "Or at least let us try."

So tempting, his whispered words filled with need, she could almost forget his heart still belonged to another. She had been an unwanted wife once, and could probably endure an eternity as an unloved mate. But why must she always be the first choice for breeding and the second choice for love?

A bitter laugh nearly fell from her mouth. Such nonsense thoughts she had, one would think her a virgin again who imagined honorable knights, innocent kisses and favors without a price. Her innocence had died with her parents, and truth be told, love had never been offered by either of her husbands, not even as a second choice.

With Math, that had been a blessing, but with Luc . . .

It was different with Luc—because he calmed Wulflings with cookies and cared when she hurt. Because he had shown her pleasure and a taste of how it could be.

She lifted her head and ran her hands over the taut muscles of his chest. His skin was smooth, likely from his Egyptian heritage, except for a soft stretch of dark hair that trailed down his stomach and disappeared below his waistband. She had an urge to follow it with her hand, and such carnal thoughts had never entered her mind with any other man.

The owl tattoo remained even after his shift; a careful execution done with great concentration and even greater skill, to keep the ink retained in his skin while fur emerged from his pores. She would consider it an extraordinary feat indeed—if it didn't constrict her heart with envy—and over a woman who no longer lived in this world.

His Koko may be dead but he had yet to let her spirit rest.

Rosa traced the outline of a wing. "Ask me that question again when you no longer carry the totem of another woman on your skin."

"Rosa . . ." He exhaled a ragged breath that would have called to her were it not for someone else. "What you ask for—"

"I know." What she'd asked for was the one thing he wouldn't give.

Koko's Journal

March 15, 1931

My dearest Luc,

I write this journal entry solely for you. Do you remember the first day we met? I waited just outside the cobbler's shop where my papa worked when ships came to port. Bangor's harbor was crowded that day, and the taverns across Devil's Half Acre filled with sailors who smelled of rum and searched for tainted women's special favors. There were many of those women to be found in the city, sickly with the disease of their trade, staying in homes made of brick, with balconies trimmed white and chimneys billowing smoke, promising more than one source of heat. My papa made me walk the streets, pointing to each and every one only to bid me stay clear. I was of an age by then to be lured into the pretty nests of painted birds, and because my skin was dark I offered their callers feathers of a different color.

Little did he know it was not the paws of a drunken deckhand that would find me that day, but those of a wolf?

My papa was inside the shop collecting his wages, while I waited outside. You stood out to me like a hawk among mewling pigeons, tall and imperious while men with white skin scurried in black woolen clothes. Did you feel my gaze on you? You must have, I think, to turn and search the crowded walk until our eyes met.

Or perhaps you heard Mr. Perkins mutter, "Gypsy." The baker smelled of yeast and owned the shop next to the shoemaker's. He shooed me away as if I were a raggedy hound begging for scraps, discouraging the good people of Bangor from buying his bread. "Brown as a filbert," he had said, though I was accustomed to worse. "Find your people and be gone from my place."

Wary, as I knew to be, I turned to run, to find my papa, only to bump into you instead. You made Mr. Perkins apologize, do you remember? Such things are not done. I may have fallen in love with you in that very moment. You waited with me afterward, until my papa took me home.

That night I dreamt I was the brown owl for which I was named. I flew over the Penobscot River; I saw ships and tall church spires, and the natives on their island mourning their lost children. I saw the cabin my papa built for my mother. And in the woods, just outside our home, I saw a black wolf.

When morning came I walked to that place in my dream. You were there, not as a wolf but as a man. My people called your kind Vukòdlak. I knew what you were, and because of my dream I also knew that you were mine.

You always will be my love, my heart, and my husband. My body is passing but my spirit remains as strong as our love. Wherever I go after this life ends, be it my Heaven with angels, or your Otherworld with tiny winged creatures who drink nectar from flowers, know that I will be there waiting for you.

~Koko

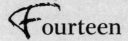

Fourteen

*Thence they plan, upon Ceridwen's last fertile
daughter, eight forsaken warriors to feast.*

CHAMBERS OF THE COUNCIL OF CERIDWEN,
HOCHMEAD MANOR
GWYNEDD, WALES

MERIN RESTED HER HANDS ON THE SCORED WOOD OF THE
Council's table and pretended to examine her nails. Unlike
the round table of Avalon, this one was narrow and long,
and forged in blood-soaked secrets and vacant chairs. Their
order ran with the nature of their beasts, not democracy. The
weak died; the strong survived; the most dominant ruled—
and his name had always been Pendaran.

William sat across from Merin, skin florid with rage, and
Neira by his side. The tedious woman had yet to stop chirping since the session began. Maelor sat silent and sullen that
he'd been called from his tower. Gweir, Edwyn and Rhys
appeared suitably irked. Bran, like Merin, looked on with
relative boredom while avoiding Pendaran's pale gaze.

All nine Council members had been summoned by him;
the eldest Guardian now that Math was dead—though

Math's demise mattered not in the hierarchy of the *Gwarchodwyr Unfed*. Stupid, narcissistic man deserved to rot in the ground.

No, it was Pendaran who sat at the head of the table, who had done so since the beginning when the Council of Ceridwen was formed. He appeared the dapper gentleman, black hair, pleasant mouth, elegant allure, but under his tailored suit beat the wicked heart of a sadistic wolf. If one dared to look long enough they would find his eyes were green, though faded with depravity. He had no family, no mate, no conscience to hinder his rule; he governed with supremacy and fear, and no Guardian ignored his summons if they wanted to remain in this world without pain.

Only Taliesin knew freedom from his dominion.

As was his right, Pendaran had claimed first initiation with Rosa as one of the eight Guardians to fulfill the prophecy. If not for Taliesin's involvement, he might have taken Rosa for himself, simply for the purity of her lineage, and most certainly denied the other seven.

And now Luc stood between Math's useless widow and the most dangerous Guardian of them all.

Merin swallowed her fear but it threatened to consume her all the same. Taliesin would hear a word when they next met for not giving her even a small warning.

"Do you have naught to say, Merin?" Neira wore a red suit with odd-shaped buttons suspiciously the color of bones, and an expression just as boldly perverted. "It is your runt who is disrupting our plans. You should have hunted Dylan down when he dared to abscond with the Bleidd."

Merin blinked slowly and forced an agreeable smile.

Oh, Neira . . . If only you knew how I dream of the day when I will kill you in your sleep.

Openly, Merin said, "How many times must I tell you this? I did not have all my wits about me when I gave birth. I had just lost my mate. Over the years I have found Luc's penchant for survival interesting enough to see where it might lead." She pretended a passing curiosity. "He has proven powerful enough, would you not agree?"

"He has the favor of Taliesin," Edwyn admitted, tossing the printed photographs that had prompted this assembly in the center of the table. "Perhaps we need to reexamine the prophecy. That boy has always played in riddles."

Merin scanned them absently.

Aemilius . . . if only you could see our son. You would be so proud. He is strong and stubborn, but he is also rational and kind, like you. But he is in danger now, the greatest he has ever been, and after all I have done to keep him safe.

Please, if you hear my prayers . . . help me! I am at a loss of what to do.

Hardly sparing Rosa's image a glance, a cowardly creature for dragging her son into this mess, Merin circulated the photographs. Luc deserved a more worthy mate than Math's widow—or the human before her.

Pure blood did not make a warrior's heart, and if her children were to survive, then their mates must be nothing less.

"He plays with us, is what he does," William leered. "Taliesin cleared the accounts shortly after sending the messages, then destroyed his phone."

Neira gave a dramatic sigh. "I have no idea what has come over Rosa. Or my Cadan." Not one Guardian responded to her chatter, perchance in hopes that she would desist. "What are we to do about them? And the Walkers? *And* the prophecy? I think we should garner all our guards and return to Avon and—"

Rhys slammed his palm against the table. "Give it a rest, woman, for the love of my sanity." He stretched his neck to the side, rubbing his right ear. "I swear on the Gods, Neira, you must have done something truly offensive in your former life to be given a voice such as yours."

Her breath inhaled on a squeak and her bottom lip trembled, forlorn as a spanked child; a tiresome pretense from a tiresome woman.

"Rhys," Pendaran scolded, "must you taunt her?"

"Haven't we all heard enough of her whining?" Rhys stood as if to leave. "Personally, I don't care to sit here and watch William pout over the loss of his little *Hen Was*. Look at him . . . One would think he fostered a shifter the way he sulks, or lost a sexual pet."

Pendaran's gaze darkened to dragon green, directed solely at William. "If I learn there's been any perversion with a child, even a *Hen Was*, there will be another empty chair at my table."

Even Pendaran had a code of acceptable behavior, low as it was. He allowed children to be enslaved under the pretense of fostering, even tortured to call their wolves—but *never* raped.

William stiffened with the insult. "I am a purist," he sneered, "not a molester. I am grooming her to be a proper servant. If she proves minimally intelligent when she comes of age, then I may train her to service other needs, but that will be determined after her seventeenth year. I will have her sterilized beforehand, of course."

"Gwilym likes his virgins," Neira twittered, articulating his name in their ancient tongue. "Is that not right, Gwilym?"

"You will call me William," he corrected her with intolerance. "The *Hen Was* have become old and disfigured, and"—his nostrils flared—"well used. I don't care to exercise the same chasm as a thousand other men."

Neira patted him on the hand. "I will talk to my Cadan and see if we can get yours back."

"Can we return to the topic at hand?" Rhys rolled his eyes to the heavens as if asking the Gods for either patience or death, with an expression that both might suffice. "Taliesin is a grown man. He has made it abundantly clear that he doesn't want our interference." He leaned over the table and grabbed the picture of Taliesin's middle finger, waving it like a flag. "Just in case you don't understand what this means, let me explain—"

"Sit down, Rhys, before your insolence turns to disrespect." Pendaran's hand rested on the crown of his knotted cane. He was as fit as an Olympian. All at the table knew the true purpose of that modified staff. Only two weapons of its caliber had been forged, then encased in carved limbs taken from the Druids' Great Oak: *Nerth* and *Cadarn*, Might and Strength. Pendaran held *Cadarn*. *Nerth*, its twin, would soon be buried with Math.

Rhys returned to his seat.

"Now," Pendaran continued once his order was obeyed. "Do you have anything useful to add, other than repeating what we already know?" Not a stupid man, Rhys remained silent. "Fine, let us then discuss our dissenters. We have allowed them too much freedom and in our folly their numbers have grown."

"They will always be weaker than us," William spat.

"Individually, of course," Pendaran agreed. "They carry too much human blood in their veins, but they outnumber us five to one. Numbers mustn't be ignored."

Rhys's gaze flicked to Merin. "There is another rumor circulating among the guards who returned from Avon," he said. "Supposedly, Merin's daughter possesses an extraordinary gift. And Dylan has sired a son who can shift. More interesting, the mother of the boy, this Sophie, retains the Serpent of Cernunnos."

Unable to be outdone, Neira leaned forward and shared in a breathless whisper, "And a hound from the Otherworld has been sighted in their woods, and later at Castell Avon. They said it protected the human."

Pendaran laughed softly. "I read Math's reports on the subject. The man's mind had softened long before he lost his head. Do you honestly believe such gifts would be given to them over us?" He gave an exasperated shake of his head. "Really, you mustn't believe everything you hear. I suspect these are simply rumors fostered by guards who fell to weaker swords."

While they spoke of her family, Merin deadened her emotions, as she had countless times to keep her children alive.

"Regardless," Pendaran continued after a long pause, "I have known Merin long enough not to discount anything that comes of her loins, even if their father was human. These rumors must be investigated further. We will continue with our plans, but after the debacle last week, and yesterday's episode at Avon, it is clear to me that our execution requires a different tactic. We shall contact them under the guise of acceptance into our fold."

"I refuse," William chimed in. "I will not mingle with the likes of them. The Cormack get, the Bleidd . . . he walked freely among—"

Pendaran slammed his staff on the floor; the resonance of wood against wood thudded with an ominous warning. "We will do what we must for the greater good of our race. If you can foster a *Drwgddyddwg* to be your whore, then you most certainly can walk beside a Bleidd."

William snapped his mouth closed.

Satisfied, Pendaran turned to Merin. She concentrated only on keeping her breaths even. "Your children have become a nuisance. Nonetheless, Taliesin is in their midst and we must tread carefully. For now, I want you to reestablish a relationship."

Her heart pounded even as it wept. Her highest wish had been granted but only as the carrier of poisoned deeds. Her children would hate her even more after this.

"As you know," she answered carefully, "I am not in their favor. I doubt they will let me beyond the door unless I break it down."

Pendaran ignored her excuses. "Make contact. That is all I ask for now. Then report back to me afterward."

She acquiesced with a nod.

"And, Maelor," Pendaran called out across the table, "you will go with Merin."

Slouching in a wrinkled suit, Maelor resembled a turned-out troll with thick brows over a bulbous nose. He had attempted to groom his hair with gel, or mayhap the sheen came from natural grease run through with a comb.

"Maelor," Pendaran repeated when the lesser Guardian turned his gaze to the floor. "My always-silent Maelor. Never ready to volunteer when duty calls. How does Briallen fare? I hope she will be at Math's funeral. If not, we might think you are keeping her locked in your tower." Pendaran grinned as if it were a jest when all in the room knew it was not. "The Continent might do her some good." His voice lowered with dangerous intent. "You have been of little use to us for some time."

The last was no mere warning; it was a sentence were he not to agree.

It prompted Maelor to speak. "I am not the proper choice for arbitrator."

Pendaran stood, approaching Maelor; he leaned forward on his staff, hovering above the hunched Guardian while he issued a string of commands. "You will go to Castell Avon in the creditable mission of checking on the Walkers. You will be hospitable. Math was our scribe, so you will ask for his ledgers. Let us see how they respond. While you are there you will investigate the rumors we have heard, and you will bring Merin and Briallen with you."

"If the reports are true," Maelor snarled, "the Norseman is there. You cannot ask this of me!"

With only a sniff to hint of his displeasure, Pendaran removed his sword from the casing of his staff and skewered Maelor's neck to the back of the wooden chair. "Why, Maelor . . . whatever gave you the impression I am asking?"

Eyes bulging, Maelor gasped blood and tried to breathe through an obstructed windpipe. The sword distended from his throat and quivered over the table in rhythm with Neira's chirping sobs. His lower half sagged while a putrid odor filled the air; with spine severed, he defecated in his chair.

Pendaran yanked the sword from the man's throat. Without

a stopper, Maelor's head fell forward and blood flowed freely down his shirt.

Bran looked across the table and caught Merin's gaze. Like Taliesin, though not nearly as pretty, he had golden hair and old eyes of the sea, turbulent and hiding many secrets beneath. Merin knew a few of those secrets. *Do not interfere,* she warned him silently. *Now is not the time.*

"And, Neira . . ." Pendaran let out a grievous sigh. "My dear, I fear Rhys may be right about your voice." Looking around for a suitable place to wipe off his sword, he opted for her red suit. "You must stop your sniveling. After all, Maelor's head is still attached. The servants shall carry him to the woods. His shift might be painful but no more than what he deserves."

Sheathing his sword, Pendaran scanned the table, pinning each Guardian with his pale gaze. "Next time one of my orders is questioned, I will not be so generous with my patience. We will meet again ten days hence and discuss the information you will bring. In the meantime, the preparations for Beltane continue. I have every confidence our lovely Rosa will be cooperative by then."

"She is not the submissive wolf we once thought," William warned. "According to Briog, she pulled power from a dead forest—*and* held it. She came with an army of insurgents and a new husband to assert her claim to Avon."

"The marriage is troubling," Edwyn said with a frown, disturbed. There were some parts of their humanity that even Council members clung to for solace. Edwyn honored tradition, if naught else.

Pendaran only smiled as if proud of his future mate. "Husbands are disposable. Prophecies are not; nor are they spun for the weak. Have faith. Ours will come to fruition." He tapped the table as a farewell. "I expect to see you all this evening. Our eldest has passed and his crossing deserves our respect."

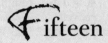ifteen

IN ALL HER YEARS OF EXISTENCE, ROSA HAD NEVER AWO-
ken to a man in her bed. Her response, though admittedly
craven, was to pretend she still slept. Nothing had prepared
her for the experience or, more important, how she should act.

He had been angry when last they spoke, and then he'd
not come to bed until after she'd fallen asleep.

His attitude must have changed at some point in the night,
because Luc had gathered her against him. And now his arm
circled across her side while his palm rested against her
stomach. More discomforting, his erection pressed against
her backside and she wasn't sure he was completely awake.

With her eyes closed, she tried to relax. But how was she
to remain unaffected when he smelled like temptation rolled
in musky pine, like warmth and desire and slumbering power.
Those sensations came again, the ones he had produced in
his brother's cabin. She almost squirmed at the memory.

She knew he had awakened when his arm tensed. His
hand moved from her belly to her thigh . . . *Did he think
that a less insinuating place?*

He inhaled. His intake of breath sent chills skittering across her skin.

"Rosa . . . ?" Her name was a husky growl.

She shivered, and then cringed, because the involuntary response foiled her ruse. "I'm awake."

He leaned in, then stilled as if rethinking his original intention. "Did you sleep well?"

"I did; thank you for asking." Was it normal to have mundane conversations while her nipples strained against her nightshirt?

"You're welcome." She heard a grin in his voice and wanted to see whether it touched his face—needed to, after last night.

Wiggling free of his arm, she turned onto her back and found that it did. "You're not angry with me anymore?"

His expression faded. "I wasn't angry. I was . . ." A sigh fell from his mouth.

"I suspect the generators will be strained with morning showers." She purposefully changed the topic to domestic matters, sensing his unease and not wanting to reopen an argument that couldn't be won. "If we want hot water we best be up and going."

"In a moment." He rose up on one forearm. He slept nude, of course. Why would he not when it would give her some relief? The owl tattoo weaved a dark pattern around his torso and down his side. He looked very much the Pagan as he observed her, with promises of carnal delights gleaming in his mercury-colored eyes.

An ache settled in her chest and it refused to part, a longing that only fed the cravings of her weakened flesh. His hair had been left unbound for the night. It fell down to mingle with hers in a tangle of golden and black fleece on sapphire-colored sheets.

It was decadent.

And sensual.

And her heart began to race as if a hundred tiny drums

beat for an ancient dance and she had yet to find the proper rhythm.

His eyes roamed her face, down her throat, lingering on her breasts covered only by a thin shirt. He reached out and brushed a taut peak, just the tiniest of caresses with the backs of his fingers. He was testing her body—*and* her willingness to accept his touch.

She turned her head and looked away, hoping to hide the incessant yearning that had taken root, reminding herself in that moment why she'd told him only the once. But the line between what she wanted and why she resisted blurred.

Simply because he kept his heart for Koko didn't stop her from wanting what he had offered her—pride be damned.

Then be mated to me . . . Or at least let us try.

Luc over William, Rhys, *Pendaran . . .* ? *Truly*, the list could go on and on, and if she had to be bound to one man for an eternity—Luc was the most appealing prospect.

"You're in need," he whispered. "Let me ease you."

"We mustn't." But even as she spoke her body betrayed her. Moisture gathered below in her feminine parts, now healed and whole and ready to be used for their designed purpose. And that one place—the one Cadan and Tesni had many names for and loved to recite simply to make her blush—*that* place strained to be stroked.

Pleasure button indeed; more like a wicked miscreant.

Luc rested his forehead next to her temple, nuzzled his face into her neck. "It can be done without risk of pregnancy."

She tensed with distrust. Granted, she knew of such things. Of course she knew, but no one had ever offered them to her, at least not a man, and most certainly not one whose touch she craved. It went beyond comprehension—to give her pleasure without asking for anything in return.

"You would do that?" The question fell unbidden from her mouth as blurred lines disappeared.

He made a sound that implied he was in pain. "Yes, I'll do that." *And so much more if you would just let me.* It wasn't said outright, merely promised in his voice. "I would have offered it last night if I knew it would produce such an agreeable response."

"If you'll recall, that is the opposite of what you proposed." She drew an unsteady breath as he slid down the length of her body, tugged off her underthings and discarded them on the floor. Rising up on her elbows to stare down at him, she asked, "What are you doing?"

His head tilted in a way that reminded her of the Great Hunts, how warriors promised their skills with haughty glares as they chased their prey across golden fields.

Slowly, he parted her legs. "Exactly what I said I would."

Anyone weak of spirit would have run; *not* weak of bodily desires, obviously. No, the latter would have done the same as her, offer the hunter what he wanted and not cared if the end resulted in her demise. If his lower half didn't hang off the bottom of the bed, she might have garnered the courage to resist. Instead she waited breathlessly to feel his hands and his fingers, startled when he started biting kisses along her inner thigh, nipping gently toward . . .

"Surely you don't mean to do . . . ?"

Oh, but he did. Her back arched off the mattress. He nuzzled at first, parting her folds, stroking circles with his tongue. And, *yes*, he found the pleasure button and he knew all too well what it liked.

This act had never been done on her before, *never*, and the indulgence was almost too intense to bear. She fisted her hands in the sheets as that glorious tension rose on a wave so great she ascended to greet it, head back, daring it to claim her.

Everything was different with Luc. It was no wonder she wanted more. He made her into a heathen writhing in a once-forsaken bed. With him she forgot the ugliness of her past, and she realized this act could be one of giving and selflessness, and therefore healing in its ecstasy.

A breeze brushed her skin. A warning. She turned her

head toward the side panel covered with purple damask. A matching drape moved away from the hidden passageway; a normal intrusion while she'd been married to Math, but only he, Mae and their porter had the key.

Gareth hovered in the narrow doorway, a looming shadow frozen in surprise. She pushed at Luc's shoulder, so close to her release words refused to form.

"Luc," she managed, though it was more of a breathless hiss. She even tried to squeeze her thighs and twist away—but his grip remained strong and his intent focused.

Without moving, his eyes rolled up to meet hers and they burned with sparks of cobalt blue fire.

He knew.

He knew Gareth watched and yet he continued to stroke her with his tongue. Oh, what a picture they must form, with her shirt rucked up to her waist and her husband's head buried between her thighs.

Rosa lifted her gaze as if called by their observer. Gareth's initial disbelief turned to anger, and then ultimately . . . lust. Anger and lust, why must they always weave an unbreakable knot?

Bold, so bold, she realized then, for him to walk into her room unannounced and expect her to be alone. And arrogant, too, as if he had the right.

By choosing not to stop, Luc denied Gareth's claim as alphas had done before the dawn of their kind.

Her release was almost violent when it came; it washed over her in wave after wave of inner contractions, not like a river with gentle currents, but an ocean during a storm that destroyed ships and carved rocks with the power of its force.

She may have cried out, was fairly certain that she had. Her hand tangled in Luc's hair. Had she been holding his head? Her heart calmed and her muscles relaxed into the mattress, enough to become more aware of her surroundings and that Gareth gripped the wooden frame of the door while Luc crawled between her thighs.

Once nestled above her, his hair hung down like a curtain, shielding her from any view but him when he captured her mouth for a kiss. If Gareth was bold for his interruption, then Luc was just as brash with his arrogant demands.

When the pleasure receded, embarrassment followed to take its place. She had lived in a different era from her Pagan-born husband and felt her cheeks burn with what Gareth was witnessing.

Perhaps Luc realized, or felt her heated skin, because he professed against her mouth, "You understand that what we do in our marriage bed is nothing to be ashamed of."

Her breath caught on a hitch because the desire in his voice refused shame. "I do with you."

"Then trust me now." He entered her in one long thrust.

"Luc—" She could not help but cry out his name as his body bowed above hers like a huntsman's weapon, imposing and primed, and piercing her with unleashed fury.

Gareth turned then, a hasty retreat that she heard more than saw, restoring intimacy to the room as his shadow faded beyond the passage. "He's gone."

"I know." Luc withdrew, shuddered, rose up on his forearms. His shaft pulsed against her inner thigh as he denied his own release. "And now he knows not to invade our privacy."

"And we have a witness to . . ." *How had he phrased it?* ". . . an active marriage." Which she suspected had been her alpha husband's primary intent.

"Yes," he said over the gravel in his voice. "It's truly sealed now, because no man would believe I stopped."

If he hadn't sounded so aggrieved, she might have thanked him for doing so. "My room was a common place to meet while Math was alive," she explained instead. "I'll have a talk with Gareth."

"And I'll ask you not to do that. He's loyal to you and deserves the respect of his position. He just needs to knock before entering our room. I trust he will from now on."

"You're right," she admitted, grateful that he was confident enough not to undermine Gareth's station. She ran her hand down his back, savoring the pull and tension of his muscles, and the way he arched to her touch. "Change will be difficult for him. More than the others, I think."

He reached out and brushed a fallen strand of hair away from her face. "You are glorious to behold in the height of your pleasure. And now, you should see how you look at this moment."

Her hand stilled on his back, halted by the gravity of his tone while uttering such pretty words. "I could say the same of you."

If ever he had resembled the Beast of his moniker, it was then, as he scowled at her with his features frozen in a mask of need.

"I'll stop in time," he said, and then entered her again.

He didn't ask. Humans asked. *Not* alphas. And his had risen to control the man. Wolves took what they wanted and claimed their mates.

She arched to meet his next thrust, and his next, because it felt good to be claimed, mindless of stupid human indecisions when her primal instinct rose to tamper them away. Her pleasure mounted again. It was easy with him, to find this place, only this time it was a gentle climbing for her, a slow build over a tender rise.

Not so for him.

He swore under his breath as his movements became frantic, harsher—closer, so close . . .

She hissed, clawing at him to move faster because her gentle climb had reached its peak and because she, too, had lost control of her wolf.

The corded muscles of his neck stood out with his strain. He made a sound, a rumble turned to a shout, guttural with a will stronger than frustration, stronger even than his wolf as he withdrew to spill his seed onto her stomach.

She watched, shocked that he had done it, but also

fascinated as that part of him, thick and glistening from her own moisture, pumped and pooled its essence near her navel. His face pinched in a scowl that would have been comical had it not been driven by a mixture of discomfort and relief.

He swore, as if he, too, was surprised by his fortitude in the end, and then collapsed on top of her.

After a long silence, one that cautioned he was contemplating an unpleasant topic, he said, "This will happen again." A warning, not an apology. "Not just once, or twice, but many more times."

She didn't argue, not when a third party had witnessed her weakness toward this man.

He rolled onto his back, pulling her with him so she lay nestled by his side only without his weight. "I've loved once," he began in a tone of a practiced speech, as if he'd mentally rehearsed this throughout the night. "Losing Koko . . ."

"You don't have to—"

"No, let me finish because I won't speak of her again. Losing Koko was like losing my only balm after a thousand years of turmoil. Koko calmed my beast; she quieted its voice." A pause. "It's the opposite with you." She tried to pull away but he only tightened his hold. "Koko and I were not mated. I'm sure of that now." He lifted her hand to examine her fingers, weaving them with his own.

"How are you sure?" Rosa couldn't help but ask.

"Because I almost broke my word to you just now." He sounded indignant. "I almost finished inside you. Even now, my wolf is"—he paused—"not pleased that I didn't. I intend to drive into the nearest town and pick up some of those condoms that humans use."

Diseases weren't transmittable to their kind, and children were rare and coveted, so what he spoke of wasn't a common item to have on hand.

She swallowed past a sudden thickness in her throat. "It

was arrogant of me to suggest you remove her memory. I won't speak of it again."

"It was only what a mate would ask," he said. "I wasn't angry with you."

"You weren't?"

"No." He shook his head. "I was hard as a damn river rock."

"Really?"

"You don't have to sound so pleased." A slight chuckle, but only a fleeting reprieve. "I want you to reconsider the offer I made you last night."

"I will," she told him. "And I'll give you a decision soon. Until Mae awakens, I've no means to null my fertility." She didn't offer him false promises, only the truth. "If I must be mated, please know that I would rather be mated to you than any Guardian."

A child was a gift; she understood that more than the Council planning a misguided ritual. Was it selfish to want her child's conception to come from love? If indeed she was even deserving of such a miraculous thing. If it was within her power, a decision she reinforced with each application of Mae's potion—her child wouldn't come from desperation and fear, or even for territories and convenience.

She didn't share her personal wants with Luc, fearing he might balk at such romantic ideals. In the end, circumstances may force a concession. And she'd spoken the truth; if forced to make a choice, she'd rather be mated to Luc.

Unaware of her inner debate, his mouth slanted on a groan of both relief and something greater, something she dared not consider because she'd begun to want it so. Regardless of her attempts, her reluctant thoughts became bold ones, and as these things were bound to do—bold ideas carried true desires. Could love come from their union? Did she dare hope for such a thing? He leaned over, gathered her close, and captured her mouth for a kiss that started tender but deepened when she responded. He toyed with her mouth until she was squirming again, only to break away to trail his lips down her neck, and lower.

"We need to check on the Wulfling," she reminded him, frightened by the potency of her longing.

"She was sound asleep in a drawer a few hours ago," he said, yanking at the neckline of her nightshirt. "But you're right. We have responsibilities that require our presence away from this room." He did not let her leave without capturing her nipple for one farewell tug of his mouth, one that would taunt her for the rest of the day.

Cadan had never felt such panic, which, if he stopped to consider the events of this downright lovely week, misplacing a child shouldn't threaten to beat his heart from his miserable chest.

But, alas, it did. Perhaps there was a place somewhere for his suffocated soul after all. He searched every crevice of her chamber, bathroom, closets and corners, only to rush into the hallway and slam into Gareth.

The porter ran his hand through his cropped hair, skewing the patch on his eye. "What's happened?"

"Audrey isn't in her room."

"The Wulfling?"

"Of course, the Wulfling." Frowning, Cadan took a step back because the man appeared . . . *ruffled?* Gareth was an imperious shadow, keeper of the night, guarding his emotions firmer than this misbegotten castle.

But *never* disheveled.

"What's wrong with you? You look positively undone."

"I saw them," Gareth said in a disjointed voice. "I saw them together. Rosa and . . . *him.*"

"Just now? Where?" Cadan bit back his annoyance on his cousin's behalf. Had her privacy not been invaded enough by Math? Still, this man was their only proven ally and deserved to be treated as such, so he kept his tone neutral. "Did you go to her room?"

"I haven't had a chance to speak with her alone," he muttered defensively. "Black is always with her."

Or I am, Cadan thought. At least he'd started calling the man by his current surname instead of the Beast. The older brother was a scary bastard, but Luc seemed fair.

So far.

However, Cadan reserved the right for judgment at a later time. For now, he tried not to associate the man with his family, if only to avoid becoming a hypocritical ass. Considering his own dear mum was queen of the Council's perverted madhouse.

Still, Cadan was allowed to be wary, regardless of Rosa's assertion otherwise. "Was he being cruel to her?"

An uncomfortable pause. "No."

"Ah," Cadan said as understanding dawned along with relief. "Luc is her husband by choice." He knew Rosa; she would have found another way had she not been drawn to him. "She may have married him to strengthen our campaign, but she *likes* him. And Luc isn't opposed. You only need to watch them together and see."

"I did see," Gareth admitted thickly. "She was . . ." He shook his head as if stunned. "I've never seen her so receptive."

He appeared more confused than bitter, which was a matter of great importance—because Cadan needed someone he trusted to stay behind for Rosa when he left. "Isn't it time to shed those scars, Gareth?" Along with the cumbersome history that bound them. "Go for a run already." He waved his hand toward the man's twisted countenance. "No human will associate your true face with that mess."

"I could say the same of you," he returned before walking away.

So true, Cadan thought, but some scars were easier to rid than others. And frankly, he quite liked his current self, messy as it was, just not the dank walls and dark memories that suffocated the very air that he breathed.

He wanted away from Avon. He wanted to dance to modern music in crowded bars with beautiful mortal men who had no way of entrapping him for eternity. He wanted—no, he *needed* to live free of Guardian demands, if only for a year. Had he not earned that right?

Once he knew his cousin was safe with this new husband, he intended to live the freedom of mortals—but a tweaked female wolf and one day of Luc's apparent kindness hadn't yet convinced him of Rosa's safety.

Once summer was behind them, he hoped, and the prophecy foiled.

Until then, he had a Wulfling to find, preferably before Tesni returned. He made another mad scramble around Audrey's room. Where would a Wulfling go? A large wardrobe stood against the far wall. He'd looked in the upper cupboard, but . . .

Walking over, he slowly pulled out the bottom drawer.

And there she was, a baby wolf rolled into a puppy ball, with her furry belly rising and falling with her breaths. The relief of finding her almost put him on his ass. Sweaters were pushed against the sides of the drawer with Audrey burrowed in the center. Tentative, he reached in and removed a wayward sleeve away from her snout.

Two distinct emotions tightened his chest; one was the burden of responsibility and the other was an inconceivable joy. Both formed an instant need to protect. So tiny, she was. This child was now theirs to shelter from harm. *She will be hunted like Rosa when she comes of age, if not sooner.*

"The Council will have to come through me first," Cadan whispered.

She made a puppy sigh and snuggled deeper into the drawer as if she'd heard.

And until he knew Rosa and Audrey were safe from Council members and beasts, he would stay to honor that vow.

Sixteen

To bear in silence, four secrets hidden, in circles of raindrops, cloak death.

THE STENCH OF DEATH HUNG IN THE AIR AS LUC FOL-
lowed Rosa to the Walkers' tombs. Puddles pooled on the
swamp-like walkways, coated in green ooze, the only vibrant
color in a mass of gray. Eight stone structures loomed on the
river's edge, reminding him of the grave sites of New Orleans,
with Celtic patterns carved on wooden doors.

A handful of guards had joined the tour, avoiding puddles
as if the slime that coated the surface came with a Walker's
life-sucking kiss.

Luc rubbed the back of his neck, feeling the same unease.
"What's in the other four tombs?"

"*Hen Was* who have passed on," Rosa said in that quiet
voice reserved for lost souls. She wore suede trousers, an
overly large sweater that bulged on one side from her sword,
and rubber boots. The sword and boots were functional, but
the others, he guessed, were a homespun attempt to hide her
curves.

Cormack followed in his human form, having gone off
the island to shift after hearing Elen was on her way. He

wore sweatpants and a wrinkled T-shirt, but stood more confident with each passing hour. Once Elen had learned of the Wulfling, Mae, and Cormack's presence, there was no point in trying to discourage her. His sister would arrive by midday.

Cormack reached over and tugged at Rosa's sleeve. She frowned at his hand gestures, struggling to decipher his awkward attempt at communication.

She tilted her head to one side, listening carefully, but her expression remained puzzled. "We're going to see the Walkers now. Is that what you're asking?"

A half-human growl. Shaking his head, he pointed to the tombs. "Ssshhh . . ." A twisted hiss rolled from his tongue, and then another garbled growl.

Luc almost intervened until Cormack had attempted to form a word. He remembered all too well the frustration of learning how to speak with the full intelligence of a grown man. It was one thing to understand words, but another skill to learn how to speak them through a new form.

Cormack tried again, "Ssshhhaaa . . ."

"Siân?" Rosa prompted immediately, almost relieved.

He nodded vigorously. Pointing again to the tombs.

Her features softened. "No, she's not here. We brought her remains across the river to a place more beautiful than this. We gave her a proper burial. I'll bring you there sometime if you like."

Placing his arm crosswise over his chest, he gave a low nod.

Suspecting his wife was the reason behind the proper burial, Luc leaned forward and captured her mouth for a quick kiss. She blinked at him, charmingly startled, and more than one guard observed the impulsive gesture. He ignored their smirks and examined the structure of the tombs.

"How were the Walkers brought here?" For all their malevolence, the tombs had been built with care and respect.

"Taliesin transported them by ship," Rosa said. "That's

all I know. The tombs were commissioned first, then Castell Avon shortly after."

"The living quarters should have been built on a separate island."

"If only we'd had that choice. The Council values their lives more than ours," she reminded him. "We were brought here to protect them, not ourselves."

"I'll discuss this with Taliesin if he remains with my brother." Permitting the Walkers to sicken their surroundings mustn't be allowed to continue. Moving them to another place might be a solution, but would that only poison more ground? Unbidden, Teyrnon's first suggestion came to mind—as did Rosa's warning. The last person to enter a tomb with malicious intent had cut off their own head. *Not* a comforting thought, as he was about to step into one himself.

"You can try," she muttered. "But I've never seen him react well when asked about them." She named the occupants, pointing to each tomb in turn. "Aeron rests in the first, then Morwyn, Nesien, and over in the far corner is Gawain."

"The ground feels warm," Luc noted.

"There are tunnels below that siphon heat. It's how Sophie escaped from our dungeons."

"You'll show me later," he said, guessing he would find them well stocked.

Nodding, she placed her hand on the door of the first tomb and slid it open. "This one is Aeron's." Her voice became hushed. "It's best if we don't stay too long. And whatever you do, *don't* touch her. I would also suggest you remove your weapons and keep them out here if you can't control your thoughts."

"Understood." Luc kept his sword sheathed but still on his person as he ducked under the doorway. Stale air greeted him inside the dark space. The open door provided the only light, a singular shaft to guide his gaze.

Aeron had been arranged on an altar of carved marble, arms to her sides, wearing a dress of blue velvet and ivory lace. Jeweled ribbons weaved a crisscross pattern through ebony black hair; a sleeping beauty, dormant between worlds, once a messenger to the Fae and now a vampire of sorts who fed on the essence of the earth's blood.

She sang a siren's death song, calling him to soothe her from an endless journey of pain. He stepped forward, drawn by her profound sorrow. Bemused, he reached for his sword and then realized what he'd done. "Shit." Fisting his hand, he turned on his heel and pushed everyone back from the door. "I've seen enough."

Rosa gave him a knowing look. "You felt her, didn't you?"

"I felt something," he admitted, running his hand through his hair. Next time he would heed his wife's warnings. "Show me the rest."

He didn't enter the other tombs, but viewed each Walker without crossing the doorways. All were arranged much the same, in formal clothing of their time, and with special care. Perchance out of respect, but somehow Luc doubted that was Taliesin's only motivation.

No, this stank of guilt.

At a loss of what to do, he swore, "Bloody hell." A few better choice words came from the other guards. He had only one certainty in this ominous conundrum. "We mustn't let my sister anywhere near here." He repeated it again, raising his voice so all the guards heard. "Until we figure out what to do with them, make sure everyone stays clear, especially Elen when she arrives. There's nothing in this place but death."

And after last week, when Elen had ripped a wolf's power from one man and given it to another, he didn't trust her not to touch.

LATER THAT MORNING ROSA'S PEOPLE BEGAN TO TRICKLE in from their secret place in the woods. Luc made his own introductions whenever he ran into a strange face, gathering a few who volunteered to watch the walls. By afternoon laughter and merriment filled the halls of Castell Avon, infectious to even his guards.

At one point he broke away and drove into the nearest city to buy the condoms. It was a task that needed to be done alone. Gareth had witnessed the validity of this marriage, so giving his wife time to adjust was a minor hindrance. Compromise was in order, because while Koko may not have been his mate, their love had been true, and her spirit still wound a tangled knot around his heart. When not in Rosa's company, and without his wolf or his need clouding his judgment, it felt wrong of him to ask of her what he wasn't willing to give himself.

Teyrnon was covering Gareth's post at the gate. When asked, the Norseman said with a shrug, "He said he needed to go for a run and would be back in a few hours."

Gareth had covered his duties with the appropriate chain of command, so Luc only nodded. "I'm taking your SUV to drive around the nearest towns. I'll be back by midday."

Admittedly, it was a relief to find the nearest city bustling with humanity, too consumed by their own lives to know the depth of this world or the secrets it held. Also realizing that he'd felt overly isolated in Avon. Rosa must make this journey with him next time, he decided. Or take a day with a friend, or by herself. With that in mind, he also found a department store and purchased clothing for her, as well as Audrey, and a few other items for Cormack.

When he returned with a handful of bags, he placed the things he'd bought for Rosa in her wardrobe and went in search of her. He was pointed in the direction of the library. As soon as he entered he knew this room was hers. It smelled of her, and was decorated with comfortable furnishings, where the rest of the castle was gilded and garish.

Rosa sat on a small sofa, with Audrey cuddled by her side. Cormack was across from her, leaning forward in his chair, concentrating heavily on the child's face. A low table was positioned in the center; open books and an odd assortment of objects lay strewn across the surface.

They made no practical sense until Audrey pointed to a round paperweight and pronounced its name slowly. "Baa . . . aaa . . . all."

Frowning as if the man were lifting heavy weights, Cormack mimicked the motion with his mouth and made a worthy attempt. "Baaaa . . ."

Rosa looked up when he approached and scooted over to make room for him on the sofa. "I thought they would get along," she said, waving her hand toward the table. "This was Audrey's idea."

"It's a good one." Children didn't judge. Luc tossed a bag by Cormack's feet. "A change of clothes if you go back with Elen," he told him. "Those sweatpants are getting old."

Cormack shook his head, tight-lipped, pointing to the table. The very image of a Celt, he carried the features of his family, with reddish hair and a stocky build. Even his glare reminded Luc of Siân, arrogant but haunted.

Luc sighed. Cormack didn't want to be a bumbling man in front of Elen. No, he wanted much more. "You are welcome to stay, if that's your choice. At least you smell less like a Guardian now."

"I noticed that," Rosa said in a grateful voice that echoed Cormack's expression.

"And these are for you." Luc handed Audrey her own bag, the largest of the bunch. Disregarding the clothes, her face beamed when she found the stuffed bear. "I'm going to ask you a few questions, though." Her head rested on the bear as she waited. "Can you remember how long you were with William?"

Rosa sent him a frown, not liking that he brought up the subject, but in his experience, at least with children, it was better to discuss things once and then move on.

"Since last snow." Her eyes regarded him warily. "I don't like William's. I don't like snow either." Her face pinched. "I don't like being alone. I like cookies and Cormack and Rosa. And Cadan and Tesni. You said I'm not going back. You said I'm to stay here."

Since winter. And she had been alone wherever William had found her. It seemed the tutor had spoken the truth, which was all he needed to know for now. "You're not going back. But now I know how smart you are to speak so well and in only a few months."

"I *am* smart," she said. "I like it here. I like you too, if I can stay. I have pretty pictures in my head when I sleep, and I eat cookies and tarts filled with gravy."

Rosa smiled at the last. "Cadan said she asked for a tart first thing this morning. I'm quite certain he gave her more than one."

"I had four," Audrey said proudly.

"I want you to stay inside the castle, though," Luc pressed. "Can you do that for me? If you want to change and go in the woods, Rosa or I will bring you."

She nodded, hugging the bear to her chest. "I can do that."

A knock sounded on the door. Luc turned but didn't recognize the man who loomed in the doorway until he spoke. Gareth had indeed gone for a run and shifted—and he had a face bards would write songs about. Shit, maybe some of the old ones *were* of him.

Gareth kept his expression stoic, making it obvious he didn't welcome comments on his appearance. "There's a woman at the gate who claims she's your sister. She has . . . *the hound* with her. Should I let them cross?"

"Please," Luc said, "let her in. I should have informed you of her visit earlier. Although I didn't know she'd be bringing Tucker with her." The porter turned to leave but Luc called him back. "Gareth, when there's time, I'd like you to consider meeting with our porter in Rhuddin Village. He's accomplished with modern technology. It's become useful for communications within our territory, but we must be careful as well. Think about it. Cell phones can be an asset but they can also be traced."

Gareth paused at the door. "I don't need to think about it. I'll learn anything that will strengthen the defenses of Avon."

Gently moving the child, Rosa stood and walked around the sofa until she faced her guard. She reached for his hand. "I'm so happy," was all she said.

He brought her hand to his lips for a brief kiss and then set it back by her side. "I'm beginning to see that." He gave a nod to Luc, turned and left.

BACK AT RHUDDIN HALL, TALIESIN WANDERED AROUND Luc's apartments. Like a shrine to a lost love, paintings cluttered the walls, exquisitely crafted yet hoarded in this private domain.

Koko's spirit kept a fierce hold on her warrior's heart.

Taliesin felt her memory in the air, not from prophecy or premonition, but by intuition and empathy.

"Koko was a lovely artist," Sophie said from the kitchen, holding a basket of baked sweets, unaware how much he treasured those simple gestures of kindness. "Though it's been almost seventy years since her passing, I think Luc may need some time before he can accept another wife."

Taliesin only shrugged. Emotional tangles were better left to the minds of humans. Wolves acted on baser instincts.

Sophie placed the basket on the kitchen table. "Are you sure you want to stay here instead of the lake house?"

"I'm sure." The lake house had a fully stocked bar and Luc drank nothing stronger than tap water. This was where Taliesin needed to be—because he had lost his other Sight during the flight back to Maine.

He needed no temptations within reach during this sudden blindness.

"I'll leave you, then." She headed toward the outer door. "Dinner is at seven. Please join us. Dylan could use the distraction."

"Porter briefed me on Luc's call." He didn't soothe her with misleading premonitions.

Concern pinched her soft features. "Yes, and my husband

is all but crawling out of his skin and I understand why. Luc may be his brother, but he raised him like a son. It's killing him not being there to check on him. And now Elen is there as well. I give Dylan another week before he takes a ride down."

Such strength this family had. Taliesin envied it as much as he feared destroying it. "I suggest you all stay put and let Luc and Rosa handle Avon."

She paused by the door, frowning. "Is that a warning?"

Swallowing a sardonic laugh, he said, "No." He couldn't *See* anything beyond this bloody room to offer warnings. "All is well, as far as I know," he tried to reassure her and then changed the subject. "What's for dinner?"

Ever observant, she cocked her head. "You've never asked me that before. Are you sure you're all right?"

"I'm fine." He waved for her to leave. "I'll see you at seven."

When the door finally closed, he sagged into the nearest chair. He couldn't tell her that he no longer had visions. It would only worry her more.

His Sight had been taken away after his latest interference. By his dearest darkest mother, he assumed. For this family, he may even humble himself to ask why. But only one place held those answers, a shimmering hell of his childhood. And the Walkers had stopped carrying his messages a long time ago.

Fuck. He ran his hands through his hair.

Would the *Beddestyr* carry one more after the fate he'd cursed them to?

Seventeen

THE HOUND WANTED TO LICK ROSA'S HAND AS IT GAL-
loped beside her. Thankfully, Mae's chamber was all but a
few doors down. *Tucker*, they called it. Large and white,
with red-tipped ears, it mimicked all accounts of hounds
from the Otherworld, but also hounds from this world; an
intimidating creature, no matter its origin.

Trying not to sound overly curious, Rosa asked Elen,
"When was the last time Tucker has eaten? I can send for
food from the kitchens."

No need to keep it hungry when one never knew what it
might eat.

Rosa received an enthusiastic bark for her suggestion.

"Tucker likes you," Elen reassured her with an apologetic
smile. "He's normally not so friendly with anyone other than
Sophie. She wanted me to bring him for protection."

"If he agreed to come, there might be a reason why," Luc
warned.

"I know." Elen gave the hound a gentle pat. "This place
reeks of life and death but no earthly in-between. It's off

balance, as if caught in a bubble of extreme mourning and excessive rapture." She shook her head. "Strange, really. I almost feel dizzy, like I've been drinking too much ale."

Rosa halted in the middle of the hallway. "Would you mind explaining what you just said?"

"This place breathes power but the source is trapped and saturating this island." She frowned, trying to give an analogy they would understand. "Like plants in a pot, over-feeding them will kill them as surely as starvation. Avon is overfed. Its roots are flooded by water. It's sitting in a bowl and rotting."

"I thought it was starved."

"It is," Elen said. "That's what comes from imbalance."

Rosa turned to Luc and caught his gaze. He shook his head. *Please don't,* was his silent plea. She sent him a look in return; *I'll talk to her about the Walkers before she leaves if you don't.*

"Is Cormack around?" Elen asked, unaware of the silent exchange.

"He's watching our Wulfling," Luc told her. "Or she's watching him; I haven't decided."

Rosa noted that he'd excluded where they were. There was dissension between Elen and Cormack. Rosa could only assume it had to do with his sudden ability to shift and Elen's involvement. It worried Luc, whatever it was, but not enough to interfere.

A frown marred Elen's forehead as she turned the corner to Mae's room. It deepened as she walked over to the bed and examined the occupant. "What is this woman's name?"

"Mae," Rosa supplied.

A wistful smile turned Elen's lips. "Maelorwen," she said, gathering the woman's hand in hers. "Is that really you?"

"Do you know her?" Luc asked.

"I believe so, but I'd like her to tell me herself because she's fully conscious."

A cackle came from the bed. "So the apprentice has sur-passed her teacher." Mae rose up on her elbows with a smirk on her distorted features, turning wider on the side that didn't bear scars. New wounds over old ones marred her face, though the swelling had come down a good deal. Her brown hair had been plaited for care, revealing more knotted flesh from burns received long before Neira's interrogation. "How are you, Elen child?"

Elen inhaled a shuddered breath. "Not so much a child anymore. What did they do to you, Mae?"

"Nothing that has not been done before."

Luc frowned over the exchange. "You seem to know each other well."

Elen spared her brother a glance. "Mae taught me all I know about plants and their medicinal uses back in Cymru. It was during the time I lived with our mother, before you and Dylan came for me. I was a bit of a nuisance."

"No"—Mae reached over and patted Elen's hand—"you were my sunshine in a vast garden of loneliness."

"I know that garden well," Elen said in a quiet voice. "I can't believe you're here. I thought you were long gone from this world."

"The Guardians have tried; you can be sure of that. But I am a jumpy old flea on their furry asses and not so easy to kill. I am the first born with the curse, did you know? *Evil Bringer*, they named me. The things they did to force the shift . . ." Her voice trailed off. "And they called *me* evil. But you know these things too . . . Do you not, Elen child? And yet here we still sit after all these years. We cannot shift, you and I, but we can make them piss in their pelts."

Recovering from her surprise, Rosa approached the bed with censure in her voice. "I was *worried* about you, Mae."

Not a single ounce of remorse entered her sigh. "You are a good girl, Rosa, with a good heart, but sometimes you are too stubborn. I like the whispers I hear about your new husband, and he was raised by a warrior with honor. This is a rare thing indeed among our kind." Her chin rose in defiance. "I will not make you any more of your potion. Math did not deserve your child but this man does. You should be upstairs with your husband making wolf babies and not worrying over me."

Rosa ignored Luc's grin. "You know it's not Luc's child that concerns me."

"Oh, pish posh, may the hangman rot." Mae gave an absent wave. "You fret too much over Sin's prophecy."

A bit offended, Rosa snapped, "Excuse me for not wanting to be a feast for eight unmated Guardians."

"If only it was warriors and not the Guardians, I would not mind so much." Mae scooted into a sitting position, fluffing the pillows to support her back. "Listen to the prophecy a hundred times and it can be twisted to suit a hundred different ears."

"So you pretended to be ill because you no longer wanted to help me?" Rosa asked again as hurt replaced the insult. "You could have just told me."

"I am done discussing that." Mae's face lit up suddenly. She made a few claps with her hands, positively giddy as she turned to her former student. "Oh, Elen child, I must show you what I can do with the poison ivy of this country. Such a shame it did not grow back home." A wistful sigh fell from her mouth. "The fun I could have had. It has the most delicious side effects when mixed with soap. Neira would go for a run, shower, and wake up again with welts on her—"

Luc cleared his throat, sending Rosa a grateful nod for her earlier warning. "I understand that you're our healer."

Mae gave him a stern eye for the interruption. "I am a problem solver, though I have been called many things in all my years: witch, midwife, alchemist, herbalist, doctor. We were burned on pyres, hung from trees, pressed between rocks, and now people of my trade work in tall buildings made of iron and glass and spin their potions in tubes instead of cauldrons. I read about these things in the magazine-books Gareth brings us. They make squares of chocolate for people to shit and I would have given them a nice cup of elderberry tea." A wide smile revealed white but uneven teeth. "Alas, I will admit I never made a potion for a six-hour erection." A dimple appeared on the unscarred side of her cheek. "Though I know of a few men who could have greatly used one."

Luc made an effort to conceal his amusement, a poor one at that, since a glint remained in his eyes that threatened to build into a laugh. "I'm glad to meet a friend of my sister, and I hope you remain here as Avon's healer and our problem solver."

Her shrewd gaze gave him a proper scan. "I believe I shall, warrior." She chortled when Tucker put his paws on the bed. "Well, look at you, beautiful boy. It has been a long time since I have seen one of these beasties." Absently, she stroked the hound's neck. "Ah, yes, the whispers have guided me well, I think. They tell me of this hound, and of the Serpent that fed well on Guardian blood, and of my Elen child." Her gaze flicked to Elen. "The whispers tell me you healed a Bleidd. Cormack, brother of Siân. He is here, as a man, so I know these things I hear are true."

"I went against your teachings, Mae." Elen looked down at her hands. "I dabbled with darkness and was given the same in return. Cormack was my friend, my only friend, and now he refuses to even look at me."

"Sometimes when the night sings, it is too tempting not to dance under the stars," Mae said with more understanding than disapproval. "He was the sunshine in your garden of loneliness, was he not?"

"He was." Elen nodded. "And I haven't seen him since it happened."

Mae gave a calculating grin. "Then you must stay for the wedding feast two weeks hence. Your Cormack will be there. I will make sure of it."

"I fear it won't matter if I'm there or not," Elen said softly.

"Listen to me now." Turning stern, Mae leaned over and lifted Elen's chin with a knobby finger. "I will not stand for this doubt I see in your eyes. You are a child of the light. You can heal this darkness."

Elen inhaled a shaky breath. "I've missed you, Mae."

"Excuse me," Rosa intervened to ask, "what wedding feast?"

"Yours, of course," Mae said, dropping her hand. "You announced it yourself when you returned."

"It was only a ruse for Neira." And Mae, Rosa realized, must have been feigning her unconsciousness even then.

"Not so much a ruse, I think. I can see the mating braid forming between you two." Her eyes roamed the space between Rosa and Luc. "It is tangled and has extra strings, but it is weaving its knot, so we must celebrate. And do not frown at me so . . . I will organize the *Hen Was*. Your marriage has given us much hope. It is a good thing you do for us. As I sit here and breathe I cannot smell a single Guardian in these walls. Is there no better reason to feast?"

"It would be a good way for our guards and staff to become united," Luc suggested carefully, perhaps sensing Rosa's unease.

"Staff?" Mae chortled. "Listen to you, warrior, so modern. Staff," she repeated, shaking her head as if it was the most amusing thing she'd heard all day.

"I'm against keeping *Hen Was*," Luc said with conviction that refused argument. "Positions will be offered with fair wages. Ledgers have already been purchased, and Rosa and I will confer who is best for what position. It's their choice if they take it."

Mae pinned Rosa with an accusing glare. "And you think we do not have reason to feast."

Truth was a difficult thing to argue with. "As long as Avon remains protected," Rosa conceded, "you can plan a wedding feast."

Mae gave an excited clap. "Wonderful. You must have something better to wear than that." She turned to Elen. "And you as well, Elen child, if you are to keep your

Cormack from the clutches of Tesni and Bethan. I hear all kinds of whispers, you know. A grown warrior still a virgin is too enticing for the likes of those two. There are bets among the guards on which one will dip Cormack's stick first. Tesni is in the—"

"Mae!" Rosa stopped her because Elen's color had drained from her face. "We don't need to know about such things."

Waving off the interruption, Mae continued. "I have just the potion for you to use on your Cormack," she said to Elen, "until you right this darkness. I will teach you today. I may not have a brew to give men big sticks, but I have one that will keep them soft as worms. It is a good recipe too." Mae cackled, then held her belly. "So many times I saw Math outside Rosa's secret door, hunched over like a portly jackrabbit with a limp pecker, bug-eyed and thumping but nothing rising in his fist."

Luc laughed outright. There was no attempt to conceal his amusement this time. Soon, though, he scowled. "Don't *ever* use that potion on me if you wish to remain in Avon."

"I just wish you had used it more for Cadan," Rosa muttered.

"It was not meant to be," Mae said, although with sadness. "In his own way, Math loved Cadan. My interference would have been suspect had he not functioned properly with him. And then where would I be? *Dead*, that is where, and no good to you now."

Elen stood as if in a daze. "I think I need to use the restroom."

"There's one in the library," Rosa said, ignoring her husband's frown. "Go down this corridor the way we came in, take a left and it's all the way at the end. You won't miss it."

ALONE IN THE HALLWAY, ELEN LEANED HER HEAD BACK against the wall to gather her composure. Her chest ached and she wanted to blame it on this unbalanced island. Unfortunately, she couldn't—because she knew how to decipher pain, and this one was considerably greener than Avon. *Tesni*, what a ridiculous name? Elen hoped she was hideous and had breath that smelled of rotten meat.

Footsteps approached to ruin her private reprieve and Elen ducked into the library only to come to a frozen halt.

She had seen him as a wolf for almost four hundred years, but only once as a man—and she had *not* been in the best of mind-sets at the time.

Now she took in her ravenous fill.

Cormack sat on a chair with a book in his lap, turning the pages with care. He focused on the words as if trying to decipher their code. A ragged T-shirt clung to the taut muscles of his back and chest. He made the furniture seem small, but then, he'd always been large, even as a wolf of their kind. Changing forms did not affect mass.

His eyes were the color of her bluest delphiniums, brighter now that they were framed by rugged features instead of fur. Like his wolf, his hair was deep auburn brown and unkempt; it needed to be shorn.

She inhaled to savor his scent. Energy had a taste and she would always know his. It changed, though—when she'd given him a Guardian's power; it melded into something of his own. Like chocolate, in its purest form it was sour, but divine once mixed with sugar. And now those fused spices rolled off her tongue and clung to the back of her throat.

She felt breathless as she never had before.

Tucker came bounding into the room and issued an excited bark. Cormack glanced up from his book. His cerulean gaze widened with surprise and then softened into what she remembered—*her friend*.

A web of memories weaved in the quiet space between them, of afternoons in her garden, or huddled under a blanket by the fire on winter nights. He loved to listen to her read stories aloud. He didn't fear her. Everyone else feared her, but not Cormack.

Until now, when all those memories turned to one hateful scowl and he pointed to the door.

Composure be damned, Elen almost crumpled to the floor, but then she told herself it was this place, this unbalanced place that pushed at her to leave, that made her want to laugh and cry all at the same time.

Neither Cormack, nor this island, would bully her away until she had one important answer from him.

Determined, she took another step into the room. "Hello, Cormack."

His scowl deepened and his arm remained fixed on the open door.

She walked around the sofa, pausing when she saw a small form tucked under a blanket. A child slept with her arm around a stuffed bear and her head on a throw pillow.

"The Wulfling?" she asked.

Cormack spared her a nod at least.

Sitting on the edge of the sofa, Elen placed her hand on the child's arm and then yanked it back. Power, much like Avon's, slammed through her.

"Extraordinary," she said softy. "This child is healthy." There was naught else for Elen to do if the child was well, so she smoothed the blanket around her tiny form. "She belongs with this place, I think." The Wulfling was the balanced version of what Avon should be. Even from that brief touch Elen had felt the human and wolf strands of their kind, weaved in a secure knot where Avon's was unraveled.

Elen looked up and Cormack avoided her gaze. A long silence stretched between them. Everything in her being resisted the urge to reach out and hug him—but she knew, could feel it like lightning over water, falling into temptation might stop her heart with its bite.

With a sigh, Elen stood. She walked over to a bookcase, keeping her back turned, afraid to watch him while she made her confession and plea. "Mae asked me to stay for Luc's wedding feast. Afterward, I'll go. I'm not wanted here." She could feel it from the island as much as from him. "I'm sorry, Cormack. I'm so sorry for what I've done to you. I . . ."

I miss you! I miss you so much I can't sleep at night.

She had vowed not to cry in front of him but tears clogged her throat despite her efforts. "Will you just tell me one thing before I leave? Do you hate me now?"

Gathering enough courage to turn around, she found his face contorted with an emotion difficult to define because it formed such a tortured mask. *Because of her. She* had done this to him. His chest rose on breaths more ragged than hers and his hands fisted by his sides.

She asked again, because she needed to know, "Do you hate me?"

He began to shake his head and her heart soared. She even took a step forward. "I can help you. I can teach you everything." Her voice sounded desperate even to her own ears, but she didn't care. "You are my friend, Cormack. My only friend. You being a man changes nothing about how I feel."

An outraged growl came from his throat. Worse, so much worse, he gave a short but distinctive nod and pointed once again to the door.

Leave! The message raged in his gaze like black clouds over a tumultuous sea. *I don't want you here!*

Staggered, she backed into the bookcase. But she had been rejected before, many times, and would be so again. Slowly, she straightened her posture and concentrated only on putting one foot in front of the other. She had received the answer she'd come for, if not the one she'd wanted. More important, she'd been a desperate fool enough for one day.

Koko's Journal

May 18, 1941

Cormack, as he often does, sat with me this afternoon while I painted in Elen's garden. I like when he visits, because in his presence I cannot resent my mortality. I simply look to Cormack and am consoled. We have become unlikely friends, a wolf and an old woman, both trapped in bodies we cannot change. We are two souls with opposite burdens, his to live forever and never know the touch of the woman he loves, whereas I have known love in all its glorious forms, but only for a fleeting time. Ignorance is Cormack's blessing; awareness is my pain. If given the choice, I would choose my burden over his a thousand times.

As I look upon my drawing of Cormack once again, my pride forces me to confess that I am not altogether happy with my work. I deliberately did not capture his true image, not as I see him. There is such need in his eyes that my drawing does not convey, consuming like the hunger of bears in spring, ferocious by nature, starving to feed, yearning to mate. Cormack's image would have been powerful had I drawn what I wanted. Instead, I relaxed his stance, softened his eyes, and even turned a wolfish smile under his pointed snout. This afternoon, after I gathered my supplies and packed them away, Cormack leaned over to view my finished work. The most peculiar sound gurgled from his throat. I am quite certain he had laughed. I am glad, for that at least.

I wish I did not know the woman who has captured his heart, but I do.

Sometimes, when I watch him look at her, my cheeks burn with embarrassment. I wonder how she cannot see it. I wonder how she cannot feel the burning in the wolf's soul that I feel.

I only know it is not my place to show her what I see. That is why I will not fix my drawing. Instead, I will remain loyal to my friend.

I will keep his secret.

~Koko

$\mathcal{E}$ighteen

ROSA EYED THE PACKAGES LUC PULLED FROM HER WARD-robe and placed on their bed, realizing she had started think-ing of it as *their* bed since this morning. "Eight boxes of them?" *How many condoms are in a box?*

He shrugged. "It was all they had on the shelf. Do you have a hidden place I can put these where no one will find them?"

She hesitated for a moment. How many more secrets of hers would he uncover? All of them, she suspected—because she wanted to share them with him. "On the floor of the wardrobe is one," she told him. "And the sixth panel on the far wall is another. Run your hand along the frame and you'll feel the latch. Gareth installed it for me."

While he hid the condoms away, her eyes were drawn to another plastic bag that promised more purchases from the human world. "What else did you bring back?"

"Those are for you," he said absently. "It's nothing much, only a few pairs of jeans. I brought four different sizes. One should fit. There's also some tops and a pair of sneakers—those I had a size for from your boots. You'll blend better wearing that," he explained. "We'll go out together next time and you can buy what you like."

Nothing much? She looked away, momentarily over-whelmed. *He offers me freedom in a bag and says it's nothing much.* "I was never allowed to mingle with mortals." Only when she went for a run was she allowed off the island, and then the route had been plotted for least human population.

"You drove to Rhuddin Village and back," he pointed out.

"That's Gareth's doing. He convinced Math to let me learn as our forest became ill. We damaged it more when we shifted, especially me. My routes were monitored and always traveled in the early mornings. Besides, by then Math had taught me not to stray."

He straightened slowly and faced her. "How, Rosa?" His tone had gone dangerously low. "How did he teach you not to stray?"

"It's not important." She made a flippant wave of her hand. "It happened a long time ago, when horses and carriages filled the gatehouse and steam engines were too exciting to heed caution."

"And you're evading my question so I think it's important." His chin lowered in that way alphas had when deciding whether or not to pounce. "Tell me what happened."

"I shouldn't have brought it up."

"But you did, and now I'll hear the full story."

"Fine." Having been the one to open this door, there was no recourse left but to parade the sordid details within. "I was never tortured, if that's what you're thinking. With me, Math was careful with his punishments."

"And you think that makes them less abusive?"

His question made her pause. "Horses aren't skittish of me as they are with some of our kind. I had one I loved very much. Her name was Eventide." Rosa remained quiet for a moment, ashamed, though she didn't know why—her impudence at the time perhaps, and her stupidity. "Do you remember the 1800s, when steam engines first came about, and the construction of the new railways that went all the way to the west?" The excitement of the times had even reached Avon. "And now we have spaceships that land on our moon, but back then a railway meant freedom." *Achievable freedom.* "I had to see it. I *had* to."

"I understand," he said softly and waited for her to continue.

"I rode Eventide to the new construction of the railway, but the journey was longer than I thought." She looked away for the last of her tale because it still haunted her to this day. "When I returned, Math slaughtered her. And for the rest of the week Eventide was the main course at dinner."

A long stretch of silence consumed the air between them. When Luc finally spoke his voice was strained, as if his beast wanted to crawl up his throat. "How did you not kill him?"

"To what end, Luc? And at whose cost? I've had Guardians more powerful than Math offer to take his place were he to die. Is Pendaran's fortress a better one than this?" A bitter laugh fell from her mouth. "I think not."

"Pendaran?" Luc's eyebrow rose over that revelation.

"He visits once a year and I've woken more than once with him standing over my bed. Silent as a ghost, I swear that man can walk through walls. Even Mae cowers when he's about."

"Did he ever touch you against your will?"

She couldn't help but smile. "I do believe Mae is right. Such an honorable warrior you are to find offense in such things." She shook her head. "No, Pendaran never touched me. Just a promise that my marriage to him would be much more satisfying than my marriage to Math."

"Pendaran can choke on his bloody promises," Luc spat, and his gaze flared.

"I thought of running that night," she admitted. "But where was I to run to? My neighbors didn't involve themselves in our affairs, and I couldn't leave others to endure the consequences of my leaving. They are my family. I thought of killing him, but that would only flood our home with more Guardians. We found a way to make peace in our own way. Cadan mostly. He had it much worse than I did, though he's flippant and pretends enjoyment; he took the heaviest burden."

He exhaled, disturbed yet pensive. "This is the reason you were initially upset by the Wulfling's presence."

She frowned. "I suppose so." Though she hadn't thought about it, apparently he had. "Innocent creatures tend to die here, and a child is as innocent as they come."

"You found a refuge to go to," he said with a tone of relief, not censure, as if he needed to hear that she'd had some small outlet of freedom. "Somewhere close, I believe. Since the castle was almost empty when we arrived and now it's crawling with people."

"Not so close. And before you go searching for it, I would prefer you waited for an invitation from the *Hen*"—she paused—"from our staff. It's their haven and their invitation to give."

He nodded. "How did you keep this place from Math?"

"We haven't had it long. It was part of our plan. We've been seeing signs of dissension, and hearing stories of rebels."

"From Drystan," he stated.

Rosa ignored his acerbic tone, remembering Taliesin had shared her connection to the alliance member. "Drystan was still active among the Guardians when my first wedding took place. He was the only one who offered to help me escape." Her smile was meant to soothe but it only deepened his scowl. "I accepted his help a few hundred years later. We formed a secret friendship, nothing more, no matter what Taliesin suggests."

"If his territory was closer, would you have gone to him first?"

"Yes, with the same original offer I intended to give Dylan. But I doubt I would have offered him marriage." She chose her words carefully, sensing his displeasure. "I've always detested being touched. I wasn't repulsed when you searched me that first time. I took it as a positive sign." She paused, reflective. "I took it as a seed of hope."

That was where it first began, this feeling of rightness that threatened to burst from her chest. And now her seed of hope had grown into a sapling.

And she would *not* let it drown like all the others on this island.

An arrogant glint darkened his eyes. "And when you screamed my name this morning, were you repulsed?"

"Not so much then, either," she confessed.

He chuckled, appeased.

Rosa went over to the bed and ran her hands over the clothes Luc had given her. "When Sophie was taken and brought here . . . I couldn't stand by and let Math harm her as he had Siân. And when Dylan took his revenge, I knew. I knew it was time to act and I did." She held up her new sneakers. "And now I have a husband who brings me gifts such as these." Her voice clogged with emotion as she sat on their bed. "Besides my swords, and Eventide, these are the most thoughtful gifts anyone has ever given me. Thank you."

Luc had gone still.

She frowned. "Did I say something wrong?"

"No, Rosa . . ." He ran his hand through his hair and a metallic square package spiraled to the ground. Had he been holding a condom? It seemed so. Bending down, he picked it up and returned it to the secret compartment. She couldn't help but feel a tug of disappointment.

After closing the hidden panel, he turned and crossed the distance between them. Sitting on the bed, he scooped her onto his lap in a position that was more of a consoling embrace. "I confess I'm at a loss for words."

Her eyes fell to his mouth when he loosened his arms. Leaning forward, she pressed her lips over his, wrapping her arms around his neck. It was the first time she initiated such a gesture. With a growl, his hand lifted and captured her head, deepening the kiss.

"Then let us be together without words," Rosa said against his mouth. "Run with me. Run with me and let me see your wolf."

"Rosa . . ." His chest rose and fell on an anguished breath. "Ask me for anything else and it's yours."

Taken aback, she simply stared. "You're serious." Baffled by his silence, she prompted for certainty, "You really don't want to run with me."

He grimaced then, as if impaled from within. "Believe me when I tell you *want* has nothing to do with it. In this moment, I want to run with you more than my honor can withstand my beast's displeasure." He untangled her arms from his neck, sliding out from under her in haste as he stood.

Her mouth hung open before she snapped it shut. No other unmated wolf would have rejected her offer—*not even Math*—and as his refusal registered the air between them soured.

Granted, her pride was stricken.

But she was also hurt, because she could think of only one reason why he would refuse. "This has something to do with *her*, doesn't it?" *With Koko.* "I'm not asking you to remove her memory; I'm just asking you to run with me."

He winced, and a trail of blood ran from his nose. He wiped it with the back of his hand. "I'll find you later," he said and strode out the door, leaving her bereft in a riot of emotions.

She shook her head in an empty room, not quite sure what had just happened.

TALIESIN FLEW TO AVON AS A GOLDEN RAVEN IN THE shimmering ether of twilight. Wide like a giant raptor, he soared above dense forests and white-tipped mountains shedding winter's last snow. The wind caressed his wings with frozen kisses of a desperate lover, clawing at him in a frantic haste of triumph.

Ah, yes . . . He had denied his true self for too long.

The brother of all things beastly was meant to commune with beasts; he was meant to fly and swim and run alongside all earthly creatures. Because he was the son of an earth mother, a goddess of transformation who balanced darkness and light, and he had been missed.

Unlike his weakened protectors, he could assume any visceral form, and not just that of a wolf. But it had been a while, and by the time he circled the wasted island of Avon, his back and shoulders screamed for rest. He angled for the Walkers' tombs and glided into the shadows. The shift back to man took but a thought and he stood naked in front of Aeron's sleeping chamber and earthly vault.

Contacting the Walkers would break his abstinence, so what was one little shift to get him to their bodily domain on earth?

When he sinned, he sinned well.

And before his thoughts generated better ways to commit his depraved deeds, he slid open the door. Moonlight filtered into the tomb, a pale embrace in the black oblivion of nightmares. Anger and guilt roiled in his gut; his own toxic cocktail of hell to keep him in his place of shame. Aeron's body remained in the position he had left her, unsullied and alone. Leaning over, he hesitated only the briefest of seconds before touching his mouth to hers.

If he had to awaken in the realm of the *Ystrad Gloyw*, the Glowing Vale of his mother's imagination, he deserved to be greeted by a pissed-off *Beddestyr*.

His mind spun into lightness, a delusion between worlds as the dank floors of the tomb continued to suck warmth from his feet. Because his father was human, Taliesin was not allowed to walk in the true Otherworld, among the emerald thralls of the ethereal Fae.

So his mother had created this space, this vale of nothingness, a valley of dreams where he could never be touched, or held, or loved. He had come here often as a child, only to leave hollow and bereft like many of Avon's broken trees and return to the controlled care of the Guardians.

And they judged him for finding succor in drink?

He wondered why he still cared, why it still hurt. More important, he wondered what the fuck he was doing here again.

A shriek worthy of a great horned owl resonated throughout his psyche. He opened his mind's eye. Outraged, black hair billowing in a wind that didn't exist, Aeron slapped him across the face.

Except her hand shimmered through his head and she screamed again in frustration. "You despicable half human. How dare you come here through me?"

"Hello, Aeron. How are you?" He stood in a forest of pink trees, on a path of purple thyme that led to a pale skyline. There was no scent of veracity, or the rustle of creatures, just the emptiness of a fabricated illusion.

"How am I? *How am I, he asks*," she ranted. "How do I look?" She shoved her fist through his jaw just to prove she had no substance. "There was a time when all I needed to do was smile at a man to bring him to pleasure, and now when one comes near me all he wants to . . . do . . . is . . . *die*!"

The last resonated like a scream.

And she wasn't quite done.

"So," Aeron huffed. "I am contained in this circle of raindrops while my spirit wanders in the Vale without contact or comfort." Desperate outrage whispered through her mind to his. "I have not tasted a single drop of wine or felt another's touch in over three hundred years because of *you*!" She lunged for him again but dissipated in the air. "You are such an arsehole."

That makes two women in one week to call him one, and possibly one more if Ceridwen deemed to accept his call. "I need a word with my mother."

Aeron reappeared by his side, sullen. "Ceri is meditating. She closed her garden as soon as you shifted and took flight. She needs to keep her mind free of painful memories."

"Nice to know my memory still causes her pain," he said bitterly.

Aeron hissed. "Poisonous greetings will not bring you what you seek." Dread thickened her delicate voice. "You have not learned from your mistakes."

He laughed, because if souls could scream, his just might. "I *am* the mistake!" He was the bastard who roamed the earth while his mother lived with her ethereal family, the result of a misbegotten affair after a long, long chase.

Leaves blackened and fell in the fake pink forest wrought by his mother's mind.

"Stop. *Please . . .* You mustn't say such things. It makes *her* despair." Eyes wide with panic, Aeron pleaded, "Control your emotions, Taliesin. Or more humans will die and forests will be laid waste."

Guilt tangled in the midst of her warning—more from her than him—and Aeron rarely exhibited such a selfless emotion.

It made Taliesin pause. "It was you, wasn't it? It was you who convinced my mother to come to earth and see me?"

Aeron lifted her ghostly hands, and let them fall back to her sides like a repentant apparition. "I was at a loss of what to do with you. You and your bumbling ways, and your pretty verses, singing tales that are not meant to be told. You were destroying yourself. The Isle of Mighty has changed. The Fairbryn of later times is not our medieval Cymru. Humans are advancing. What you say is no longer passed from the mouths of bards and twisted with each song—or scrolled into pretty pictures by cloistered monks. Communication among the humans has become too dangerous for your drunken ways and slurred prophecies."

"I'm well aware," he reminded her. "*I'm* the one who lives among them."

Aeron tilted her head, regarding him with translucent

resonance. "You almost speak as if you care. Is it possible that you have seen the error of your ways?"

"I've always cared." *Too much.* It was the reason why his vodka-scented siren sang such a sweet, sweet song.

"Only when it suited you," Aeron continued with her tirade. "You would not listen to us. We are your mother's messengers and you would not even give us an audience. Ceri risked everything to come and see you—and how did you greet such a sacrifice?" She paced on ground that didn't hold her tread. "Drunken beyond comprehension, that is how. You told your mother to bugger off."

Actually, I believe I told her to fuck off. And she left every human in Fairbryn ill because of it.

The last was meant to be a thought, but in the Vale, potent thoughts became words.

Aeron fisted her hands in frustration. "When the Mother of Darkness and Light weeps—*things die*! The death of the humans devastated Ceri. She cannot even look at me anymore without the memory causing sorrow—because I am her messenger. *Because I was the one who brought her there!* I am no longer allowed to walk between worlds because the risk is too great. None of us are. You have cursed us all, Taliesin, with your depravity and unforgiving ways."

"I'm not unforgiving." He would accept the former but not the latter.

"For a Seer, you are sometimes blind."

"On that, we agree," he said, reminded of the purpose for this visit. "You knew me as a child, Aeron. You saw the people my mother created to raise me. Look at what they have become. Look at what they do to preserve something they should never have been given."

"It is unfortunate," she concurred with an elusive frown. "Your Guardians could not handle the power of the Fae in their veins. It tainted their minds, twisted it into malevolence instead of good. It is another one of your mother's laments. Another betrayal of her family for you."

"There are some who can handle it," he defended. "I've come here for them. My foresight is gone. The prophecies I once foretold are no longer clear to me. All I See are faded reflections, like the Vale." He exhaled, and while his breath had no substance, his shoulders caved with the weight of his concern. "I've come to ask for guidance."

Aeron turned thoughtful. "If you have lost your Sight, then there is something that Ceri does not want you to See. I wonder . . ." A smile widened her face then. "A Tree of Hope must have grown among these people you seek guidance for." She opened her arms wide and spun around in a giddy circle. "A Tree of Hope may just set us free."

Her shadow stumbled to a halt in front of him. "You must not interfere, Taliesin." Her chin lowered in a stern warning. "It is why your Sight has been taken. I am sure of it. Ceri does not trust you with something this precious."

A cloud appeared to darken the dusky pink forest. His mind turned murky. He was being kicked out of this realm, having stayed beyond his welcome. Not even fit for a council with his darling darkest mother, or even trusted with something as promising as hope.

Soon, his senses saturated with sight and sound and the musk of the tomb. He awoke to the pressure of stiffened lips and the dankness of his life.

"Yes, a Tree of Hope might set you free," he whispered to Aeron's unresponsive shell. "Or doom us if it dies."

If it was true, not even he could fault his mother for assuming he might kill it.

It was what he did to everything good in his life.

Koko's Journal

January 12, 1942

The room is spinning and my heart is aching. I think I have had too much of Enid's special mead. It makes me bold, as if I wield a mighty sword and not a simple pen, bold enough to write what I will not speak aloud. Come morning I will find the courage to remove this page. Or maybe my courage has become as fleeting as my final days.

Remember me.
When I pass and you live on,
Remember me.
When you lie with another woman,
Remember me.
When you wed again,
Keep my image close to your heart.
Remember me.
And if this woman can run like a wolf,
Let her run alone with the wind.
Remember me.
That is all I ask.

~Koko

Nineteen

Luc began to hunger for her. He began to crave her touch, to listen for her voice when she walked the halls. Four days had passed since he'd left Rosa in their bedroom holding her new sneakers, four days of chaste nights and cold mornings and torturous indecisions.

Like Avon's broken bridge, they had come to an impasse and neither of them was willing to jump over the turbulent waters.

Worse, it was his error to fix. And he was losing control, torn between honor and need, and need was winning this faithless battle to preserve Koko's only request.

Agitated, he searched Castell Avon. The afternoon sun heated the inner bailey. He nodded to the guards as he passed and scanned the yard, taking note of the building that held the generators.

A clanging of swords echoed over the soft hum and he followed the sound to a clearing in the broken woods. Rosa circled Cadan, wearing her jeans and sneakers—and a feral grin.

His blood rose to stimulate a baser organ as he watched his warrior queen.

Cadan wielded her mother's sword, and Rosa held the one Luc had given her, gaining confidence with each stroke. Griffith, one of Isabeau's men, leered from the side, along with Cormack; both men held a look of intense longing but Griffith's was directed solely toward Rosa, while Cormack's was for a skill he didn't possess.

Gritting his teeth, Luc tasted iron on the back of his throat.

Mine, mine . . . mine! echoed through his thoughts with livid impatience.

"Halt," Rosa announced, holding up her hand and lowering her weapon. She turned to Luc with a questioning gaze. "Is there something you need?"

Yes, my mate.

"Leave us." He glared at all three men. Only Cadan hesitated.

"I'm fine," Rosa assured her cousin, not hiding her annoyance as the area cleared.

Slowly, he approached her, ignoring her frown as he made a motion for her to lift her sword. Her scent had deepened from exertion and it taunted his wolf. "You're skirting away too soon," he instructed, searching for a neutral topic. "Size can be as much a disadvantage as it is an advantage. Would you like me to show you some countermoves?"

She lifted wary eyes the color of violets. "Yes."

It was her first concession of closeness since he'd refused to run with her—and he intended to take full advantage. "You can use momentum against your attacker." He showed her how to wait and pull, then shift to counter his move. She was a quick study, but he was older and more skilled. He taught her a pivot strike. Predictably, she fell forward as all students did on their first try, and he followed her to the ground, turning her so he took the weight of her fall.

She laughed—and the air between them suddenly emptied of resentment and grew in desire. "You planned that."

"Maybe." He rolled her beneath him, positioning himself between her thighs, allowing the harsh evidence of his need to press against her through the confinement of their clothes. He knew she felt it by her hitched breathing. "How long are you going to avoid me?"

"Run with me," she taunted in a husky voice. Her lips trailed down his neck to rest by his ear. "Run with me and I'll accept your offer."

"Rosa—"

"Before you say no," she interrupted, "understand that this is not an easy submission for me to make, and what I'm asking for is so little for what I'm offering." Her tone suggested she'd made a concession, and that she'd wanted more but would settle for a union of their wolves in a flight through Avon's forest. "Afterward, we'll try to conceive."

Flooded by pleasure and pain, he groaned. "My brother is mated to a human. And they don't run together."

"I'm not just human." A simple truth that refused argument. "*We* must answer to our wolves."

"I can't—" His beast shredded his chest with his denial. Not that it mattered; his heart was already torn.

A feminine growl greeted his ears and prompted his darker half to attack outright in complete accordance with her frustration. She rolled out from under him, grabbed her sword and stormed away without another word. He let her go, certain that sharing his promise to Koko wouldn't help his cause—or ease her anger.

And his wolf . . .

His wolf didn't care about a mortal long dead; it wanted to claim its very alive mate and seal their bond.

When he knew the area was clear, he spit out the blood that had crawled up his throat from his shredded innards. Consumed with hunger and lust, he watched it soak into the barren ground; blood into dust when he could have life. To deny Rosa a run was to deny the very nature of their wolves.

Rising to a standing position, he kept his head bent in shame. "I want her," he whispered to the woman who'd taught him how to love. "I'm sorry, Koko . . . I'll never forget you. *Never.* But I ache for another and I don't know how much longer I'll last."

The anguished plea eased his beast, knowing its master's resolve was weakening to an instinct more powerful than honor.

ON THE EIGHTH NIGHT OF ABSTINENCE, LUC BROKE LIKE tinder ready to catch flame. Rosa would hear his promise to Koko and know his dilemma. It was well past the waking hours, she had yet to come to bed, and he refused to spend another evening of proper conversations about Avon's defenses, antics of their precocious Wulfling and the training of their guards and staff.

Their battlements were secure and he needed his wife. Humbling, how he could go almost seventy years without the physical comfort of a woman and now he couldn't even last a fortnight.

An open staircase wrapped around the south turret, and he ascended the stairs, having learned over the last weeks the places she liked to visit most. The banners of Math's house had been replaced with ones that touted a wreath of thorny rose canes around a silhouette of a black wolf. At least the residents of Avon welcomed their union, enough to herald it from their home, although Rosa must have approved the new crest.

He found her standing on the parapets, a somber silhouette against a midnight sky. An emerald cloak whipped about her shoulders while her hair danced in the wind, golden strands teasing the night.

She stole his breath.

"Summer approaches," she said as he drew near. "I can taste its scent on the breeze. It's as if I can hear the Council's whispers and they are calling my name." Her shoulders rose and fell on a heavy sigh, preparing him for her next revelation. "Just so you know . . . I've spoken with Mae. She's agreed to make more of my potion after I told her you wouldn't run with me."

Mates ran together; to deny one was to deny the other. It was why Mae had agreed to Rosa's request, and why he contemplated his argument before making demands he had no right to make. Did Koko know this when she wrote her last drunken and desperate plea of him?

"It will be ready in the morning," Rosa continued in his silence. "She's teaching Elen the recipe."

He fisted his hands by his sides, trying to calm an anger she didn't deserve. Before he implored her not to take it, he shared, "It was the only request from a woman I loved. I won't apologize for that, but I will for the pain it's caused you, and for the distance it's created between us."

"I think I hate her." Her words were hardly audible, even to his ears. "And I hate that I do."

He could think of no adequate response, other than an offer he once gave. "Ask anything else of me, Rosa, *anything*, and it's yours."

"You have already fulfilled the terms of our arrangement, above and beyond my expectations." Disenchantment weaved a heavy line through her voice, tainting her praise. "But I would have the one thing from you that I didn't have the foresight to request."

She turned to leave but he snagged her arm. Her cloak whipped back to reveal a long nightshirt underneath, molding against her curves by the wind.

"Lie with me." Luc dropped his lips by the sensitive skin just under her ear, while the hood of her cloak feathered against his cheek. He resisted the urge to nip the column of her neck, to brand her as he should. "Give me a chance to foil this prophecy before you take that potion."

"Run with me," she returned, "and I will. Our staff has invited you to our place beyond the river." She leaned back, her expression fierce and demanding. "It's an hour away. Join me." Her eyes flashed with challenge. "Join me if your wolf has the bollocks."

Twisting her arm out of his grasp, she fled toward the south turret. Her cloak billowed behind her hasty retreat as she disappeared down the spiral staircase after her fiery proposition.

He hissed. *Bloody hell . . . Yes*, his wolf had the balls, and so did he as a man.

Lifting his face to the crescent moon, he howled in the wake of her glorious exit.

You are a wicked one, are you not, my wife—to issue such a challenge and then run?

Wicked and defiant with the knowledge of their wolves, knowing that he could do naught but give chase—promises be damned.

Blinded by instinct, he hunted her trail, followed the scent of vanilla to the river beyond the wall, where the shallow waters broke over open rocks. He crossed the currents to find her waiting for him in a field surrounded by evergreen trees.

Kissed by moonlight, she beamed an invitation like a beacon for a starved warrior. The air carried her siren's call and lightning bugs danced in the wavering weeds. Slowly, while he watched, she let the cloak drop from her shoulders and pile around her feet.

"Leave now," she warned. By the naughty glint that entered her gaze, and the smirk that turned her lips, her notice was issued with the purpose to tease. "If you don't want to see my wolf, turn around and return to Avon."

Her grin became a triumphant smile as he remained frozen in place. She tugged the ties of her nightshirt, letting the thin material caress her skin as it glided to the ground, a mere whisper in the night that could fell even the mightiest beast.

With her hair loose about her shoulders, she stood naked, daring him to pursue or turn, but forcing him to make a decision as she widened her arms and called the elements of the forest. The potency of the approaching summer rolled off the mountains. Even the air stilled in that moment of sacrifice, as it gave its very life force to a magical being. The scents of pine and earth hovered like a cloying fog, waiting to be consumed. She manipulated its energy with the ease of an alpha and fed it to her waiting wolf.

He watched in awe.

Rosa shifted like a dancer, a graceful ballet of molting skin and sinew re-forming over broken bones, without even a gasp or a growl until a golden wolf regarded him with burgundy eyes. And in that moment he was forced to face what he'd already known but chose to ignore: No unmated man with wolf blood in his veins would resist her lure in that final reckoning of undeniable—and rare—power.

Poised in that same knowledge, she gave a taunting nod, turned, and ran.

Tortured, he buckled to his knees and understood that he was the prey in this chase, helpless to a huntress of his will.

"I'm sorry," he whispered to another's memory and began his own change, barely removing his clothes in time for his beast to explode from within, victorious in its master's weakness. It was a brutal shift, comparable only to when the Guardians had marked their presence in Rhuddin Village. He fought with his wolf to keep the ink in his skin, barely preserving that one final promise.

Within minutes he was breathing sharper scents, viewing the shadows through keener eyes, and hunting her trail with a night creature's heightened senses.

Forest paths provided a maze of discoveries as he caught up to her and they loped across packed clay floors and hurdled over fallen limbs together. How had he thought to deny her this?

How had he thought to deny himself?

Before long, they came upon a hidden village, although he had never seen such an ensemble of enchanted makeshift homes since the old forests of Cymru. There were hills with arched doors and trees with peeking chimneys—a haven for their kind.

He listened, circled the dwellings, satisfied to find them deserted, and contented to know he was alone with his mate. He leapt upon her, nipped her neck, and received one in return. They rolled on the moss floor, panting from play. It would go no further than chaste frolic. Because their minds were human, even the mere idea of sexuality in this form was as abhorrent as rape, much like exerting dominion on an innocent creature, unheeded by wolves but not by humans with a conscience.

He was the first to initiate the change back to humanity. The forest here was abundant with life, far enough from Avon to thrive. Once he started calling the elements, she rode the power and they shifted together.

Looking to the clear sky, they remained on the bed of moss. The cool air felt good against his heated skin. He was almost hesitant to fill the air with a voice, but his need over-rode peace.

Rolling on top of her, he captured her wrists in his hands and held them above her head. It was time the huntress met the hunter.

"I ache for you, Rosa." He dared not look to the sky, for if Koko's spirit soared above in the form of her owl, she might just shit on his head for what he was about to confess. "I ache for you as I've never ached for another."

Her eyes fell to his chest. Even in the darkness his tattoo contrasted against his skin. She didn't complain, or even comment.

Instead, she wrapped her legs around his waist and braided her fingers through his. "Prove it to me."

Shaking, he edged the head of his shaft against her opening. Slick, she was so slick and ready for him. He thrust at her command, faltering only when her warmth grasped him with its tight fist.

Nirvana . . .

If there was one, this was it.

He nuzzled his face into the waves of her hair and growled next to her ear, "I think of you and I get hard."

He withdrew and thrust again. "I catch your scent and my mind wanders."

And again. "I hunger for you."

And again, embedding his shaft as far as it would go, holding it there for his final assertion, "And no matter how many times I'm inside you, I still feel starved."

"Luc—" She arched, widening her legs, bracing her feet on the forest floor to meet his thrusts. Her hands clutched his, searching for a lifeline in her tumultuous fall. Like a piston, her hips jerked and he felt her inner muscles tightening with her release, milking his shaft with pulsing contractions.

He waited for her climax to end. He waited for her to understand his intent. "I'm not stopping, Rosa. From this night forth, I'll do everything in my power to foil this prophecy."

She had set the terms when this chase began and he was claiming his reward.

Neither words, nor thought, nor even the barest hint of restraint formed after his final edict. He just rode her stretched heat and understood why Celts worshiped women, because in that moment he was a slave to her vessel. When the tightening gripped his shaft, he groaned her name. A low growl vibrated from his chest as he spilled his seed, the most blessed form of claiming on this magical night.

Afterward, she brought him to her private cabin surrounded by a curtain of willow reeds. Charmed by her place, and her excitement in showing him, he simply had to have her again on a narrow cot. And while she dozed, he browsed her odd assortment of magazines and modern books. Later he learned that Math had censored Avon's library. Within the week he intended to bring her to the mortal world and let her buy her fill from the nearest bookstore.

Her life would never be censored again. Not on matters they could control and that didn't bring danger to Avon. And under no circumstances would he allow her to feel trapped as his wife, or his mate.

"HA! I WIN THIS ROUND," ROSA ANNOUNCED, PANTING in a rush of laughter over her husband's flummoxed expression. A few cheers went up around the crowd. What started out as a training session in the inner bailey became a serious workout. Admittedly, Luc had her on her bottom a few times, because he fought without rules, but then, so had Rosa's mother.

"That's fifty bucks you owe me," Teyrnon shouted to Cadan.

Rosa glared at her cousin. "You bet against me?"

"You're out of practice, Rosabea." He gave an unrepentant shrug. "And Teyrnon owes me a hundred and fifty."

After sheathing her sword, she bent forward with hands on knees to catch her breath.

Using her distraction, Luc pulled her on top of him and they tumbled to the ground. Their audience cheered as he rolled on his back and she straddled his waist. "And this one is mine," he taunted the crowd, sitting up to claim her mouth for a debauched kiss.

She should not have allowed his public antics but couldn't help but whisper against his mouth, "Is that my prize, or do I get a better one later?"

He gave a soft growl. His lips moved to her ear. Softly, he said, "If we're handing out boons, then I must remind you that I get three to your one."

The laughter fell and voices hushed. Luc gave her a gentle tap to move but Rosa had already begun to scramble to a standing position. Gareth broke through the circled guards, holding a folded letter. His expression left little doubt who the sender was, and the formal seal of the Council confirmed her suspicion, with a horned serpent stamped in blue wax.

"It's addressed to Rosa," Gareth said as he handed her the parchment. "It was delivered by overnight express in a separate box."

Strange, how her heart refused to beat like it had ceased to exist. Her seedling of hope had just been hit by a hard frost, edging its leaves in black.

Rosa slid her hand under the seal and read the few lines, then handed it to Luc. "It's from the Council," she confirmed to the waiting crowd.

"Is it a declaration of war?" This from Teyrnon.

"It's an announcement of their arrival tomorrow evening," Luc clipped as he read the proclamation. "They want to check on the Walkers and discuss their continued care."

"We should cancel the wedding feast," Rosa said. Even now the great hall was decorated in swaths of linen and golden leaves for tomorrow's festivities.

Luc's brows snapped together. "Let them witness our celebration." His eyes lifted to hers with warning. "Is this not what our plan has always been?"

Sadly, she said, "Yes, but I was getting used to my castle without their stench." Grumbling in agreement, the guards began to disperse and she held her husband back with a hand on his arm. "Would you walk with me, Luc?"

He regarded her with a questioning frown. "Of course."

"I have something I want to show you and I need your advice." Then she found her cousin in the crowd. "Cadan," she called, "I would like you to come as well. This is as much your business as it is mine."

Turning at her voice, Cadan winked at her. "Now I'm curious."

Twenty

ECHOING CADAN'S SENTIMENTS, LUC FOLLOWED ROSA through the great hall. On the far wall sat three chairs on a raised dais, the center one larger than the sides, with wolf heads carved into the oaken arms and navy velvet cushions to pad Math's ass.

"The thrones need to go," he told her. He had been meaning to mention them earlier but now seemed as good a time as any.

She waved her hand absently. "Burn them on a pyre for all I care. Nothing good came of those chairs."

Behind the thrones, she pulled back a large curtain, gathering the folds to rest in the corner to reveal a hidden panel that covered a fortified door.

Cadan had gone still when she pulled out the key. "Why do I need to be here for this?"

"You are my only family, Cadan. The only family I have left who cares about me."

"As you are for me," her cousin whispered.

"I am the reason you came to this place . . ." Her voice

trailed off. She swallowed, gathered her composure. "As far as I am concerned, half of this is yours." She fitted the key in the lock, turned and opened the door.

"Shit," Luc muttered, running his hands through his hair as he viewed the contents within. Jewels, goblets, crowns, silver plates, gold bars, baskets of coins, rolled tapestries and scrolls lined the shelves on the inner walls. "Why does it not surprise me that Math had a vault behind his throne room?"

Rosa shrugged. "He was a king for over two thousand years."

"And he liked to collect rare and pretty things," Cadan added with scorn.

"Shit," Luc repeated again for lack of a better word. "I should have been shown this earlier."

Rosa just blinked at him, unrepentant. "I didn't trust you earlier, and now I need your knowledge of the mortal world. I want to secure this before the Council comes tomorrow. They may ask for it. Can we liquefy it?" She frowned. "I believe that's the term I read, and separate it into different banks or comparable storing facilities. They will also want Math's ledgers."

"Not in a day." Luc shook his head. "And the artifacts will be problematic. I'll ask my brother. We have accountants in Rhuddin Village who may know. Porter is good with this type of thing."

"Half of it's Cadan's," she pressed.

"I want nothing to do with it," her cousin sneered and turned to leave. Halfway across the hall, he paused and then returned. "You know what? Bugger that. I earned it." He took Rosa's hand in his. "We earned it. Thirds, Rosabea. How does that sound? A third for you, me, and the rest to govern Avon." Cadan sent Luc a wary look. "That's if your new husband doesn't claim it all."

"I'm not a pauper," Luc informed him, understanding his ire was a personal one. Luc had lived only four hundred years shy of Math; he had his own wealth, and it was secured much better than this. "Rosa keeps what she came into our marriage with."

True wealth was not material riches—but family, friendship, land to live, freedom and love. However, it did provide the means to support and protect what mattered most.

Cadan relaxed. "Is a third of this enough to run Avon?"

"Yes." Luc cleared his throat to hide his amusement. "Yes, I believe it is." Or a large and needy country for centuries.

However, the naïve question made him realize that Rosa hadn't been the only one cloistered from the modern world. And it was time they both became acclimated. "I'm bringing Rosa into Manchester to do some shopping this afternoon. Would you like to join us, Cadan?"

"We shouldn't go now." Rosa barely contained her disappointment. "Not with the Council members here."

"They're watching us, I'm sure," Luc told her. "Let them watch. Avon is secure, Manchester is only a two-hour ride, and we mustn't act frightened."

Cadan made no attempt to hide his opinion. "Piss on the Council and whoever's here . . . I'm coming with you."

And a reminder of freedom was what both his wife and her cousin needed.

After Rosa secured the vault, a bellowing shriek echoed through the throne room, followed by scampering feet and an outraged chef. Audrey dashed to hide behind Rosa while Walter waved his bloodied hand.

Picking up Audrey and settling her on her hip, Rosa asked, "What happened?"

"The Wulfling bit me," Walter accused, florid with outrage. "And almost destroyed your wedding cake."

Tesni turned the corner then, offering an apologetic grimace. "I'm sorry. I thought she was napping. She's a slippery little eel, that one. A baby alpha, if you ask me."

Audrey hid her face against Rosa's arm, leaving a smear of butter-scented frosting.

"Is this true?" Rosa asked.

"He said I can't come to the feast anymore." Audrey peeked out long enough to point an accusing chubby finger at Walter. "He said the Guardians are coming. I want cake. I want meat pie." Her lip trembled. "I want to come to the feast."

"Walter is right," Luc told Audrey in a firm voice, agreeing with Tesni's suspicion about her being an alpha. "There will be people there who'll want to take you." He turned to the chef, knowing he lacked the ability to shift. "Go find my sister and Mae. They'll care for your hand."

"I believe you've become a bit overindulged," Rosa said, but not without kissing the top of the child's head to soften her discipline. In return, Audrey absently rubbed her hand along Rosa's upper arm, a tactile form of seeking comfort and affection.

They were bonding, Luc thought, and the evidence of Rosa's natural acceptance formed a powerful grip around his heart.

"You'll have cake," his wife continued, "and you'll have meat pie, but you mustn't come to the feast, and you must ask before you take."

"Why?" Audrey's voice was small, confused and *irked*.

"Because it's the proper thing to do," Rosa asserted. Her tone now was that of an alpha guiding her young. "And if you make a mess, you need to clean it up. And you must apologize to Walter afterward. Do you understand?"

Wide eyes blinked innocently. "I don't know what *apologize* means."

"Now, that's not true," Tesni supplied. "I heard you teaching Cormack all the variations of that word yesterday when he ate one of your strawberries."

"I like strawberries. I like Cormack too." A heavy sigh came from a small chest. "And I like Walter because he makes cake and cookies. I'll say the sorry word to him."

"Let us go clean up your mess." Tesni held out her arms and Audrey switched holders.

"Thank you, Tesni," Rosa said, and as the room cleared,

she turned to Luc with determination to protect her home and the inhabitants within. "I'll show you Math's ledgers if you like. They're an accounting of all the Guardian descendants, but I'm learning he knew very little."

"Has the Council seen them?"

"Of course."

"Then we'll hand those over if asked and hide your treasures this afternoon."

MEMORIES WERE LIKE SEASONS, WEAVING PATHS OF interlocking journeys. Some were harsh and draining like winter while others were bountiful and healing like spring. But the day Rosa spent in the mortal world with Luc and Cadan was like summer, glorious and free. They ate hot dogs and fried potatoes, drank Coke and purchased clothing that smelled of chemicals, but she didn't care, and then Luc brought her to a bookstore two stories high. *Oh, goodness gracious*—that was what the woman had said when Rosa had dragged filled carts to the counter. Luc fit eight boxes of beautiful tomes into Teyrnon's SUV. The rest were being shipped.

And on the following night she wore a black dress for her wedding feast, belted by her scabbard and sword. She'd found it in a cluster of department stores called an outlet mall. Tesni arranged the top of her hair in a plaited coronet intertwined with pearls, while the back curled to hang about her shoulders. They walked together to the great hall where music reached the upper floors. Bethan and Tobias had dusted off their lyre and flute and filled the castle with haunting melodies. Soldiers made bawdy jokes and even Gareth laughed as new memories were made, happy ones despite the looming shadow of the Council's visit.

"You wear a somber color this night," Tesni said with a teasing lilt to her tone when they entered the hall. "But look, it turns your husband's eyes a very lovely blue."

"Yes," Rosa agreed. "Yes, it does." She felt sensual and uninhibited—and wished the Guardians weren't coming to dampen the joy of the evening.

Luc approached with a feral grin and kissed her temple in greeting. His suit and shirt didn't match his sword but the way he wore them fluttered her heart.

"What a daunting pair we make in our formal clothes and weaponry." She flipped a loose curl over her shoulder, sending him a half-turned smile. "I'll look forward to removing yours later this night."

"Don't tease," he warned. "I don't need additional distractions."

The porter from Rhuddin Village arrived before the Guardians.

Luc glowered at the man. "I called for advice—*not* for you to come here."

"Llara and her army are at Rhuddin Village, along with a few of Isabeau's guards," Porter informed him. His shaved head reflected the light from the flickering sconces, brandishing the Celtic cross of his Irish heritage. "Your brother has been a right surly thing. I've been ordered to set up your communication system and not be returning until it's complete so he can talk to you freely."

The feast was served. They sat at tables arranged in rows, filled with platters of roasted meat, crusted pies, and honeyed vegetables. The wine, ale and mead had been reserved for a later time. Even so, as the night progressed, Elen acted intoxicated. After her third hiccup, Porter grabbed her goblet, sniffed, and then shook his head as if confused.

"It's this island." Elen giggled. "I feel so dizzy," she slurred.

Ever watchful, Gareth hovered close. "Are you well?" he asked Elen.

"Maybe I should get some fresh air." She stood, weaved and grabbed the back of her chair. "*Whoa . . .* room is spinning."

Gareth responded by scooping her up into his arms. He carried her away from the table and paused by Luc's chair. "I'll bring her to the library and return shortly."

Luc gave a nod as they passed. "Don't look so worried," he whispered in Rosa's ear as he leaned down. "Trust me when I tell you my sister can protect herself if need be. She enjoys it here, and Elen gets so little enjoyment in her life."

"We've all gotten used to her gentle presence," Rosa told him. "And Mae adores her, but it's odd how the island influences her."

"I don't want to go to the library," Elen protested as she was carried away. "Cormack's in the library with Audrey and"—she hiccupped—"he hates me."

The Guardians arrived shortly after Elen and Gareth disappeared around the corner. Teyrnon filled the main entrance, appearing stunned, as if someone had just broadsided him in the head with a rather nasty club.

Merin, Briallen and Maelor glided into the great hall with only a glare as a greeting. They wore modern clothes of discreet colors and styles to blend while traveling.

Inappropriate, as her cousin tended to be in tense situations, Cadan leaned over to Tesni with a mischievous smirk turning his mouth. "Look at the Norseman. I think he wants to eat Maelor's wife."

Tesni sent a conspiring whisper, "Yes, but in a good way or a bad way?"

Cadan sniggered softly. "Both, I think."

"Hush," Rosa ordered them. Once they started on this route, it was difficult to veer them away, and now was not the time for such antics, especially with her husband still as a Walker in his chair.

Tucker came bounding into the room, leapt on the dais that formerly held three thrones, sat back on his haunches—and watched. It was then that Rosa noticed an eerie difference from earthly hounds, as if iridescent waves ruffled the air as it breathed. And there was nothing quite as unnerving as witnessing a hound from the Otherworld stand sentry over three Guardians who had invaded her home.

"Let us do our task and leave." Maelor glowered at the hound in displeasure, stalky and unkempt, with his massive arm tethered to his petite wife. Briallen stared ahead with unfocused eyes, her red hair hanging loose down her back. Her skin had a pallid tone as if malnourished or stretched thin.

"I must say that for once we agree." Merin scanned the tables with a serene gaze, landing on Luc. "We will not stay long," she announced. "We have come to see the Walkers and request Math's journals." She turned to Rosa. "Pendaran has also sent you a gift for your upcoming ceremony."

Under the Guardian's gaze, Rosa felt pinned to her wooden seat. Assessed like an anomaly of nature who didn't deserve to live. "Thank you, Merin," she said. "But I cannot accept such a generous offer. Please tell Pendaran that I'm married."

Pendaran knew, of course; it was why they were here. Merin's annoyance flared in her gaze. But Rosa had mastered the art of misleading pleasantries a long time ago. "I'm surprised Neira and William didn't share this news already, but no matter, so long as he knows the ceremony is no longer viable with me."

"That is a most unwise decision," Merin returned.

Luc stood, pressed his knuckles against the table and leaned forward, lowering his head as if he might actually lunge. "You will also inform Pendaran that Rosa and I are mated."

Inwardly, Rosa cringed. It was not good to tempt fate with a lie. In her experience it stopped it from coming true. Rising next to Luc, she said, "Let us then view the Walkers together and you can be on your way."

It was a macabre procession to the tombs, Teyrnon with his sinister scowl and Luc void of all emotion, the false boredom of a troubled heart as he helped Rosa slide open the first door. She chose to show Nesien because he tended to be the least malevolent of the four.

The Walker was displayed in English country clothes, with a plain overcoat and fitted breeches and boots. A leather-bound book rested under his crossed hands, a sentimental gesture from the person who had arranged him on the marble slab.

With a slight grimace, Merin ducked under the low overhang, her nostrils flaring at the stale odor.

"Nesien was a bore of a man," Merin muttered absently. Wearing slacks and a spring jacket, with her golden hair twisted in a serviceable knot at the nape of her neck, she viewed the shell of Nesien with passing disdain. "He could talk of human history for hours if you let him. But he did not deserve a fate such as this."

With Luc guarding the doorway, they were alone inside the tomb. Rosa felt compelled to warn, "Don't touch him."

"Do you think I am stupid?" Merin snapped. Her gaze fell to Luc and suddenly her expression held more shadows than this half-alive grave. "You mustn't insult Pendaran by refusing his gift. It does not matter if you are married, or even mated. Pendaran will see the prophecy through and destroy anyone who stands in his way."

"Save your threats for someone who'll cower to them," Rosa said with conviction. "I'll never be ruled again by the Council's dictates." She made a motion for Merin to exit before her. "I'm allowing you to see the Walkers because it's a rational request, no more."

Merin's hand snaked out to grab Rosa's arm. This time, unlike with Briog, Rosa was prepared. With a heady flash of metal through leather, she unsheathed her sword and pressed it against the woman's neck. Nesien answered with his own song, flooding the enclosure with promises of death were she just to swing the weapon his way.

"Ah, you are your mother's daughter." A slow grin spread across Merin's face, eerily like Elen's but twisted with hostility. "I had wondered."

With lips peeled back, Luc charged inside. "Leave," he

ordered, head bent, eyes flashing as he gripped the hilt of his own sword and poised it above Merin's head. "Leave, or I'll let my mate slice your throat."

Merin released her hold. "I have seen enough." She brushed by Luc with a cursory comment. "You carry your father's weapon well."

A muscle tensed on the side of his neck while his gaze followed her retreat. "You wouldn't happen to know how it found its way to me."

She turned at his voice. "I have no idea what you are talking about." Blue eyes lifted, stark with warning. "Pendaran has ears in the wind."

He opened his mouth but snapped it closed when a lantern's light edged around Aeron's tomb.

"Move aside, Norseman," Maelor spat. "This place reeks of weakness. I have done Pendaran's bidding. We are going home now." His wife stumbled alongside him until she righted her footing to his pace on the pathway.

"Briallen," Teyrnon called after them, his hands opening and closing by his sides, stance ready. "Say the word," he growled in outrage on her behalf.

Briallen stiffened. "Do not address me." She tightened her hold on her husband's arm and continued walking.

Before she left, Merin studied Rosa in impassive silence. "This may have begun as a dangerous scheme, but I think a true marriage has formed. You must know this will not end well. Pendaran will contact you soon, I am sure. If you choose not to cooperate, be prepared for his wrath."

"Such warnings should be issued by him," Luc said in a cutting voice. "Not by his messengers."

A bitter laugh fell from Merin's lips. "Pendaran does not give warnings."

Koko's Journal

— — —

January 14, 1931

She stood in the center of a snow-covered field, shrouded by a red cloak, a contradiction of both purpose and nature. Her features were veiled and yet adorned within the boldest of colors; I believe she wanted to be seen. When I first noticed the woman, I thought she was Elen. I even waved and called out her name, but once she turned I realized my grave error.

Regrettably, I stumbled back in surprise. In hindsight, I wish I had shown more composure, but how is one supposed to react when hatred is perceived within a familiar blue gaze? When Elen had never looked at me so?

It was a new experience for me, this hatred. I have faced ignorance, of course, from the people in the cities who only see my brown skin and know naught of my family's honors.

Sometimes they even watch me with fear in their eyes, and gather their children close as I pass, as if I plot to steal their babes in the middle of the night.

I knew the woman who held such vile sentiment toward a stranger must be Merin, the mother who would have killed my husband to see her older children live among the powerful ones.

Luc does not speak of her. The very mention of her name brings angry words from his lips, which saddens me, because anger is born of pain. I despise the woman, I now realize, for the heartache she caused my husband. Children should never know a mother's rejection. It steals their joy; it hardens an essential part of their heart.

I would have voiced my feelings aloud had she not departed like a cardinal on the wind in winter. I was left standing alone with only a fleeting glimpse of red over snow. I pray she never returns. I only wonder why she came at all.

~Koko

Koko's Journal

—

January 21, 1931

After a week of pondering over Merin's visit, I have a curious thought that demands purchase. I must write it down, even if it angers you, my dear husband. When you read this one day, please remember this: Such as anger is born of pain, so too is hatred. One cannot hate if they have not loved! I will not begin to presume what

Merin's motives were for coming here, to her children's home where she is not welcomed, I only sense that she must carry a great burden of sorrow in her heart, and I hope one day you will find forgiveness in yours.

~Koko

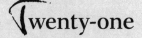wenty-one

THOUGH IT WAS NICE TO BE CARRIED, AND HELD WITHOUT fear, the jarring motion of Gareth's strides didn't help with the spinning of her head.

"I should leave this place," Elen told him, only to receive silence in return.

He was a stoic man, this porter named Gareth.

"It wants me to," she rambled, too dizzy to care that he may not welcome a discussion. "I can feel it. This island wants me to leave. You must wonder why I stay."

Another long pause.

Her arms were wrapped around his neck and it was not her fault that his power soared to be read. Honor among depravity was rare, and his scars ran deeper than the ones recently removed from a shift. She wouldn't share her findings, but felt better knowing her brother's porter possessed a pure heart, albeit a troubled one.

"I don't presume to wonder over anyone else's reasons but my own," Gareth eventually said.

But she sensed the lie. He watched all, and considered

all, because he prided himself on being the protector and porter of this home. It was his purpose. He was lonely, though, and his emptiness almost equaled hers.

"People don't fear me here," she offered, because he was carrying her and therefore forced to listen. "They talk to me and invite me for tea. At home, everyone fears me." She sighed. "I do miss my garden, though."

"We've known the leadership of Math. Nothing you do would compare."

"I doubt Cormack agrees."

"I'm not so sure." Gareth lowered her, holding out his arms for her to right her balance. "Which is why you're going to walk into the library on your own two feet."

"I think I can manage that." Elen concentrated on her footing, taking slow steps. She giggled again, not a dignified greeting to Cormack's scowl. Audrey knelt on the floor, unpacking new books from Rosa's shopping excursion.

"Avon has unbalanced her somehow." Gareth gave a brisk explanation to Cormack. "I don't think it's good for her to be around the Guardians in her current state. Can you stay with her?"

Cormack's gaze narrowed with concern, or at least Elen chose to believe it was concern rather than annoyance. After a sharp nod, he motioned for Gareth to leave.

"I got kicked out of my brother's wedding reception." She hiccupped, slapped her hand over her mouth.

"Me too." Audrey looked up, interested now. Her trimmed hair feathered around her pixie-like features as golden-green eyes commiserated. "Did you eat Walter's cake?"

"No, I didn't have any cake." Elen slouched into the nearest chair.

Audrey seemed pleased by that, padding over with a book in her hand. "Want to read to me?"

"I don't know if I—"

The child crawled into her lap and the room stopped spinning. Leaving her with Audrey, Cormack busied himself by a serving cart and returned with a pitcher of water and a glass.

He filled the glass and shoved it in her face. "Drink."

It was the first time she'd ever heard his voice. Dark and husky with just a word. She accepted the water with gratitude, needing to soothe a suddenly parched throat.

"It's this island," she told him. "Somehow Audrey balances the effects." She handed him back the empty glass. "I feel better now."

Wiggling into a comfortable crook, Audrey opened the book and pointed her finger. "Read this word to me."

Flushing under Cormack's inspection, Elen looked down—then frowned. "Oh, well . . ." She cleared her throat, hedging. "What is the name of this book?" She flipped it over and read the title, *Oxford Dictionary of Modern Slang.* She scrambled for an excuse not to read the word, suspecting this strong-minded child would use it often.

And the next time Walter denied Audrey of cake, she might be inclined to call him a *fuckwit* in return.

"This book is boring. Let's find another one," Elen said, picking Audrey up, because she was an innocent with power, and therefore an equalizer to this island—and Elen wasn't letting her go while in the same room with Cormack. "How about this one? *Where the Wild Things Are*," she read. "I think this one is very fitting for you, Audrey."

AFTER CHECKING ON ELEN, ROSA FOUND LUC STANDING on the balcony outside their bedchambers deep in thought. The last days of spring were almost at an end and warm evening breezes carried the scents of summer to her island. From where he stood, he could see beyond the river and across the vale to the mountains outlining a starred horizon. It was why Rosa had chosen this room as hers from the day she came to Avon.

The balcony connected to Math's former apartments, and

for the first time she smiled at that thought, because come morning Porter would begin ripping it apart to refurnish it into a media suite. Divine justice, in her opinion, for the lair of a dictator who'd denied all connection to the mortal world.

Leaning against the doorframe, she admired the view of her husband. "I doubt the Guardians will return this night."

But soon.

He only nodded in the meager light that spilled from the open doors. Shadows contoured the outline of his muscled form. He presented an intimidating silhouette, with his back bare and his hair loose about wide shoulders that tapered into a taut waist. His pants rode low on his hips and his feet were bare.

She hesitated before joining him, because she felt his internal conflict, and because he was a proud man who wasn't comfortable sharing his thoughts on emotional matters. Regardless, she went to him, wrapped her arms around his waist and rested her cheek on his back.

His stance relaxed on a sigh of comfort. He entangled his fingers within hers and they remained silent for a time. As the evening began to chill, he shared, "It was the first time she's ever spoken to me."

In almost two thousand years.

"And I put a sword to her throat," Rosa said without triumph, running her cheek over the hard planes of his back. If she could ease this hurt from him, she would, but that was not the reality of the world they lived in. "I checked on Elen."

"As did I, and almost everyone in this castle. Their acceptance is why she doesn't want to leave." He squeezed her hands briefly. "She needed their kindness tonight."

Rosa didn't invade further on the subject of Merin. Like with her first marriage, some matters shouldn't be needled. "Elen seems perfectly fine as long as Audrey is with her, which I find curious."

"Innocence with power is rare and my sister is sensitive to such things. Audrey balances the effects of the Walkers."

"Perhaps, but I'd like Elen to view them before she leaves. She may give us some insight on how to help them."

He didn't answer immediately. "I'll ask her. Porter predicts he'll be done by the end of the week and I've convinced Elen to go with him."

"Shouldn't they leave before Beltane?" Rosa asked with concern. "Tonight's visit was only an information excursion for the Council. They will return."

"I know," he said. "Don't fear for Elen." His voice held calm conviction. "Fear for the Council if they cross her, or threaten anyone she cares for. It's her choice to stay and I'm grateful."

"As am I." She placed a kiss on the grove of his spine, inhaled his dark scent. "So let's not talk any more of the Council tonight, and finish our wedding celebration properly."

He exhaled softly. Shifting his weight, he turned so her hands now rested on his chest. His gaze held hers with stark need.

She wouldn't define the emotion she felt from him—such things were too precious to mark with words—but she would answer his need with her own. Rising on her toes, she gently touched her lips to his. A soft groan vibrated up from his chest, as if her touch had called his deepest ache. He lifted his hands to anchor her against him, turned his head and caught her mouth for a devouring kiss. She felt the wild pounding of his heart as their embrace became a frantic tangle of tongues and limbs and desperate breaths rasping for air.

Gentle was not his mood this night.

Trailing his hands down her back, he lifted her—and she was forced to wrap her legs about his waist or be dragged as he pressed her against the outer wall. Stone bit into her back from the open scoop of her dress but she didn't care, reaching between them to fumble with the closure of his pants while he ran his palm under her skirt and gathered her new underwear in his fist. The weak seams provided poor resistance and the silk material tore with a mere twist of his wrist.

Locking one arm around his neck, she helped him ease his shaft into her opening. "Luc—"

His mouth swallowed her words as his flesh invaded her core. "Shhhh . . . No more talking tonight."

"Easy—" she hissed, and he did pause, waiting for her body to stretch to his size. This position was starkly invading, with no footing to use as leverage against the pressure of his size. All her weight surged down only to shove his shaft higher, pressing against organs that were not meant to be pressed unprepared.

But he smelled like untamed power, and his forehead rested on the wall behind her head while the corded muscles in his neck strained from his will to wait for her.

It was not long before her body softened and prepared to take him. Squirming, she gripped her arms around his neck and whispered, "Move."

And he rode her to pleasure, surging without restraint, and shaking with the raw urgency of his claiming. And when his release finally gripped him, he roared her name.

She could only hope that Pendaran did have ears in the wind.

TWO DAYS LATER, IN THE COUNCIL CHAMBERS AS SCHEDuled, Merin clenched her teeth as Pendaran trailed his hand up her arm, resting his fingers by the curve of her breast. Darkness was seductive and he had mastered the allure.

His musky autumn scent cloyed to the air like the rotting husk of a broken tree, a once-beautiful thing wasted by power-hungry greed.

He leaned down and whispered, "Explain to me, Merin, why you chose to allow Rosa to refuse my gift?"

She ignored Neira's delighted leer. "I gave her leniency due to Taliesin's involvement."

Maelor glowered at her from across the Council table.

Undeterred, Merin continued. "I am beginning to find Taliesin's contentious behavior tedious." It was not a complete lie, because his silence had now begun to threaten the safety of her children. Moreover, Pendaran would accept no other excuse but the one that involved his foster son. She added affront to her voice to make it more believable. "Also, Rosa suggested we speak with Taliesin on the new developments of the prophecy. Was I to tell her that he does not speak with us anymore?"

Predictably, when confronted with evidence of Taliesin's hatred, he lashed his anger elsewhere. "And how did your reunion go with your Beast?"

"As unpleasant as you would expect," she said dryly.

My heart is still weeping.

Pendaran chuckled, amused by the second revelation. "We are at a quandary, then, are we not?" His grip tightened momentarily before releasing. "And I understand your frustration." He walked around the table, pausing behind the back of each member as a reminder of his authority. "Taliesin's fascination with peasants is getting tiresome, and his association with our dissenters is unacceptable," he exclaimed like a weary father with a misbehaved child. "We can only continue as planned. If Taliesin has an opinion on the matter, then he had better come to me personally."

"What of the rumors?" Neira chimed in, not willing to let Merin escape censure that easily.

"Maelor," Pendaran prompted. "Your comrade has asked a question. Are you not going to answer her?"

"A hound from the Otherworld resides at Avon," Maelor supplied, his voice a dark grumble that matched his countenance. Snot hung from his bulbous snout as he tried to wipe at it but was ineffective.

Closing his eyes briefly, Pendaran stroked the crown of his staff as if tempted to rid himself of the man properly this time. "And your investigations into Rhuddin Village? What did you uncover?"

Merin pinned the troll with a glare. *Don't say a word. If you do, what I threatened on our journey home will come to fruition; this I promise you. Do you want your wife in the Norseman's company?*

"I saw no evidence of the Serpent," Maelor mumbled. "I watched from the forest, and listened to the villagers' gossip. Dylan's mate kept to the house, but their boy is a shifter. I witnessed it myself."

Rhys sat forward. "A shifter from a human mate?"

Merin gave Maelor a smile that made greater men empty their bladders. Did he not know she weaved convincing lies? "Briallen seemed taken by the Walkers. I even felt one of them respond to her presence. She may be a good overseer to their care at Avon."

Pendaran slashed his hand in impatience. "I want to hear more from Maelor. We will discuss the Walkers later."

Refusing to look at Merin, Maelor spewed her secrets like a bumbling coward, fearing Pendaran's sword more than her, or even the loss of his wife. "The people of Rhuddin Village are timid of Elen. Their gossiping confirms Math's reports. They say she ripped a wolf from one of us and gave it to a Bleidd. We watched Avon before sending the notice of our arrival. Cormack was there, not as a wolf but as a man, and fumbling with a sword like a boy . . . like he had never held one before. I knew his mother. He has the look of her. The hound from the Otherworld resides with them. There is power in this family."

Slowly, Pendaran turned his pale gaze on Merin and she knew in that moment her time was limited. She shrugged absently, having been prepared for this day since birthing Luc and begging her sister to give him to Dylan. "Why would you assume that anything that comes of me would be weak? Even my Beast holds more power than many of our Guardians."

His nostrils flared. "You have let them run free without our authority!"

"I did what I was bid to do," she claimed with inarguable truth. "I have acted on *your* orders. Even when you demanded I put Elen through the gauntlet to force her change. I tortured my daughter at *your* bidding."

"And she never called her wolf," Pendaran said absently, deep in thought. "But perhaps she called another power."

"The hound may be a sign," William supplied. He tried to act aloof but his desperation bled through. "I wonder if we are meant to have the ceremony at Avon."

Merin laughed bitterly then, unable to gather enough cleverness and lies to fight the idiocy of this Council. William did not give a whit about a hound or signs; it was an excuse to be closer to his lost ward. And Maelor was an oaf.

Bran was her only ally in this room and he could do naught but hold her gaze with shared misery.

Pendaran cocked his head, pondering over the idea. "I will think on this tonight. In light of this new information, it may be time to remind our dissenters of our power before they become unruly." He waved his hand absently. "You are all dismissed. I will contact you in the morning." He halted by Neira's chair and ran his hand around her neck. She visibly shivered with both pleasure and pain. After the death of her mate, Neira's only release came through other methods. A sinister smirk turned his lips. "Except for you, my pet. I have found this evening most unsettling and I am in the mood for your distractions."

Wary, Merin stood to leave; she expected a sword in her back—or through her neck—but only received a final decree.

"Merin," Pendaran called after her. "I trust you will continue to be loyal to the Council's rulings."

She refused to look back, almost preferring his sword, because the game continued and she hardly had the will to make another move. "You insult me by suggesting I would not."

"I am glad to hear your vehemence . . ." His voice trailed

off with purpose, a warning not to object or he would have a head more precious than hers. "Because I believe it is time that I met your daughter."

LYING IN BED, LUC LISTENED TO THE SOFT BREATHING of his wife. He wanted to awaken her in pleasant ways. Except on this morning a wolf nestled between them, curled and content, hindering him from their usual morning activities. He eased out of the blankets and was on his way to the bathroom when he noticed flowers sprinkled around Audrey's paws.

He stroked his hand across her muzzle. "The day has arrived and it's time to change."

Rosa stretched at his voice, scooting against the headboard into a sitting position. She smiled when she noticed their visitor. "When did she sneak in?"

"Around four."

Tilting her head, Rosa picked up a blossom and began examining it in her hands. "Where did these come from?"

"I'm not sure."

Audrey arched her back, peeked open an eye. A cloying scent filled the air, a brief warning before she changed forms right on the bed.

Luc barely had time to blink. "Is it always this easy for you to shift, Audrey?"

Her face brightened. "Change is easy here."

Luc looked to Rosa.

"We all shift off the island," she answered his silent question. "It takes too long to call enough life to change. A child may require less." Rosa held up a blossom. "Do you know where these came from, Audrey?"

"I told you this already," the child sighed with impatience. "I see pretty pictures when I sleep. Elen says the word for them is dreams. The lady in my dreams said you would be sad today. She gives me flowers for you. For hope."

She jumped from the bed and scampered to the door. "I go wake up Elen. I want to wear my princess dress again today."

As their Wulfling dashed out the door, Rosa swung her legs over the bed, stood to pull the coverlet up and then sucked in her breath.

Luc followed her gaze to a red stain and his chest tightened. "Rosa—"

She dashed to the bathroom as he helplessly waited for her to come out. And when he saw her face, he knew—it was a look he'd seen Koko wearing many times.

"I've not had my woman's flow in over three hundred years," she whispered. "Because I've never gone this long without taking the potion. I had hoped . . ."

"I'm sorry." Such a stupid sentiment for when there was nothing better to say and yet he said it anyway. He wrapped her in his arms and kissed the top of her head. "We have a lifetime, Rosa."

"But do we?" After a shuddering breath, she withdrew from his arms and went to the hidden alcove. Filled vials of Mae's potion sat untouched beside the condoms. She retrieved the items she sought and closed the panel.

"Summer is only a few days away." She met his hardened glare with one of her own. "I'll do this now when I know there's no babe."

Luc clenched his hands as anger roiled in his gut.

"I would like you to leave," she said. "I don't want you here if all you have to offer me are doubts."

"Wait another day," he implored.

"No." She entered the bathroom and quietly closed the door.

Unable to sit and wait while she harmed herself, he stormed out of the room. Knowing his wife was in pain and unable to come up with a good enough argument to stop her.

Mae hovered at the bottom of the stairs.

Their problem solver, as she liked to call herself, had an uncanny way of lurking in the midst of trouble. Her gaze narrowed as he brushed by. "What has happened?"

"I ran with her," he spat, unleashing his frustration on the woman who provided his wife with this noxious solution. "Why did you remake her that potion?"

"Ah," she whispered as her scarred face fell with understanding. "I see. This is sad news. I had hoped the run would break this tangled line I see over your heart. There is a strong spirit that does not want to share you even in death."

"Don't," he warned. Koko did not deserve this blame.

"Do not look at me so," Mae scolded. "You know it is true."

He growled at the insult. "I know no such thing. I've—"

"You have held on to your old love—that is what you have done. And now you have hurt the new." Mae's gnarled finger pulled back the neck of his shirt, slapping her hand against the ink outlines of his tattoo. "It is this thread that hinders your mating knot."

"Your riddles annoy me," Luc thundered, unable to face the accuracy of her accusations, and the consequences Rosa suffered because of him.

"I will forgive your insolence, warrior, because I know you love our Rosa. You would not be so upset by her pain did you not."

He remained silent because her claim felt accurate.

"We are human, with human needs and emotions," she pressed. "But we cannot deny our wolves. Our beasts are too possessive to share. Only two hearts can form one true match, and you are carrying a third. A child of our kind is only conceived with an unhindered pairing." She gave a disgusted wave of her hand. "The Council has forgotten our ways. They twist prophecies to suit their ambitions."

"I've seen mated couples who loathe each other," Luc pointed out, not sure whether he believed her theory.

"Ah, but that is not how they began. I am an old soul, and I have seen much. Love and hatred are born of the same passionate seed."

"You should share your notions with Rosa."

"You think I have not?" She huffed with impatience. "She

is as obstinate as her mother, that one, and she is young. Stubborn minds do not listen well. They need to experience everything for themselves."

His frustration turned to dread. "I don't know how to help her," he confessed.

Mae gave his cheek a gentle pat with her bent hand. "This spirit that tangles you . . ." She paused with empathy that softened her reproach. "Remember her, honor her, but you must let her go if you want to keep our Rosa."

Heart-burdened, Luc returned to their room. Rosa sat on the bed, leaning forward with her face in her hands. She looked up and he knew without words.

The potion had been taken.

Snagging the end of the coverlet, he wrapped her in a bundled cocoon and carried her out to the balcony, sitting down with her in his arms. He didn't know what she needed from him, but leaving her alone was too painful to bear.

So he held her.

After a while, she whispered, "It's time to make a decision. The Council is coming for me. We either leave Avon or call our allies for help." She added with determination, "I want to stay and defend our home as we originally planned."

"As do I. And I've already made the calls. We'll make a stance against the Guardians now, or they will follow us wherever we go."

"They will follow me, you mean."

"Yes." With acceptance came outrage, and he knew that Mae was right. The thought of losing this woman in his arms was too agonizing to contemplate. He loved her.

Burying his face in her tangled tresses, he inhaled a scent that had become more precious to him than life. She had awakened him from a half-lived existence and he wouldn't fail her now. "We will keep what's ours safe," he vowed.

And I will keep who is mine.

Koko's Journal

—

July 2, 1945

Yesterday I journeyed up our great mountain and knelt under the cherished tree of my husband's people. The night bathed me in moonlight and sorrow. His oak wept leaves that carried unanswered wishes, and still I prayed one last desperate prayer. I dared both his Gods and mine to listen, for this prayer was my first unselfish one.

I did not pray for a child, my body is too old and broken for that now, nor did I pray for immortality, for a love too pure to end in one lifetime. I prayed for Luc, for I fear my spirit, even as my body passes, will remain with him.

I prayed for the strength to let him go.

~Koko

Twenty-two

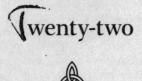

TROUBLE ALWAYS CAME TO AVON IN THE MIDST OF CIR-
cles and rain, Rosa reflected with some acrimony. On the
eve of summer the Guardians arrived. The sky released
angry tears like her mood as she paced on the parapets of
her castle. Soaked through from rain, her jeans clung to her
skin and her sword swung with her strides.

By midday, the Guardians began to circle the river,
ordered by the Council, she assumed, to prove their loyalty.
They waited on the outskirts of her island, across the moving waters. A wall of shifters in their human forms, impassive faces touting a variety of weapons, swords and axes
with shields, or simply garrotes and anything that served to
separate a head from its body.

Guns were of no use to their kind and fire would evacu-
ate the island but it might harm the Walkers. If they kindled
an aggressive flame, her dead island would burn—so they
waited.

To act openly without the cover of darkness or trees was
the most frightening declaration. The Council intended to

see this prophecy through with their interpretation at all costs.

Pendaran stood by the gatehouse on the opposite side of her bridge, with seven men forming a procession of warriors who had come to feast on her, four of whom she recognized as Council members even from a distance.

She bloody well didn't care who the final three were because none of them would be inside of her.

Unfortunately, her vow weakened as more Guardians arrived and the rain cleared to reveal summer's first moon. Was she selfish to put so many lives in danger for her cause? Fisting her hands by her sides, she chased her weak thoughts away. This stance was about freedom, and the right to live without cruelty.

Even so, tension filled the air, heavy with the pungent odor of adrenaline and power and the musk of rising wolves. Her battle-worn warriors were ready to fight. As a precaution, Luc had requested more guards from their allies. They circled the castle and the lifeless woods. Even her people had stayed, willing to risk death rather than lose their first taste of freedom, or run and leave her to fight this final battle alone.

She loved them for it, even as she feared the consequences.

Luc, Porter and eight guards walked the wall beside her, while the rest filled the yard and held their assignments at the base of the bridge. There was no sign of Gareth or Teyrnon, or the four guards positioned at the gatehouse and the shallow end of the river.

"Rigged that damn bridge with explosives, I should have," Porter muttered. "But I figured fire and torn limbs would only be pissing them off." His gaze was feral and ready for conflict. "It would've done my soul some good to watch that bastard fly."

"He's waiting for me to come to him," Rosa said with rancor.

"We only need to hold the Guardians for another hour," Luc clipped. "Dylan and Llara's army are on their way."

Pendaran laughed as if he'd heard, the resonance amplified on the wind. His cloak billowed about his parted stance, catching on his staff as he lifted it to the sky. A blue light glowed from the crown of the twisted vines.

"What is he doing?" The question had come from Griffith, one of the guards from Isabeau's territory.

"I don't know—" But even as she spoke Rosa buckled against the wall. A sharp pain gripped her abdomen and a yearning called her to go to him, incessant and undeniable. "I . . ." She gritted her teeth. "I think he's pulling me somehow."

"What?" Luc hovered, his voice thick with anger and sudden apprehension. He wrapped his arms around her, firm and strong, anchoring her.

She bit back a moan and clawed at the rock wall, blinded by the pain of resisting a summons.

"Dark magic," Porter spat. "Pilfered pieces of his soul to the evil one, he has. Casting a spell. No good will come of this."

"Call the forest, Rosa," Luc ordered. "Now!"

"I cannot," she hissed, squeezing her eyes against the assault. "Not on this side of the river. My forest is dead. There's nothing to call."

"Fight this," he demanded. "Do *not* allow this asshole to take you from me. Do you understand?"

She coughed. A choking laugh fell through her tension. "I'm trying not to."

A disruption below drew Luc out of her arms, and without his support she took a step toward Pendaran. With her submission, the pain eased enough to view the cause of the distraction. Cadan and Tesni tussled on the ground with a tiny brown wolf.

"They are trying to hold Audrey back," Rosa ground out

through clenched teeth. And they were taking a brutal beating while struggling not to hurt the child.

"Marked the Wulfling, the bastard's done." Disgust filled Porter's voice.

"Shit," Luc muttered when Elen walked into the outer bailey as if in a trance. "Pendaran is summoning all powerful females." A possibility he hadn't prepared for, and his anger spread to the guards.

Another guard swore behind them. "Like a perverted piper, he lures children and women from their homes."

Shouting incoherent sounds, Cormack lunged from the castle and dove on top of Elen. A wild cry filled the air, muddled between human and wolf as he buckled into a shift so violent he collapsed into a ball, stunned. Elen wiped at her face as if blinded by tears but kept walking.

"No," Rosa corrected. "He's beckoning all *unmated* females with power. He wants me, but is getting more than he assumed were here."

A tic pulsed against the muscle of Luc's jaw as he clenched his teeth but he didn't refute her theory.

Another screech echoed through the yard as Audrey broke free of Cadan's hold, tumbled several paces out of reach, limped from her fall and then took off toward the bridge.

Tesni stumbled after Audrey, bloodied down her arms and holding her neck. She looked up and found Rosa, her gaze desperate and beseeching as she screamed for help. "We cannot stop her without hurting her!"

Cormack struggled to his feet in wolf form but with the same dilemma as he tugged at Elen's skirt, locking his haunches until the material tore. More guards dove to help Cormack only to meet a shift just as brutal. Canine cries echoed throughout the bailey and carried to the wall. Cormack suffered another ruthless shift, twitching naked on the ground as currents racked his body.

"I'm going down." Rosa turned from the parapets. "She'll

take out our entire guard this way and I cannot let Pendaran have Audrey or your sister."

"You stay here!" Luc shouted. "I'll go down. Pendaran will only pull you with them."

"No," she cried. "They'll be taken in my place. I could never live with myself if I don't act to help them. *Never.* And the pull doesn't seem to be affecting me as badly as them. I can resist him," she promised. "I *will* resist him."

His lips pressed in a thin line, reading her conviction. "You'd better," he commanded, displeased but not arguing with her resolve. "You get Audrey. I'll try to stop Elen. She may listen to me."

Accepting the logic of his order, she ran down the circular stone stairs, through her bailey and across the yard to where Audrey fought Cadan's hold. Rosa fell to her knees and grabbed the pup by the scruff of the neck, issuing a low rumble of displeasure, hoping the Wulfling would comprehend her alpha's command over Pendaran's.

Audrey stilled and dropped the hunk of Cadan's side from her jaw. Rosa gathered the pup in her arms and turned toward the forest. The bridge could be seen through the trail at this distance. Another wave of the dark summons almost pulled her, but as she'd begun to suspect, it didn't affect her as much as Elen and Audrey.

Rosa wasn't mated, she knew she wasn't, but perhaps what had begun between her and Luc lessened Pendaran's influence.

A mere fledgling to such power, Audrey began to wiggle violently and then lunged, forcing Rosa to ease her hold or break the Wulfling's legs. With the extra leverage, Audrey clawed Rosa's neck and chest and twisted to the ground.

The tumble and chase brought them to the river's edge. Frantic, Rosa dove and rolled with the Wulfling before she crossed the bridge, grasping the pup's forearms in a death grip as she stood.

If necessary, she would break her legs with her hold rather than let her cross that bridge.

Elen remained on Avon's side, her face wet with tears as she fought not to step off the island. Luc hovered over her, cradling her in a tight hold, talking low near his sister's ear. Ordered not to touch, the guards formed a protective circle around the pair.

Luc's gaze found Rosa's and held with stark warning. "The compulsion is affecting Elen most. I don't know how much longer I can contain her."

Rosa lifted her chin to Pendaran's satisfied smirk. He had a look of a well-fed cat who had caught three mice in one trap.

Pendaran raised his voice in greeting. "Rosa." William and Rhys stood by his side with triumphant expressions, feeding off her struggle like parasites. "So glad you could finally join us. Who is that lovely creature you have in your arms? Even from here I can feel her power."

Rosa tightened her grip on Audrey's legs as they began to twitch at his voice. Since the secret of her nature was out, William should face the weight of his actions.

Her lips turned in a slow smile. Tilting her head, feigning curiosity, she yelled over the rushing waters, "Did William not tell you of the Wulfling? First Taliesin and now William. Does anyone communicate with you, Pendaran?" The head of the Council stilled and her smile widened. "William was hiding her for at least three months. How could you not know of this? Her name is Audrey. She's mine now, by the way."

"This is your *Hen Was*?" Pendaran turned to William, his face florid with rage, and for a moment the spell he cast eased. Audrey relaxed in her arms and released a whimper, trying to crawl up into Rosa's neck and hide.

The roar of her river swallowed their voices and Rosa started easing backward. Heads turned on the opposite side as the conversation was retold and spread down the lines. There was dissension in this mix of Guardians who had been called. Some leered with the hunger for blood in their eyes—but some watched with disgust.

"I was training her for the Council." William sputtered excuses loud enough to carry.

"Save your lies!" Pendaran's nostrils flared. "I can taste your fear. You intended to hoard this child until she came of age." Heat burst through the air and sizzled when it hit the river. "You are a traitor to the Council and belong with the other traitors."

Eyes mad with panic, William took a step back. He darted desperate glances as Guardians flanked him, halting a retreat.

"Hang him with the others until I decide his fate," Pendaran ordered. "I do not tolerate lies," he spat. "Especially from those I keep company with."

Rosa's eyes followed the macabre procession of William being carried to the outer woods. He didn't fight, accepting a lesser punishment rather than an immediate execution.

But as their final destination came into focus and her mind registered what she saw—a gasp tore from her throat and her lungs refused to draw air.

Luc's gaze must have tracked the same route. A low growl erupted from his chest in an ominous tenure. "Is that Gareth?"

"And Teyrnon," Rosa choked out. And the other missing Avon guards.

"He will die for this," Luc vowed, his voice thick from his beast, echoed by the guards in their midst.

Hung by their necks, Avon's loyal guards dangled from trees, red as skinned game and coated in their own blood. Even to this day a noose was the Guardians' most efficient disabler, and the ones made for their kind were constructed with wire and razor edges. If the quarry shifted, it tightened. If they struggled, it tightened. And increased weight sent the sharpened wire edges through their necks like a garrote.

They must remain completely still if they wished to keep their heads.

A hush weaved throughout the crowd, but death only bolstered death, and Rosa clung to Audrey with dismay as the musk of anticipation mounted. A protective impulse raged within her, a blinding fury for this child and for her people. But the child was an innocent and must be brought to safety first before she could help the others.

Acting on instinct, Rosa assessed her possibilities. Avon's guards and allies had emerged from the forest. Luc had Elen locked in his embrace. He shook his head, letting her know his sister was unmovable.

Audrey. She mouthed her intent, then turned toward the trail and ran. Cadan was there at the end making his way to her, more bloodied than Tesni and missing an ear. His red hair was caked and matted to his head.

"Take her while Pendaran is distracted," she ordered, handing off the Wulfling. "Lock her in a bathroom if you must, but don't let her out until this is over." She didn't tell her cousin about Gareth and Teyrnon, because there was nothing he could do and she needed him focused for this task.

Nodding, Cadan clutched the child and finished the retreat. Rosa waited until he disappeared into the outer bailey.

Calm clarity washed over her once the child was safe. She stood on the trail of her broken forest and lifted her arms, calling its power. Trees that barely budded each year wept their only leaves.

It tried . . . Oh, how it tried to give its very last breath but offered no more than a meager cough while limbs broke like skeletons in a storm.

Desperate, Rosa reached out to another source on her island, one she had never dared breach. Trusting Elen's knowledge that Avon was overfed, there was only one place that might be the root. She sent tendrils of inquiry toward the tombs of the Walkers, probing with open invitation.

They answered with a force that buckled Rosa to her knees—jubilant, as if they had been waiting three centuries for this day. Never had she felt such a response from them.

They flooded her with pent-up frustrations, with laughter and hope, death and tears, ready to be used in any capacity other than nothingness.

Life filled her very essence, dark and light. She channeled it, savored it—allowed it to bleed from her skin. Dirt and rock scraped her palms as she crawled to a standing position. With careful strides, she returned to stand in the circle of guards who surrounded Luc and Elen.

"What have you done?" Luc's narrowed gaze flared blue.

"Walkers," was all she could manage because they began to overwhelm her. She wasn't Elen; she couldn't give away the power she received. Her wolf paced and the shift was almost on her.

With that dangerous thought, the culmination of an intuition that had formed when she called the Walkers, she regarded Elen in hopes of finalizing her idea.

"No," Luc said, reading her intent.

"Let her decide." Rosa held out her hand to his sister.

Elen's gaze fell to the offering, rimmed red and heavy-lidded with anguish. "Are you sure?" she croaked out on broken breaths. "I might hurt you."

"I'm sure. Show the Guardians that it's us they need to fear. Show them that our family cannot be intimidated. Let us try to prevent this war. Can you do that?"

Concentration tightened Elen's face, not so gentle in that moment. "Oh, yes . . . I can do that." Without hesitation, she snagged Rosa's hand and Luc was repelled when the connection formed.

And time stilled.

Or perhaps becoming a conduit to otherworldly control cooked Rosa's brain. She ground her teeth as currents traveled through her body. Elen fed, and fed, and the island began to breathe life. Sepia tones and starved dust became emerald greens and lush earth.

Rosa felt the Walkers sigh with relief as the pressure evened out, like a boiler releasing steam. Vines burst from the ground. Moss formed like a carpet around Elen and rolled out to the river's edge. Guards hedged away from the engulfing stream.

But Rosa accepted it. And in doing so, the earth at her feet wasn't the only thing that healed. She felt the familiar tugging on her female organs, similar to the time in Elen's cottage, only more forceful. Her abdomen cramped, twisted, and then eased. She also felt another urge and knew in that moment she was fertile.

Under summer's first moon.

Guardians began to recede, wary of the unknown, and a realization that the rumors they had heard were true. They feared losing their power more than combat or death.

Pendaran watched with curiosity—*not* concern.

One Guardian, bloodthirsty and too primed to retreat, sent out a battle cry and charged the river. Others followed, as was the frenzy that fed all wars. Even her guards responded. Some fell into the rushing waters; some waited with weapons raised. The clash of swords filled her ears, and the scent of iron cloyed her throat, becoming thicker as Guardians made the cross to this side.

In dismay, Rosa pointed to Pendaran. "You," she shouted over the hysteria and dismemberment, daring him as much as beseeching him. "This is your doing. Stop it if you have the bullocks."

His eyebrow rose at the challenge, and his lips quirked as if charmed, but he didn't raise a single sound of protest.

Instead, Pendaran stepped onto the bridge. And Luc waited for him on the opposite side with a handful of warriors, sword unsheathed, lips peeled, and chin lowered.

Pendaran stared hard at the barricade with irritation. "It is time for you to die, *Beast*."

It was then that a figure in a red cloak broke away from the Guardians. She made her way toward Pendaran on the bridge. Her hood caught in the wind and fell back as golden hair twisted in wild disarray from the river's tumult.

Pendaran frowned at Merin's approach. "I did not call you."

"There was a time I admired you, Pendaran." Sadness carried with Merin's voice. "You once knew honor but now you are seduced by darkness. You rape all that is good about our kind." A slight pivot into a dancer's stance was her only warning before twisting in an arc. Her red cloak flared like a cardinal in flight descending for the kill. "This is a wretched day but perhaps a new beginning."

His eyes widened as her sword descended. Snaking backward at inhuman speed, he barely avoided the blow. And Merin's arm circled wide as she missed her mark with a snarl.

Pendaran shook with rage. "How many traitors will fall from my Council today?" Swinging his staff in an arc, he unsheathed his weapon; they circled each other like two birds of prey in a waltz of death.

Luc lunged toward the bridge to help his mother. Blood flowed from a long gash down his sword arm and coated his fist. More Guardians reached the shore through the turbulent waters, and with brutal control he fended them off.

But a fourth Guardian emerged and Rosa knew this one all too well. Features rabid with vengeance, Briog dragged a sword from the river's edge, rose with a savage scream and charged Luc's back.

Riding the Walkers' power, Rosa pried her hand out of Elen's grasp, unsheathed her sword and countered Briog's attack with a rush of heightened strength. The Guardian rode his own adrenaline and swung with crazed frenzy. She fell back but not in time to miss a thrust to her side. Luc pivoted when he heard her cry out, shouted for her to duck, and removed Briog's head in a swift circular strike.

As Avon's guards fought off more Guardians, she leapt onto the bridge alongside her husband.

Merin spared them a piercing glare. "Get back! You will not die this day. Not after all I have done to keep you alive."

Her focus remained on Pendaran as she revealed that secret. "What? Does that surprise you?" She countered again, spun, ducked his swing and charged. "You should have known that anything I want dead"—she aimed for his sword arm instead of his neck—"will die."

Arm severed, Pendaran's sword fell to the floorboards still entangled with his dismembered fist. Head lowered, his gaze turned dragon green, as merciless as the forgotten winged beasts. "Just as you should have known that *Cadarn* is not my only weapon."

He began to chant and the river churned.

Twenty-three

BLIND OF HIS SECOND SIGHT, TALIESIN SAT CRUMPLED outside Aeron's tomb with his face against his knees and gravel riding his bare ass. As soon as Luc had made the call, he had come on the wind. He had begged to speak to his mother—*begged*! Only to be denied access and exiled from the Vale with screaming threats and dire warnings not to interfere.

To do nothing. That was the extent of his purpose—*absolutely nothing.* While those who had shown him kindness fought and bled because of his existence.

And now he sat like a cobbled coward, while the stench of blood coated his throat.

But if he interfered, if he helped—would he trigger an even worse fate?

A soft whine alerted him of a visitor, and a wet nose poked his arm. He looked up and met Tucker's sorrowful gaze.

"How many rivers must run red for my worthless soul?" he asked the hound, who bared his teeth at the question.

"How can I listen to them suffer and do nothing? It should be me instead of them."

A kind of peace washed over him the moment the words fell from his mouth. Tucker growled, sensing his intentions as he stood. The hound grabbed his wrist with his jaw but released when Taliesin accepted the assault without contest. He did not need an arm for what he planned to do.

Sitting back on his haunches, the hound issued a canine wail that echoed through the island and maybe even into the Glowing Vale. As the haunting sound continued, storm clouds rolled in to cover the moon.

Taliesin didn't shift. He could have marched to meet the battle as a golden stag, or flown in the form of a raven or eagle. But he chose to walk as a man, naked and unarmed, bared to his soul. He no longer wished to continue in this existence if it meant the death of everything and everyone he loved.

The roar of battle filled the night, and then softened as warriors started shouting his name. He walked by Elen, who forced three Guardians to shift with just a touch, and change again to human form when they attacked with claws and teeth, too stunned to move after the second shift. Stepping onto the bridge, he passed Luc and Rosa holding off three guards. Spray from the river coated his bare skin, tainted by Pendaran's incantation.

Swords lowered and Guardians watched as he crossed to the center of the bridge.

And Merin started shaking her head.

Taliesin smiled at her, a final token of friendship, and for all she sacrificed to keep her children from the men and women unable to handle the blood of the Fae in their veins. "Whatever happens, Merin, it's been my pleasure to know you."

Blue eyes so like Elen's implored him to leave. She knew him, more than the others. *She knew.* "Sin—"

"I'm done," Taliesin said.

Pendaran turned, disorientated and riding the influence of his malevolent curse. "Taliesin . . . ?"

"No more, Pendaran." Taliesin bent down and retrieved *Cadarn*, kicking the dismembered hand to the river. Pendaran accepted his weapon with his left hand, not his sword hand, but Taliesin trusted he would make do.

His former tutor sent a questioning frown as Taliesin opened his arms and lifted his face to the sky. "If you need to take life . . . then take mine."

Nature arose in his vicious defense, trying to wash him away from danger. Lightning burst from the sky in angry shards. Waves churned off the river and pounded the bridge in swells.

Legs wide, neck exposed, Taliesin waited. And when no deathblow came, he opened his eyes.

Pendaran stared, dumbfounded with indecision, and horrified as any parent, teacher or guardian when faced with a child's willingness to end their life.

There was a time when their kind had fought in battles, fearless of death and confident they would be reborn again to live another life. That confidence had receded when their power had grown. Now not one of their kind welcomed death, since this life offered them partial immortality.

Taking advantage of his distraction, Merin raised her sword.

"No!" Taliesin shouted at her. "No more death. Not even his."

She beseeched him with pleading eyes. "How can you ask this of me now?"

"I'm asking." Taliesin watched her struggle to ease her stance, her chest rising and falling in frustration, but she lowered her weapon.

"Leave!" Taliesin shouted to Pendaran. "If there was ever a part of you who cared for me as a child, just leave."

Baffled, Pendaran remained frozen. "But your prophecy . . ."

"Words." Taliesin laughed with bitterness when he thought about that stupid poem. "Just the words of a drunken asshole. I can't even remember reciting the bloody thing."

A commotion of more warriors rounded the entrance. Dylan and Llara stood at the forefront with fifty-plus more men and women called to fight against the Guardians.

Sullen, Pendaran gave a dignified nod. "I will leave today as you request, Taliesin, but I expect contact from you by next week." One-handed, he sheathed *Cadarn* into the vines of his staff. "If you choose not to apprise me of your wishes, how am I to know what they are?" He waved his weapon toward the river and looked to the sky. "And now I have this media cleanup to deal with," he chastised as if the battle had been their fault and not his. With his scolding delivered, Pendaran walked past Merin with a sneer and made a motion for all to follow.

As the Guardians retreated, Luc scanned the river's edge and along the trees. In a glance, he counted eight deaths and several maimed, three of whom where Avon's guards. Too many, but it could have easily been more if not for Elen and Taliesin's interference.

The injured began to shift, able to now that his sister had healed Avon. Dylan and Llara cut down Gareth, Teyrnon and the other guards. A passing Guardian did the same for William.

Sitting on the ground, and unable to speak, the Norseman offered the retreating Guardians his middle finger. He shifted as soon as Llara peeled away the wire noose.

Eyes dark and sunken, Elen made her way onto the bridge and settled next to Luc, refusing to look at their mother.

"You okay?" He gathered her close for a quick embrace.

"Aren't I always," she whispered with irony.

His free hand found Rosa and clutched her to him with a desperation he hadn't felt since Koko's passing.

He'd almost lost her. Had he not turned in time, Briog would have had her head.

Fisting her hair, he captured her mouth. "Next time," he growled against her lips, "I want you to stay in the bloody castle."

"Let us pray there isn't a next time," she said without agreeing to his order, but returned his embrace with equal passion.

A flash of red alerted Luc to Merin's approach. Lifting his head, he gathered Rosa close to his side and nodded to his mother. His throat thickened as she reached out her hand as if to touch him and then pulled it back.

Fighting for composure, Merin cleared her throat. "I loved your father more than my own life," she professed. "And every child that came from our union I considered a blessing. *Every* child. It hurts me to look at you, Luc, because you remind me of him. Aemilius would have been proud of you this day." Her chest rose and fell on a broken breath as she looked to his sister. "And he would have been proud of his Elen. As am I."

And with that, she turned to leave.

"Where are you going?" Luc whispered over the gravel in his throat.

"Home," Merin said. "I, too, have people to protect and accounts to settle. Pendaran will want my head now that he knows. This is not over," she warned. "He is too blinded by his power. He *will* retaliate. And next time he will come in shadows and on the wings of dragons."

Before Merin left, she paused in front of Taliesin. With a disparaging growl, she slapped him hard across the face. "Don't *ever* scare me like you just did!"

His cheek bore the mark of her hand as he leaned down and kissed her forehead. "My home in Newport is yours."

"You should have let me kill Pendaran," she clipped.

"And then you would be no better than him." His tone lowered, but not enough that Luc didn't hear. "Stay for a while with your children."

"I cannot." Merin's voice trembled. "Look at their faces.

They need time, and even then it may never be enough to right what I have done."

He reached out and caught a tear. "Think about my offer."

"Mail me the keys," she said. "I expect Pendaran's interest will turn to Elen now that he has witnessed her gift. Protect her," she ordered in a mother's desperate tone. "Because if she is harmed by Pendaran—it will be *your* fault for not letting me kill him." She nodded to each of her children and walked away.

Dylan, having made his way onto the bridge, blocked her path. "Mother," he greeted softly. "I still remember the day Father gave you that cloak."

Her stance weaved slightly, as if she'd expected cruelty instead of kindness and was suddenly off balance, but spite was not Dylan's way. Merin lifted her arm to reveal a threadbare patch sewn into the inner lining. "This is all that remains of the original, but it brings me comfort."

Struggling for an adequate response, Dylan simply said, "All this time, and you never let us know."

"I wanted you to live." Her voice carried only conviction and sadness. She garnered the courage to place her hand tentatively on her firstborn's arm. "When you are ready, contact me. Taliesin knows the way. There is much I need to share." After Dylan gave a sharp nod, she jumped to the ground in a fluid leap and disappeared around the carriage house.

Luc understood why his brother allowed their mother to leave—because Merin was right. The things she had done needed time, for Elen especially. Giving his wife a kiss as he unwound his arm from her waist, Luc shrugged off his jacket and handed it to Taliesin as he strode by. "To cover your ass, unless you like dangling in the wind."

He accepted the offering with a smirk. "Be careful, warrior; I might think you care."

Luc gave Taliesin a nod of respect. "I'll remember what you did for us this day." Then he closed the space between him and Dylan, welcoming his brother with a rough embrace that needed no words.

AS THE AREA CLEARED OF GUARDIANS, ROSA LEFT HER husband alone with his siblings. She made her way toward the edge of the trees where Gareth and the others remained. Relief at seeing them alive tightened her chest. Most had shifted, but her porter remained on the ground as a man, his eyes dark with self-censure. A bloodied metallic noose glinted in the dirt by his side. As she approached, he lowered his head.

She knelt down next to him, taking his hands into her lap. "You need to shift."

"The Guardians jumped me before I had a chance to sound a warning." He coughed and fluid rattled in his lungs. "I failed you."

"No," she said softly. "Why would you think such a thing? You were outnumbered and yet you still fought, for me, for us and for Avon." Shaking her head, she repeated, "No, Gareth, you have *never* failed me. It is your loyalty that gave me the opportunity to begin this journey, and now we are free."

"Free?" he questioned, cynical as always. "For now, perhaps."

"Yes." She sighed, knowing he spoke the truth. "For now. But until the next battle begins we will live as we choose." She stood then, assuming the role that came naturally to her. "Go for a run," she demanded, sensing he required acceptance more than sympathy. "I need my porter strong."

The slightest of smiles tugged at his lips before he winced. "You've learned to issue orders well." And he didn't sound displeased.

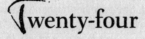wenty-four

*For barren not, under summer's first moon, comes the
prophecy they most seek.*

BEFORE DAWN GREETED THE DAY, AFTER WOLVES RAN AND
the fallen were honored, after warriors rested and a Wulfling
was calmed and put to bed, Rosa and Luc walked their
rebirthed island alone.

Wildflowers lined the trails: daisies, yellow irises and
blue forget-me-nots. New leaves rustled in a forest kissed
by hope and promise. Rosa entwined her fingers through
her husband's and led him to a private glen where meandering streams formed a pool.

On the edge of the forest, skirted by moss, grew a new-
born tree with lush green leaves, glimmering in the shadows
of night. A tiny bird clutched a tender branch and sang a
lovely song before flitting away.

"Luc, did you see that?" she asked, breathless. *Life has
returned to Avon.* She brought his hand to her lips and
placed a kiss inside his palm. A prelude to a gift she planned
to offer him before the sun chased away the moon. "You
have given me more than I dared hope for."

"And you've given me something I never thought possible." He folded his fingers as if to capture her gesture. "You've taught me that I can love again."

Her heart raced and her chest filled with wonder. Smiling, because her happiness demanded a response, she kicked off her sneakers and peeled away her jeans, slowly stripping while he watched. She gave her husband the vows she should have given him when this marriage began. "On this night I offer you my heart, my home, and all that I hold dear, because I cannot imagine having them without you."

Like the stars in the sky, his gaze shimmered iridescent silver with promises for eternity. "And all I want is you, my wolven queen."

Wading into the cool waters, she washed off the filth of the day and waited for him to join her. Her side was still tender from Briog's one good strike but not enough to hinder her plans. He caught her under the water's surface, dragging her to him for an unbridled embrace of love almost lost. His mouth captured hers, trailing kisses down her neck until his forehead rested against her shoulder. They held on to each other for a long while, with feet curled in the graveled bottom waters, absorbing the magnitude of the moment.

After a time, a heavy sigh fell from his lungs and a shudder racked his body.

He wept, she realized then. As the scent of elements rose, of healed earth bursting with life's most precious gift, her husband wept. For an instant she thought moonlight and shadows teased her eyes, because his tears were black as ink trailing down his chest.

And then she realized it was her husband's greatest proclamation this night.

As he bled Koko's tattoo from his skin, she whispered, "Fulfill a prophecy with me, Luc. Love me under summer's first moon."

* * *

RAW FROM TWO BRUTAL SHIFTS, AND THEN A THIRD, COR-
mack went to Elen's room as a wolf. He refused to deny her
a friend this night. Because of Merin's appearance, he knew
she hurt. The doors were locked but he'd convinced Mae to
let him in. As a wolf, he was adequate—and not the bumbling oaf of a man who could barely walk a straight line, or
talk around his own thick tongue.

When the door quietly closed, he padded over to the bed.

Elen slept on her side, cocooned in blankets. A row of
pillows lined her back. It was how she'd slept when he'd first
met her, as if squares of encased feathers could protect her
from the nightmares of her youth.

With his teeth he dragged the pillows from the bed. She
slept in a loose shirt and undergarments, but the shirt had
ridden up to reveal her spine with two jagged scars, the only
physical evidence of her mother's torture. Merin had pinned
her down and shoved rods under her skin in an effort to force
a wolf that never came.

The mattress sagged under his weight as he jumped on
the bed and settled along her back.

She stirred, and then inhaled. "Cormack . . . ?"

He nuzzled into her tumbled hair. Her scent had lessened
in this place, but he caught a whiff of the moonflowers that
bloomed at night in her garden, pure and white, and sweeter
than honeysuckle.

Elen turned, stroked her hand over his side. "I'm so sorry,
Cormack . . . for hurting you again." Her voice clogged with
her tears. "I couldn't resist Pendaran's summons."

He growled softly from the memory of that putrid ass
who had dared to call her, and his own inability to protect her.

"Do you hate me?" she asked again, as she had in the
library.

He was not ready to show her his true feelings, so he vowed them silently . . .

No, Elen . . . I don't hate you. I love you more than the air that I breathe. And if I had to choose between the two—I would choose you.

Unaware, she fell asleep with her face buried in his neck as his fur absorbed her tears. Come morning, Mae cracked open the door and Cormack slipped from Elen's room without waking her. She was returning to Rhuddin Village with Dylan today and Cormack wasn't going with her.

She wanted a friend. He wanted more. Next time they met, he would be the adequate man she needed—the warrior she could love.

Padding to his chambers, he grabbed a belted bundle of jeans and carried them in his muzzle to the Avon forest. The scents greeted him like an orchestra of nature, rich and pure.

The shift hurt like a son of a bitch. Gritting his teeth as the final bones snapped into place, he wasn't sure whether he would ever get used to the change. Luc had promised that he would—but Cormack wasn't convinced. Tugging on his jeans, he went in search of Porter. The man had announced his plans the evening before and should be doing a final perimeter check of the island.

Gravel bit the freshly formed soles of his feet as he took a shortcut through the graveyard of the Walkers. Cormack slowed when he noticed the doors of the tombs hung ajar. One Walker sat on the ground with his head between his legs, his body racked with sobs. Another sat in a puddle of water, slapping the surface like a child might do in a wading pool.

Aeron, the female, was wrapped around Porter. The newly dense forest barely concealed their location.

And Aeron's voice carried. "Do you want to die, warrior who bears a Celtic cross?"

Porter frowned down at the armful of an awakened Walker. "Not in this century, I don't."

Head thrown back, Aeron laughed as women do when they drink too much wine. Her hands roamed downward.

Porter muttered, "You're getting a wee bit cozy down there, aren't you, now?"

She giggled, obviously pleased with what her wandering hands found. "May I pleasure you?"

Dumbfounded, Porter just blinked. "*Bloody hell . . .* Are you trying to torture me, because I'm thinking you are?"

"Not in a hurtful way." She lowered to her knees and rolled up her eyes. "Please . . ."

A groan fell from his mouth, and his hands fisted in her hair. "Am I supposed to be saying no to an offer like that?"

"No, you should not." Aeron gave a smile that promised heaven with a kiss. "What is your name, warrior who bears the Celtic cross?"

"Porter."

"Your given name," she clarified. "Do I not deserve to know that at least?"

He hesitated only briefly. "Finnbarr," the porter of Rhuddin Village hissed between his teeth. "Just call me Finn."

Finn, was it? It suited him better than Porter, but Cormack suspected he'd had a valid reason for guarding his given name—*until now*. With some Irish luck, Aeron might even keep his secret. If not, it wouldn't be the first time a man had fallen because of a female. And this modern society considered women the weaker sex. *Idiots*.

Knowing Finn would be in no mood for interruptions, Cormack pivoted and searched for another who'd serve his purpose. Besides, it was an act he had seen many times before. As a Bleidd he'd been invisible to their kind. Since he couldn't speak their secrets, people ignored his presence—everyone but Elen.

Cormack nodded to Mae as he returned the way he came. She sat next to one of the Walkers, patting his hand. A crowd began to form around Tesni as she led the one named Gawain to the outer bailey. It was a gift, perhaps even the greatest given this day, to see the *Beddestyr* walk again in this world. Perhaps their kind wasn't doomed after all.

When Tesni noticed Cormack, her pretty face spread into a wide smile. She'd offered him what Aeron had Porter. And, *yes*—he'd been tempted. However, he'd been waiting four hundred years for Elen, and he was *not* going to risk losing his only chance with the woman he loved by tiddling with anyone else.

It was Elen's hands, and Elen's mouth, he wanted on his flesh—almost as much as he wanted his on hers.

Entering the castle, he found Teyrnon, Cadan and Gareth sharing a pitcher of ale in the dining hall; all three men were healed after shifts and quiet with their cups.

Cormack pointed to Gareth's sword, moved his tongue to form words, and fisted his hands in frustration. His speech never formed the way he heard it in his mind.

"Teach," he finally managed. "Me."

It was Teyrnon who lowered his cup. "Teach you to use a sword?"

"Yes," he growled. "To fight." *Teach me to defend Elen.* Because he had no doubt Pendaran would return for her.

And when he does, Cormack vowed, *I will be an adequate warrior for all her needs.*

Maybe then she could love him as more than just a friend.

INSIDE CASTELL AVON, TALIESIN STARED AT A MISCHIE-vous child with eyes the color of copper and leaves. He sat in Avon's library, with Luc and Rosa snuggled on the opposite sofa, while Dylan waited for Elen to say her farewells before bringing her home to Rhuddin Village.

Audrey blinked at him, tilted her head. "You made the lady sad."

His lips quirked. Yes, there had been many sad ladies over the years because of him. And some of the women—bless their naughty hearts—hadn't been ladies.

Still, her question made him curious. "What lady are you talking about?"

"The lady in my dreams." Audrey held up her fisted hand and spread her fingers to reveal a crumpled leaf. She padded over to Rosa. "She said this is for you. She said it's from your tree."

Unease settled on Taliesin's spine, a tingle of awareness despite the absence of his Sight. "Can I see the leaf, Audrey?"

Shaking her head, she said, "It's Rosa's leaf, from Rosa's tree." She returned to stand next to him, crawling into his lap.

And he was awakened in the Vale.

With Audrey in his arms.

The child pointed a pudgy, iridescent finger to where his mother stood. "The lady is over there."

Ceridwen wore a light blue dress, plain and cinched at her waist with a gilded tie. Her fair hair hung to her waist and her heavy-lidded gaze regarded him with wariness and sorrow. "I will not listen to cruel words, so mind what you say to me now if you ever wish my company again."

Cobbled before he spoke—was that not the entirety of their relationship?

How she still had the capacity to surprise him was as unsettling as this new development. Shaken, he managed to state the obvious. "You've assigned me a new Walker."

"The others are useless." She made a disparaging sound. "It is my wish that you will not be as cruel to a child as you were to them."

Acid churned and he swallowed his reply, but it was some time before he could speak without rancor. "What have you done with the others?"

"Their services have been terminated." She returned his frown with one of her own. "If you have no respect for their warnings . . . what use are they to me?"

"So you killed them," he said through clenched teeth.

Her eyes widened. *"What?* No, I have sent them home," she snapped. "Why do you always assume the worst of me?

Aeron is accosting the porter of Rhuddin Village at this very moment." She shook her head. "Finnbarr may not be able to walk come morning. Such a good boy, too . . . I always liked him. *He* respected his mother."

Finnbarr O'Connor was *not* a good boy. Decent, *yes*—but also hot-tempered and prone to finding trouble.

"Finn will be fine, I'm sure." The news made Ceridwen's little zinger less irritating. "Having them awakened was worth losing my Sight."

"Do not act like a martyr, Taliesin. I took your Sight from you in an attempt to stop you from interfering." The spectral forest darkened with her mood. "But, alas, you have done your worst damage without it."

"I stopped a war," he felt compelled to point out.

Unimpressed, she made an absent flick with her hand. "Your Sight is returned. See what you have done."

His throat clogged as images flooded his mind's eye and he foresaw what his interference wrought.

"Pendaran was *meant* to die," she raged. "Merin, blessed be that warrior's heart, she would have broken the darkness and balanced the light had you not stopped her. And now it will grow like a poisonous weed. The war you thought you ended has just begun—*because* you interfered."

Too stricken to speak, he let out a ragged breath as guilt and denial roiled in his gut. In the midst of his turmoil, Audrey patted his cheek. He held the child on earth and in the Vale; therefore he actually felt the gesture.

"The lady is mad at you," Audrey whispered. "Did you do a bad thing?"

"Yes, I did a very bad thing, I'm afraid." He was good at doing bad things.

After another soft pat, she nodded with understanding. "You should say the sorry word. Sometimes it works. Sometimes it doesn't. But it's not so hard to say, so you should try."

Taliesin looked to his mother. She appeared absorbed—though in a way that suggested she dared not move for the importance of his reply. Even the imaginary air in this forsaken Vale stilled as if waiting.

Some words were harder to say than others, especially if they forgave a lifetime of abandonment. But he was no longer a boy left in Pendaran's care and he could atone for his own misdeeds.

Chagrined, he offered, "I *am* sorry, you know."

She closed her eyes briefly. "As am I, Taliesin . . . As am I." Her lip trembled slightly, much like Merin's when she refused to watch her children suffer because of her presence. "I cannot cry. I will leave for a moment. Rhiannon is teaching me meditation techniques. Stay in the Vale! I will not be away long . . ."

Ceridwen disappeared for a short time and when she returned she seemed more settled. "Already you listen to this Walker better than the others. I think Audrey will be a good match for us."

"The Council will hunt her," he said as concern grew.

"Which is why I have already given her a message to deliver when the time comes." She approached slowly. Her hand whispered over the child's hair. "Do you remember the message you are to say if someone tries to take you?"

Audrey nodded. "I am *Beddestyr*. I am a messenger of Ceridwen." She enunciated each word carefully. They had practiced this more than once. "If you take me, you will be reminded of why she is also known as the Crone."

"Perfect, my sweet child." His mother clapped. "That was perfect."

Audrey beamed.

And, yes, even Pendaran would honor that announcement. The risk of it being true wasn't worth the wrath of the Crone.

With conviction, Ceridwen ordered, "I want her fostered by Rosa Beatrice, wife and mate of Luc, son of Merin, *Penteulu* of Avon, and keeper of the *Beddestyr*." She held up her arm toward the end of the pathway where a sapling shimmered, tiny like Audrey. "Rosa brought forth a Tree of Hope, the first of its kind in over fifteen hundred years. She will protect this child from the darkness."

Awed, when very little caused such a sentiment these days, Taliesin had to ask, "It exists in both worlds?" He had killed the last living Tree of Hope on the day he'd condemned the Walkers to their three-hundred-year coma.

"Yes. It exists on earth and in the Land of Faery." A soft smile touched her face. "It is a gateway, a small one, but it weathered your storm. Let us hope it can weather a greater one to come."

"I'm tired of the storms," Taliesin admitted.

"I know." She lifted her hand to touch his arm, but like all their other visits in the Vale, touches were just whispers and apparitions. "I felt your heart on Avon's broken bridge and it has taken another piece of mine. Humankind is gifted with free will and choice—and they are tangled in their own war of good and evil. The demons cast from their heaven want the very essence of their souls, while you are torn between worlds and must answer to both. If you interfere with their gift, darkness grows and light ebbs—"

"And the earth becomes unbalanced," he finished. Because of him. *Again.* "I messed up."

"Yes," she readily agreed. "This one was not good, Taliesin." A stricken look folded her features. "Elen, daughter of Merin, will face a great trial ahead. Pendaran will come for her in the arms of seduction and it may be stronger than the pure love she was meant to have. And Cadan . . ." She sighed as her spectral forest wilted with her sadness. "He will have his own challenge to confront when he seeks freedom outside of Avon."

Taliesin's chest constricted when he viewed their future. *Why is evil always drawn to pure hearts?* "And I can't help them," he choked out with resentment.

"No, human blood runs in their veins as well as Fae, and we mustn't interfere with their free will. But . . ." Mischief entered her gaze and the Vale crackled with anticipation, like the warmth of sunbeams on a frosty morning. "I have been given a gift, and when given a gift as precious as hope, I am inclined to give one in return."

Wary, because Taliesin couldn't foresee this gift—and that could only mean one thing: it was pure Fae. "Is the gateway large enough for travel?"

"It serves well enough." Merriment lightened her spectral image. "Might is not determined by size, Taliesin, but by fortitude and honor. We lost this battle, but we shall see who wins the next."

Oh, What a Mighty Creature Hope Befalls

ELEN BROKE GROUND IN HER GARDEN WITH FEROCIOUS jabs of her shovel. Sweat pooled on her spine and her arms throbbed but she continued the task, needing the mind-numbing escape of planting a tree and not thinking about Cormack.

Or the fact that he had snuck out of her room before dawn—and then refused to return with her.

Something flowering was in order, she decided. A lilac perhaps, because it had been a vexing few days and nothing made her feel better than a tree that blossomed every year to remind her that life also brought peace and beauty and not just turmoil and ugliness.

A bird flitted about, landed on a branch of a nearby apple tree, turning its head sideways to watch her work. It was a winter wren, small and perky, with brown-and-white-striped wings and a creamy white throat under a dark beak.

Odd, though, how the top of its head glinted gold in the sun.

Dropping her shovel, Elen approached slowly for a closer look. Eye level, the wren lifted its chin in a haughty gesture. It held a square object in its left talon. The glinting bit on top of its head looked very much like a crown, an *actual* one of gold and not yellowish feathers.

Elen stilled, for this was no usual bird. The energy that reached for her was greater than the entirety of a healthy forest. "Should I welcome you to my garden, or should I be afraid?"

A glimmering cloud whirled around the wren to reveal a tiny woman with iridescent dragonfly wings edged by dark brown veins. She was lovely by human standards, but rather plain for an extraordinary creature; her coloring matched the bird, with creamy skin and striped brown hair, curled short and tucked under her coronet.

Elen blinked, squeezed her eyes shut and opened them again.

The woman with wings remained.

"What are you . . . a faery?" Not the most intelligent inquiry—but she was surprised and therefore deserved some lenience. A sighting of the wee folk hadn't occurred, as far as she knew, since before the Guardians were given the ability to transform to wolves.

The woman lowered her tiny chin and issued an indignant glare; it was far more disconcerting than her size should allow. "We have much work to do if you cannot even tell the difference between a faery and a pixie." Like a wren, her voice came out in piercing overtones and was clearly amplified.

"You're a pixie," Elen whispered, daring to take a step closer.

"You look disappointed. What were you expecting? Pink hair and sparkles? Beauty comes in many forms. And mine, you will learn, is knowledge."

"I'm not disappointed."

"Now you lie," she clipped. "And I tolerate lies even less than stupidity."

After receiving two scoldings in under a minute, Elen became less enchanted. "What are you doing here?"

"I am your new teacher, Elen."

"What are you going to teach me?" She had a doctorate from Harvard and had apprenticed under Maelorwen. She could perform modern surgery and turn a man's stick as soft as worms. But she was always willing to study new things, especially from the Fae.

"Our kind has given you a powerful gift." A delicate snort carried. "You must learn to do more with it than run rivers of moss and force transformations, especially if you are to fight the darkness that wants you. And you must learn to control it."

"There's a darkness that wants me?"

"To be sure, but we will get to him later." The pixie hovered before settling into a cross-legged position on the branch. "First, let me introduce myself." Apparently, the item she held was a miniature-sized book. She flipped the pages, searching. "I found two books of use to me in the library of Castell Avon: *Etiquette for Travelers* and *Oxford Dictionary of Modern Slang*. I had them transcribed to my size," she explained while tilting her head over what she read. "It says here that teachers of this time and culture are assigned a prefix before their name of Miss, Mrs. or Ms., depending upon marital status. My personal relationships are none of your concern, so you will refer to me as Ms. Hafwen. Do you understand?"

Elen could only nod.

"Good," Ms. Hafwen said. "Now, I will need a home, because it is inappropriate for a student and teacher to reside in the same dwelling." Her wings began a whirling motion before she lifted off the branch and hovered around Elen's garden. "You will build this home for me out of stone, mortar and wood." Her voice carried sharp in the wind like a bird's song. "Nothing elaborate; one turret, a window and a door is all I need. Here," she announced, "under the hydrangeas in your shade garden."

"Okay," Elen agreed when pinned with a glare.

"It is my understanding that *okay* means *yes*." She waited for verification.

"Yes."

Still, the pixie hovered as if expecting more.

"Yes, Ms. Hafwen."

She gave a nod of approval. "Thank you, Elen. You will build it today." She flipped another page of her tiny book. "You and I have much to do. There is an axiom I found . . ." She flipped yet another page, pursed her lips, paused and frowned over what she read. "Mother fuc—" Inhaling a sharp breath, she caught herself before finishing the crude but common saying, and then gave an indignant sniff. "That is disgusting!"

Elen laughed; she couldn't help herself.

Ms. Hafwen huffed, "I do not know what it is about humans and their fascination with inbreeding. That was *not* the modern adage I wanted. Where is it . . . ? Ah, here it is: *Work your arse off.*" She gave a satisfied smile. "I like that one."

Why did Elen suddenly feel as if her quiet world had just started to spin like a merry-go-round and she needed to hang on or be thrown off?

"Elen," the pixie announced with glee, "you and I are going to work our arses off."

The way Ms. Hafwen pronounced *arse* rather than *ass* ruined the impact—but Elen dared not contradict this formidable creature.

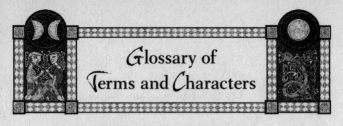

Glossary of Terms and Characters

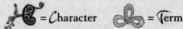

= *Character*   = *Term*

AERON

Walker; once a messenger to Ceridwen in the Otherworld; earthly body remains in Avon while spirit is trapped in the Vale.

ANNWFN; OTHERWORLD; LAND OF FAERY

Homeland of the Welsh Celtic deities, similar to *sídh* of Irish mythology, where the *Tuatha Dé Danann* reside, the land of faery and magical beings.

BaBBaɪ joh; WALKER

Once messengers to Ceridwen in the Otherworld. Four known Walkers still exist; all have lost their power to walk between worlds.

BELTANE; MAY DAY

A Celtic holiday to celebrate the beginning of summer. Ancient Celts believed that the barrier between our world and the Otherworld was opened this day and that the Gods visited to bestow fertility blessings.

BLEIDD; WOLF

A Guardian descendant born or trapped in wolf form who cannot change to human; human intelligence exists within the wolf.

BRAN

Original Guardian; member of the Council of Ceridwen.

BRIALLEN

Guardian who resides in Wales with her husband; wife of Maelor; mate of Teyrnon.

CADAN

Son of Neira; cousin of Rosa; Math's former lover.

CASTELL AVON; RIVER CASTLE

A castle on the island of Avon; commissioned by the Council of Ceridwen as a wedding gift for Rosa and Math.

CERIDWEN; CELTIC GODDESS

Welsh Celtic goddess, worshiped by ancient Celts as the great sow goddess; though less recognized, Ceridwen was also revered as the goddess of wolves; known to brew potions of transformation and knowledge; Earth Mother of Darkness and Light; master of animal transformation; birth mother of Taliesin.

CERNUNNOS; CELTIC GOD

Welsh Celtic Lord of Animals; worshiped by ancient Celts as the Great Hunter; commonly depicted in Celtic artifacts with horned animals, such as the horned snake of Celtic tradition, and the stag; honored by ancient Celts as the leader of the Wild Hunt where spirits of the dead were carried to the Otherworld.

CORMACK

Brother of Siân and Taran; close friend of Elen; born in wolf form without the ability to transform to human; human intelligence exists within the wolf; given the power to shift by Elen in the first battle of the Dissenters' War against the Guardians.

COUNCIL OF CERIDWEN; GOVERNING ASSEMBLY OF ORIGINAL GUARDIANS

A self-proclaimed governing body compiled by the nine surviving Original Guardians.

Council members in alphabetical order: Bran, Edwyn, Gweir, Maelor, Merin, Neira, Pendaran, Rhys, William.

CYMRU; WALES

Homeland of the Original Guardians.

DARON

Leader of the Ontario territory; views the Original Guardians with disdain.

DEWISEDIG; CHOSEN HUMAN

A human mate of a Guardian or Guardian descendant whose offspring can transform into a wolf.

DhмABBоBBмᴀ; EVIL BRINGER

A derogatory description of Guardian descendants born in human form without the ability to transform into a wolf. The name was created by Original Guardians, fearful of their loss of power.

DRYSTAN

Leader of the Blue Ridge Highland territory of Virginia; views the Original Guardians with disdain.

DYLAN (AD 329–)

The alpha wolf and leader of the Katahdin territory; husband and mate of Sophie; father of Joshua; eldest brother of Luc and Elen; son of Merin.

EDWYN

Original Guardian; member of the Council of Ceridwen.

ELEN (AD 331–)

The healer of the Katahdin territory; sister of Dylan and Luc; daughter of Merin; cannot shift into a wolf but can manipulate nature.

FINNBARR (AD 1682–)

Also known as Porter; head of home security of Rhuddin Hall of the Katahdin territory; has a tattoo of a Celtic cross in honor of his Irish mother; cannot transform into a wolf.

FRANCINE (AD 1955–AD 2013)

Mother of Sophie; human; killed in the first battle of the Dissenters' War against the Guardians.

GARETH

Porter of Castell Avon; tortured by Math for taking a mortal lover; wears patch due to damaged eye; not allowed to shift and heal.

GAWAIN

Walker; once a messenger to Ceridwen in the Otherworld; earthly body remains in Avon while spirit is trapped in a dreamland between worlds.

GₘₐₕABₑBₘₒₕ; GUARDIAN

Descendants of Original Guardians who follow the command of the Council of Ceridwen.

GмıнАВьВмон UⅅbaB; GUARDIAN, FIRST IN ORDER; THE ORIGINALS

An Original Celtic warrior appointed by Ceridwen to protect her son Taliesin; taught how to draw energy from the earth to transform into wolves; served Taliesin as a child; age at a very slow rate. The oldest surviving Original Guardian was born 95 BC. There were forty-eight Original Guardians; only nine remain to form the Council of Ceridwen.

GWEIR

Original Guardian; member of the Council of Ceridwen.

HAFWEN

A pixie sent to earth to teach Elen how to use her gift.

Haⅅ Waı ; OLD SERVANT

Slaves to the Original Guardians and the Council; Guardian descendants born without the ability to transform into a wolf; age at the same slow rate of an Original Guardian.

ISABEAU

Leader of the forest region of Minnesota; family was tortured and killed in the house of Rhun while serving the Original Guardians.

JOSHUA (AD 1995–)

Son of Dylan and Sophie.

KALEM

Leader of Alaskan territory; views the Original Guardians with disdain.

KOKO (AD 1868–AD 1946)

Luc's deceased wife.

LLARA

One of four leaders who occupy the territories of Russia; views the Original Guardians with disdain.

LUC BLACK (AD 342–)

Youngest brother of Dylan and Elen; son of Merin; husband of the late Koko; banished at birth by his mother for being born in wolf form; raised by Dylan; known as the Beast of Merin.

TBa MabaDEAaED

Also referred to as the *The Mabinogi*; a collection of Celtic folklore from medieval Welsh manuscripts, including *The White Book of Rhydderch* and *The Red Book of Hergest*. The first translation of *The Mabinogion* into English was by Lady Charlotte Guest in the mid-nineteenth century.

MADOC

Leader of the mountain regions of Montana; captained the ship that brought Luc, Elen and Dylan to the New World; views the Original Guardians with disdain.

MAELOR

Original Guardian; member of the Council of Ceridwen; husband of Briallen.

MAELORWEN

Also known as Mae; witch who lived in the hills when Dylan and Elen were children; taught Elen the medicinal uses of plants; the first Guardian descendant born without the ability to shift; tortured by the Guardians; currently resides with Rosa in the White Mountains territory of New Hampshire.

MATH (62 BC–AD 2013)

An Original Guardian; former leader of the White Mountains territory of New Hampshire; former husband of Rosa; loyal to the Council of Ceridwen; executed by Dylan.

MERIN

An Original Guardian; mother of Dylan, Elen and Luc; resides in Wales as a member of the Council of Ceridwen.

MORWYN

Walker; once a messenger to Ceridwen in the Otherworld; earthly body remains in Avon while spirit is trapped in a dreamland between worlds.

NEIRA

Original Guardian; member of the Council of Ceridwen; mother of Cadan; aunt of Rosa.

NESIEN

Walker; once a messenger to Ceridwen in the Otherworld; earthly body remains in Avon while spirit is trapped in a dreamland between worlds.

NIA

Leader of the northern New York territory;
views the Original Guardians with disdain.

 PENDARAN

Original Guardian; head of the Council of
Ceridwen.

 PADJAKBK; HEAD OF FAMILY

Leader of a territory; alpha wolf.

 PORTER; RESPECTED SERVANT

Head of home security.

 RHUDDIN; HEART OF TIMBER

The name Dylan chose for his territory,
located around Katahdin, the highest
mountain peak in Maine; the northern end
of the Appalachian Trail.

 RHUN (58 BC–AD 2013)

An Original Guardian; killed by Sophie in
the first battle of the Dissenters' War
against the Guardians.

 RHYS

Original Guardian; member of the
Council of Ceridwen.

ROSA ALBAN (AD 1702–)

Widow of Math; wife of Luc; leader of the White Mountains territory of New Hampshire; parents were killed while protecting Rosa from the Council of Ceridwen; the last pure-blooded unmated female shifter.

SERPENT OF CERNUNNOS

A flexible sword in the shape of Cernunnos's horned snake, forged in the Otherworld as a gift for Taliesin. The wearer of the Serpent is given a heightened perception of their surroundings and a connection to beings of the Otherworld.

SIÂN

Dylan's ex-lover; eldest sister of Taran and Cormack; threatened a pregnant Sophie in the woods the night Sophie left Dylan; the woman who gave Sophie her scars.

SIN

See Taliesin.

SOPHIE (AD 1975–)

Wife and mate of Dylan; mother of Joshua; daughter of Francine; the first human to give birth to a shifter in more than three hundred years; her aging process has slowed since carrying Dylan's child.

TALIESIN; "SIN" (42 BC–)

Son of Ceridwen; possesses powers of transformation and prophecy; Sophie's former employer. Taliesin spent much of the medieval ages intoxicated; therefore, it was during this time that many stories of his antics were documented by humans. Though the Original Guardians were assigned by his birth mother as protectors, Taliesin views most of them with disdain.

TARAN

Deceased sister of Siân and Cormack; mother of Melissa; killed by Rhun in the first battle of the Dissenters' War against the Guardians.

TEYRNON

First in command of Luc's guard; mate of Briallen; Guardian descendant with the ability to shift; father was human of Norse descent; homestead destroyed by the Guardians in the late 1600s for daring to live outside their rules.

TREE OF HOPE

A gateway between earth and the Otherworld.

VALE

See also *Ystrad Gloyw*; an ethereal dreamlike world between earth and the Otherworld.

WILLIAM; GWILYM

Original Guardian; member of the Council of Ceridwen.

WULFLING

Wulflings begin as infant shifters, often deserted by the death of their parents while in hiding; left to fend for themselves; without the company of humans they are unable to learn by example; instincts of their wolves often become more dominant than their humanity.

Yɪ ʝ ʜaB Gʙɪɒɴ, GLOWING VALE

An ethereal dreamlike world between earth and the Otherworld.